Christmas at
The Beach House Hotel

The Beach House Hotel Series – Book 4

Judith Keim

Wild Quail Publishing

This is a work of fiction. Names, characters, places, public or private institutions, corporations, towns, and incidents are the products of the author's imagination or are used fictitiously. Any resemblance to actual events, locales, or persons, living or dead, is coincidental.

No part of this book may be reproduced or transmitted in any form or by any electronic or mechanical means, including information storage and retrieval systems, without permission in writing from the author, except by a reviewer, who may quote brief passages in a review. This book may not be resold or uploaded for distribution to others.

Wild Quail Publishing
PO Box 171332
Boise, ID 83717-1332

ISBN# 978-0-9982824-5-9

Dedication

This book is dedicated to those who share the spirit of Christmas or the holiday of their choice, making the world a little more peaceful, a little more fun for even a brief amount of time.

our guests, making the hotel a first-class operation, are gone. No complimentary items in the room, no morning newspapers, no treats available to them. And last Christmas was a freakin' nightmare—cheap decorations, no bonuses for the staff, no community Christmas Party, none of our usual holiday fun. No wonder our return guests no longer feel a part of our family, the wedding bookings have cratered, and the locals are staying away from the restaurant."

"I'm tired of this kind of thing continuing to happen," I snapped. "We've tried talking to the new owners about our deep concerns, and it's done absolutely no good. I don't know what else we can do about it."

"I do," growled Rhonda. "We can take back the hotel. We have that contractual right, remember? That hotel was my home; we built it into something unique, and those SOBs are turning it into an ordinary, chain-style hotel where no one gives a damn about our guests."

"Take it back? Do you mean it?" Excitement surged through me in tantalizing waves. God! I'd missed running the hotel with Rhonda. Though our contract specified that we'd retain a minority interest in the business and would act as consultants, the new owners had scoffed at every suggestion we'd made. They'd even indicated in sometimes not so subtle ways that we should go home and take care of our families.

I felt a huge grin spread across my face. *It would feel so good to get rid of them!*

"It won't be easy, but, Annie, we gotta do it! Are you in?"

"Oh, yes," I said with growing determination. "It's time to stop this nonsense. Things have gone from bad to worse after Aubrey Lowell took over the management of the hotel."

"Yeah, what a little punk! Let's get rid of him and all the others!" Rhonda's voice changed, became tentative. "Will Vaughn be okay with your doing this? I think Will might fight

CHAPTER ONE

My cell phone rang. *Rhonda.*

Staring out my kitchen window at the palm fronds rustling in the sea breeze like impatient children wanting to run and play, I picked up the call from my best friend in Sabal, Florida.

"Hey, Mrs. Grayson! How's it going? Those two little ones driving you crazy?"

Rhonda laughed. "Annie, I swear Willow is teaching Drew every one of her 'terrible two' tricks, but she's so sweet with him, I don't mind."

I couldn't help chuckling. Willow was two and a half, and Drew, thirteen months younger, was fascinated with his big sister and tried to mimic her whenever possible. They were darling together, but a real handful.

"Listen, Annie; we gotta talk. This mess at The Beach House Hotel can't go on like it is. I just got a call from Stephanie Willis from Connecticut. She was furious because, for the second year in a row, they couldn't get a reservation for Columbus Day weekend. She and Randolph have always been loyal guests of the hotel. What in the hell is going on?"

I let out a sigh of exasperation. "I'm not surprised a bit by this latest news. Ever since we sold it, The Beach House Hotel has deteriorated from the elegant, discreet, seaside resort we created to a commercial enterprise that is all about dollars, not class." The sale, almost two years ago, to the investment group of Peabody, Lowell, and Logan had turned out to be big disappointment to both of us.

"Yeah," said Rhonda. "All the finer touches we provid

me on this, but honestly, Annie, after staying at home for two years with the babies and with him thinking he's the biggest stud around, I'm afraid I'll get pregnant again. And at my age, it isn't as easy as it was when I had Angela. I love my babies, but I'm too old to have more."

I held back a laugh. Rhonda was in her mid-forties and her husband, Will, ten years older. But Will was so taken with the idea of having kids in his fifties that, given a choice, he would have many more.

"So, what about Vaughn?" Rhonda persisted. "Can you convince him it's the right thing for you to do?"

I hesitated, knowing he wouldn't be thrilled. Vaughn loved having me spend time with him in New York while he filmed *The Sins of the Children*, the soap opera he'd starred in for several years. But I missed the hotel's work environment and interacting with our guests. Fresh resolve rose in me. "Vaughn and I will work it out. The hotel is my baby as much as yours. Let's do it!"

"All right! Before I chicken out, I'll call Mike Torson right now."

"Let me know what we need to do next." I ended the call hoping Rhonda and I weren't making a big mistake. Together, we'd made a few.

After I hung up, I couldn't contain my excitement. Raising my arms in the air, I did a little dance across the kitchen floor.

"Me, too, Mommy!" cried Robbie. He jumped off his chair and grabbed hold of my hands.

Laughing, I twirled in circles with him. As I looked down into his shining brown eyes, my heart surged with love for him. At almost five, he was a darling little boy with dark hair, a sturdy body, and a sweet nature. Liz was still the best sister any little boy could have, but at the time his parents, my ex, Robert, and Kandie, were killed in an automobile accident, she'd been unable to offer Robbie a secure home. Vaughn and I had been so right to adopt him.

As if my thoughts about my daughter had prompted it, my phone rang. Still chuckling from our crazy dance, I picked up the call from Liz.

"Hi, sweetheart! How are you?"

"I'm busy with Chad's business, but I need to talk to you about my wedding. I'm not sure Chad and I want it at The Beach House Hotel—not with the way things are being handled there. Would your feelings be hurt if we changed our mind and tried to hold it at the Ritz?"

The Ritz? Telling myself not to overreact, I drew a deep breath. "What if I told you Rhonda and I are going to try to take back the hotel?"

"Really? Mom, that would be great! The Beach House Hotel is not the same kind of place it used to be. If you buy it back and make it the way it was when you and Rhonda ran it, I'd be thrilled to have the wedding there."

"Don't say a word to anyone else about this. We just made the decision today, and I haven't even had a chance to discuss it with Vaughn."

"Oh ..." Liz let the word drift into silence.

"I think I can get him to agree on this," I said, not at all certain I could.

"For what it's worth, I think it's important for you and Rhonda to do this on many levels. Vaughn is pretty used to having you around, though." Liz paused. "Good luck with everything. Here comes a call on the customer line. Gotta go."

I couldn't help the frown I felt form as I ended the call. Maybe I was being too optimistic about making our new plan work. I had my family to consider.

My cell rang again. I checked caller ID. *Mike Torson.*

"Hello, Mike. How are you?"

"I'm fine, thanks. I just got off the phone with Rhonda. Are you in agreement with her to exercise your right to buy back the hotel?"

"You bet," I answered, fired up again. "Under the new owners' direction, the hotel has really gone downhill."

"Even though it is within your right to do so under the contract you signed with them, you understand there will be resistance, don't you?"

"Yes, probably because they are more intent on making money than giving the guests an unforgettable experience." I couldn't hide the distaste in my voice.

"Well, yes, there's that. Also, they won't want anything to mar their reputation, so we have to be very discreet in how we pursue this," Mike said in his usual calm manner.

"I understand, but Rhonda and I want the chance to make things right. We invested the money from the sale, so we should be able to handle the purchase of it."

"You have the right to buy the hotel at a fair price, but we're going to need people on our side to do property inspections and an appraisal. The investors will have valuations done on their own, which will, no doubt, be substantially different from ours."

My stomach twisted. Peabody, Lowell, and Logan was an investment group from Boston that played hardball. Though Mike Torson was a clever and persistent lawyer, the battle might get nasty.

"I understand," I repeated, though I was certain there would be unpleasant surprises.

"Shall I begin to prepare?"

"I'll reconfirm with Rhonda, and we'll get back to you tomorrow. But, yes, this is what we want." I didn't mention that neither Rhonda nor I had discussed it with our spouses.

I hung up from the call and checked my watch. Vaughn was flying in from New York that evening, and I had approximately two hours to prepare my case.

After quickly calling Rhonda to give her an update, I checked on Robbie, who was happily splashing in the pool with Elena Ramos, our young, trusted nanny. I waved to them and then went into the bathroom to take a shower. Might as well look my best.

As warm water sluiced over my body, I felt my shoulders relax and my mind open. Vaughn was a good man, a kind man, who'd been happy to have me at his beck and call these past two years. I'd been more than pleased to do that because, even after two years of marriage, I was still crazy about him. Anticipating the intimate moments ahead with Vaughn, my fingers trailed my body. He was such a good lover—generous and giving.

After rehearsing my approach to Vaughn on the plan Rhonda and I had come up with, I got out of the shower and dressed in a blue blouse that Vaughn had once said matched the color of my eyes. I brushed my straight, dark hair until it lay smoothly inches above my shoulders. Giving myself a critical look in the mirror, I thought maybe I didn't look too bad. Vaughn sometimes teased me about being a hot babe, but I wasn't that. I smiled at the memory, though, and slipped diamond earrings into my earlobes. It would be so good to have him home.

When I walked out onto the lanai, Robbie called to me from the pool. "Look, Mommy!" He stood on the edge of the deep end of the pool, made sure I was looking, and then jumped into the water.

"Good job!" I called to him as he bobbed to the surface. At age two and new to the house, he'd almost drowned in the pool. Now, two and a half years later, he swam like a little fish.

"You sure you don't mind staying with Robbie while I pick up Vaughn at the airport?" I said to Elena.

She stood and faced me. Her dark eyes sparkled, and a smile lit her pretty face, framed by thick, straight hair that she wore in a ponytail most days. Over the last couple of years, she'd become like another daughter to me. And with Elena dating the boy Liz was once infatuated with, it seemed like family when we all got together. I couldn't imagine not having her around.

"I don't mind at all," said Elena. "Troy is due here for Robbie's swim lesson. Afterwards, Robbie can come with us when we go out for hamburgers."

"Sounds great. He loves to be with the two of you." I gave Robbie a quick hug, not minding that I got a little wet, patted the silky head of Trudy, our black and tan dachshund, and headed for the garage.

On the way to the airport in Ft. Myers, my body hummed with anticipation. With Vaughn gone so much of the time, each homecoming seemed special. I still found it amazing that of all the women he could have chosen after his first wife died, he'd married me. With Robert, my ex, pulling the old stunt of leaving me for the younger, voluptuous receptionist in our office, my self-confidence had been destroyed. But the relationship between Vaughn and me had a depth of tenderness and commitment I'd never known. I treasured him. I treasured us together.

As agreed, I waited in the baggage claim area for Vaughn to arrive. Hearing a commotion, I looked up. Vaughn was stepping off the escalator into a small crowd of people who'd recognized him, even with his doing his best to hide beneath a Yankees baseball cap. Some were holding up pieces of paper for him to autograph. He obliged a few and then quickly made his way toward me.

As he neared, I took a moment to study his tall, broad-shouldered form. His black curls and snapping brown eyes, familiar to fans across the country, looked wonderful, especially when a happy grin crossed his face when our eyes met.

I hurried forward to greet him.

People stepped back as he swung me up in his arms, heedless of the curious onlookers. In the past, I might have frozen with embarrassment, but I'd learned to live with the attention he got. I didn't necessarily like it, but I managed.

"Hi, darling! Glad you're home!" I murmured into his ear.

He beamed at me as he put me down on my feet. "Not as glad as I am. Where's Robbie?"

"He and Elena are waiting for Troy to show up for Robbie's swimming lesson, and then they're going to take him out to dinner. You'll get your big greeting from him when we get home."

I loved that Robbie and Vaughn were so close. With his children from his first marriage grown, married, and starting families of their own, Vaughn was happy to have a second chance at fatherhood.

He took my hand, and we headed for the baggage conveyer belt to pick up his luggage. As soon as he grabbed his suitcase, we hurried out of the airport terminal.

Vaughn slid behind the wheel of my car, and we headed to Sabal, twenty minutes south.

As he drove, the wind ruffled his hair—the dark, soft curls I loved to finger. He turned to me with a smile. "What's new since we last talked?"

"There's something I need to discuss with you after you're

settled at home. I thought we could take a walk along the beach at The Beach House Hotel and talk there."

His eyebrows lifted. "Something serious?"

"Something unexpected, but important to me."

He narrowed his eyebrows into a V and cast a suspicious look my way. "Something about The Beach House Hotel?"

Willing myself not to blurt out anything, I simply nodded. "As I said, we'll talk where we can have some privacy away from the house."

"Hmmm, doesn't sound good to me, but I'll play along."

My nerves did a foxtrot inside me. I was eager to please him, but the hotel had been part of my life before I'd met him, and I'd missed running it. If necessary, I'd fight him for the chance to go back to it.

After playing with Robbie in the pool, Vaughn took a shower and changed into casual clothes.

"Ready to go?" he asked, approaching me in a golf shirt and shorts that nicely showed off his buff body. In his early fifties, Vaughn kept himself trim for the show. "Thought maybe we could have a drink at the hotel before coming home for dinner. What do you say?"

"Sounds good," I responded. "Robbie will be fine with Elena and Troy."

"Troy pop the question yet?" Vaughn asked.

I shook my head. "We're all going to get after him if he doesn't do it soon. Poor Elena has been waiting for weeks to officially receive the engagement ring they selected together."

Chuckling, we went out to the pool area to say goodbye to the others, and then we climbed into Vaughn's silver sports car and headed for the hotel.

As Vaughn drove through the gilded, wrought-iron gates

onto the hotel property, I glanced to my right, at the little house I owned and now rented to the hotel. I loved that house. It had been such a source of pride to me to have my own place after Robert had robbed me of my home and my job. Rhonda's wish ... no, demand ... that I join her in converting her seaside estate into a small, boutique hotel had been my salvation. It had come with a ton of work, especially on my part, handling the finances and smaller details of setting up the hotel and running it.

I took a moment to study the hotel. Clad in pink stucco and with a red-tiled roof, the building extended along the shoreline like a lazy flamingo. Oversized, carved wooden doors stood guard at the top of wide, marble stairs. Potted palms sat next to the doors, balancing their height, softening their edges. Flowering hibiscus lined the front of the building, their bright blossoms a nice enhancement.

We came to a stop in the front, circular driveway and waited while a young man hurried to help me out of the car.

"It's still lovely, Ann," said Vaughn, gazing up at the building.

I remained silent. It was a beautiful place but without the polished look of welcome that Rhonda, our employees, and I had given to it.

"Welcome to The Beach House Hotel," the valet said in a bored tone of voice, holding the car door open for me.

Tears unexpectedly stung my eyes as I remembered how Rhonda and I used to run down the steps to greet our guests, our arms outstretched. I chided myself for being overly sentimental and got out of the car.

Vaughn handed over the keys and walked around the car to meet me. "Ready?"

I took his arm, and we climbed the front steps together.

Pausing in the front entry, I recalled the first time I'd seen it, when Liz and I had visited Rhonda and Angela on a Thanksgiving several years ago. It had seemed so elegant, so open, so welcoming.

"Hello. Can I help you with something?"

I smiled at the young man behind the desk who obviously didn't know who I was. Tim McFarland, Bernhard Bruner, and Jean-Luc Rodin, our former Front Office Manager, General Manager, and Chef, had either been fired or quit during the past year, leaving poorly trained staff behind who were inconsistent in providing continuing, professional service.

"No, thanks. We're going to take a walk along the beach before having a cocktail."

"Enjoy," the clerk said and picked up a phone that had started to ring.

I led Vaughn out onto the pool deck, doing my best to ignore the loud rock music, the pool packed with kids, and the gossipy tones of the mothers supposedly watching their children. I loved having families at the hotel, but the clientele that now came here to take advantage of hotel package deals were people who wouldn't tolerate or appreciate anything understated.

We left the pool area and walked onto the beach.

Stepping onto the soft, warm sand, I drew deep breaths in and out, reminding myself that, to convince Vaughn of the need to take over the hotel, I had to remain calm.

Vaughn grabbed hold of my hand, and we walked up to the edge of the water. Waves caressed our toes in gentle, cool laps that kissed the shore and pulled away. We closed our eyes and breathed in unison.

This ritual of allowing ourselves a peaceful moment with the sounds and feel of nature around us had begun shortly after we met and continued to be an act of bonding. We'd even used a scenario like this as part of our wedding ceremony.

Moments later, I opened my eyes and turned to Vaughn, my heart swelling. "I love you."

He grinned. "Love you more."

It was a game we liked, and by playing it, we both won.

As we headed down the beach, I splashed in and out of the water's frothy edge. It lay on the packed sand like spun lace wrapped around seashells both broken and whole, little treasures the Gulf had offered up. Seagulls continued to cry and whirl above us, white and gray bundles of feathers dancing in the air.

We'd gone about a mile when Vaughn stopped walking and turned to me. "Okay, I'm curious. What did you want to talk about, Ann?"

I faced him, my shoulders stiff with determination. "Rhonda and I want to buy back the hotel. Our contract states that we have only a couple more months when we can do that."

"But things have changed since you sold it," Vaughn said. "You both have husbands and responsibilities as mothers. And what about the freedom for you to travel with me?"

"We're distraught at seeing the hotel become ... ordinary. It's our baby, and now they're making it ugly. Besides, during the past two years, Rhonda and I have learned a lot about running a hotel on a larger scale with more staff, and I'm certain we can set things up in a way that gives us almost as much freedom as we have now."

"Aw, Ann, I know you want me to say 'go for it,' but I can't. Not yet. Give me some time to think it over. I know it's your decision, but I want things to be right between us. I want Robbie to have the mother he's had for the past two and a half years."

I stared out at the water moving back and forth

rhythmically as it had always done, as if telling me that my life should continue in the same steady pattern. Ellen, Vaughn's first wife, had been a model, stay-at-home mother. But that was over twenty years ago, and times had changed, roles had changed.

"What does Will have to say about this?" Vaughn asked. "I can't imagine he'd be happy about it. He loves having Rhonda at home with the kids."

"True," I said, "but she, like me, is unwilling to let our hotel go to ruin."

"I wouldn't say it's in ruins," protested Vaughn.

My sigh held back words of frustration. "Let's go have that drink you talked about. When you look around the hotel, I think you'll have a better understanding of what Rhonda and I need to do. We've already talked to Mike Torson about it."

Vaughn's eyebrows rose in an arch. "You have?"

Unwilling to back down, I nodded. "He'll handle everything for us. It won't be easy, but I'm willing to fight for it."

His brow creased with worry, he studied me. "Let's head back and go inside. We'll talk later."

I followed Vaughn into the hotel hoping he realized how serious Rhonda and I were about getting our baby back.

CHAPTER TWO

I rose early, tiptoed out of the bedroom, and let myself out of the house. Having private moments in early mornings like this was a good time to settle things in my mind. Last night, Vaughn and I had agreed not to ruin his homecoming by further discussing the matter of Rhonda's and my buying back the hotel. We'd agreed instead to talk about it this morning when we could have more facts and figures before us.

Breathing in the humid, late-September air, I walked down to the end of our sweeping lawn on the edge of an inlet of water that served as a small bay for the few houses that surrounded it. I sat down on our wooden dock and dangled my feet over the edge, listening to the water meet wood in rhythmic laps. The sun was rising in the sky, a yellow orb that would bring another day of early autumn heat. But for the moment, the warm air felt good on my skin.

My thoughts settled on Vaughn. Last night, our lovemaking, as always, had been a fabulous experience—sexy, fun, satisfying. I was so grateful for him. He'd brought love into my life and had made it possible to live in a warmhearted lifestyle I'd never thought possible. Was I selfish to want that and more? A troubled sigh escaped me.

"I thought I'd find you here," said a familiar voice, trying unsuccessfully to whisper.

Startled out of my reverie, I turned as Rhonda approached me.

Rhonda's bleached-blond hair was tied in a knot behind her head. Dark brown eyes full of intelligence and humor snapped happily at me. Though she'd lost some weight helping to take care of two toddlers, Rhonda still thought of herself as heavy and continued to wear colorful caftans as much as possible. Her language, too, was colorful and straightforward to the point of bluntness. Once people got used to this, her loving heart won them over.

"Have a seat," I said glumly.

Rhonda's brow furrowed. "Uh, oh. Things didn't go well with Vaughn?"

I lifted my shoulders and let them drop. "We decided to postpone any decisions on the issue until today. How did your talk with Will go?"

Rhonda groaned as she lowered herself onto the dock beside me and then gave me a devilish grin. "Well, I thought he was going to yell and scream about it, but I let the children loose on him when he got home. He loves it when they cling to him, ya know, but only if it isn't too much, if ya know what I mean. So, by the time the kids were in bed and we finally had a chance to discuss it, I think he felt sorry for me."

I felt a smile spread across my face. "And?"

"And as long as you and I finance it and arrange the running of it to allow time for our families, he said he'd go for it. We're lucky, Annie. We both have enough help in the home to make it work. Vaughn has to agree with that."

Fighting my worries, I nodded. "Yes, but it's more than that for Vaughn. He likes me to be with him in New York as often as I can. You and I both know if we buy back the hotel, my time with him in the city will be limited."

Rhonda put an arm around me. "We'll make it work, Annie. I promise."

Silently, I bobbed my head. I'd loved working with Rhonda, but in the past, I'd borne more than my share of the load, and I didn't think that would change.

"Ah, here's double trouble," said a deep, low voice that viewers across the country loved to listen to.

I looked up to see Vaughn heading toward us.

He took a seat on the other side of me from Rhonda. "Discussing the hotel?"

"Yeah," Rhonda said. "Will's on board. How about you?"

"Ann and I have yet to discuss it in depth." He studied me. "The decision isn't mine to make, is it?"

I shook my head. "But I want to make the right one for us."

He lifted my chin and kissed me on the lips. "Then choose what you want to do for you. Though it's inconvenient at times, you permit me to do what I want. I realize I need to do the same for you."

"Really? You don't mind?"

He cocked an eyebrow at me. "I didn't say that, but I'll go along with it as long as it doesn't destroy our family life. We have a great, little guy at home who needs you, a wedding coming up, and a couple of grandchildren on the way who will want to get to know you."

My relief came out in a long, happy sigh. I clasped my hands together and turned to Rhonda. "Okay, partner. Let's call Mike Torson. I think we ought to pull our old staff together again. What do you say, Rhonda?"

Her smile lit her face. "I say it's about frickin' time."

Vaughn and I laughed together. Rhonda was Rhonda, and we loved her.

I jumped up from my place on the dock and helped Rhonda to her feet. "Let's go!"

As we hurried toward the house, I looked back at Vaughn. He stood, watching us.

I lifted my hand in a little wave.

He smiled and waved back.

--ooo--

After placing the call to Mike Torson, I sat in my office and studied my business partner and best friend.

Raised by a straight-laced grandmother in Boston, I'd been shocked by my first meeting with Rhonda. Now I could laugh at the time Rhonda had told me that the black, one-piece bathing suit I was wearing made it seem as if I was going to a beach funeral. But back then, her bluntness had made me uncomfortable.

"Whatcha' grinnin' at, Annie?" Rhonda asked.

"Memories," I said, still smiling. "We've come a long way, baby!"

"You bet your ass! Now let's get our hotel back."

After Rhonda left, I went into the kitchen for a cup of hot coffee. Vaughn had already made Robbie his favorite breakfast—scrambled eggs and cinnamon toast.

"Get that call to Mike done?" he asked.

"Yes, we're all set to begin our fight." I poured myself a cup of coffee before taking a seat at the table opposite Vaughn. "I know we're right about doing this."

"I hope so," he said. "I have a feeling they won't easily give up the hotel. There's no other place like it in this part of Florida or anywhere else."

I reached across the table and gave his hand an affectionate squeeze. "Your support means a lot to me, Vaughn."

He grinned. "I know. I love you."

"Mommy?" said Robbie, watching us closely. "I love you too."

"Oh, honey," I said, rising and giving him a hug. "What would I do without my boys?"

"What about Trudy? She's a girl," said Robbie.

At the sound of her name, Trudy wagged her tail and gazed up at me with a hopeful look.

I patted her head. "I love her too. We girls have to stick together. Right, Trudy?" At my attention, her entire body seemed to wiggle.

"When are we going in the boat, Daddy?" Robbie asked, finishing the last of his toast.

I glanced at Vaughn.

"Thought we'd take a little sail around the inlet," he said. "Want to come?"

"Sure." It had become a ritual for us to sail together on at least one of the days that Vaughn was home. Vaughn had taught his older children, Nell and Ty, how to sail from an early age and delighted in teaching Robbie. "A good sailor makes a good man," he'd told me when he'd bought the boat with the house.

Outside, Robbie skipped ahead of us with excitement as we walked down to the water's edge. I couldn't help laughing at him. His yellow life jacket surrounded his body like a turtle's shell. Being with my family like this was one of my greatest joys.

The boat was a day sailer—simple to handle, a good way to learn how to use the wind to one's advantage. I'd never had the opportunity to sail as a kid and had grown to love the serene feeling of having the wind brush my skin as I settled back in the boat and lifted my face to the sky.

Moments later, I watched from the bow of the boat as Robbie, sitting next to Vaughn, handled the tiller. A sense of satisfaction filled me. We'd given Robbie a chance to experience many things in life that otherwise he might not have had the opportunity to do.

Vaughn looked over at me and grinned like a schoolboy with a few mischievous ideas. Being home with us, enjoying one of his favorite things to do, he became like a kid again.

As I enjoyed the lazy, autumn morning that would soon

give way to the heat of the day, I felt my shoulders relax and drew in a deep breath. Even the seagulls above us seemed to simply hover or glide through the air above us with spread wings that appeared too listless to flap.

"Ann?"

I opened my eyes and gazed at Vaughn.

"Remember my telling you that Lily Dorio might be brought into the show on a more permanent basis? It's a done deal. She starts filming with us next month as the mayor's new girlfriend. It was a last-minute decision to hire her due to the insistence of Roger Sloan. Some sort of payoff, if you ask me. Maybe for Lily allowing Roger and Darlene to adopt the little girl she and Roger had produced."

I swallowed hard, trying to stop the panic that filled me. Lily Dorio was an actress who'd once publicly accused Vaughn of fathering a child with her in an effort to hide her affair with Roger. Bad acting to say the least. I detested her—she was shallow, selfish, greedy, and not a little bit in love with my husband.

"You know it doesn't mean a thing to me, right?"

I swallowed my protest and nodded. Vaughn's question wasn't a casual one—it was a test of our faith in each other. Being in show business had its perks and its problems.

Vaughn covered Robbie's hand and helped him maneuver the boat to come about so we could head home.

As we approached the dock, Liz walked down to greet us. Looking at my daughter, I filled with pride. Tall, with long blond hair, blue eyes, and an athletic body, Liz was an attractive young woman. More than that, she was a kind person, a woman with brains who knew how to use them to make life better for herself and those around her. She'd always felt bad about turning Robbie over to us. When, at her father's request, she'd earlier signed a paper giving her custody of her brother in a crisis, she'd had no idea of what it really would mean to suddenly have the care of him when she, herself, was still in school. In addition, her father had left her with no financial ability to support a child.

"Hi, Lizzie!" cried Robbie, climbing out of the boat and onto the dock. "Daddy and I sailed the boat."

Liz gave Robbie a hug. "Good job! I saw you!" She smiled at me. "Have time for some girl talk?"

"Sure," I said, joining her and Robbie on the dock.

"Hold on, Robbie," said Vaughn from the boat. "You have to help me put things shipshape on the boat. That's part of a sailor's job."

Robbie's lips formed a pout.

I ruffled his hair. "Better listen to Daddy. He's right."

As Robbie turned away from us, I looped my arm through Liz's, and we walked up to the house, comfortable with each other.

In the kitchen, Liz slumped down into a wooden chair at the kitchen table.

"What's wrong?" I asked.

"This wedding is becoming a huge problem. Since I was little, I've always wanted a small, intimate wedding on Christmas Eve. I thought we were all set with it at The Beach House Hotel. Now they're giving me the runaround about the reception we wanted in the private dining room. I learned that Aubrey Lowell has canceled my reservation so he can hold his own private dinner there that night. And when I called the Ritz, they're booked for weeks before and after that date. What am I going to do?"

My lips pressed together with anger. How dare Bree Lowell do that to us! Liz was my daughter, and I still owned a percentage of the hotel. I forced myself to speak calmly. "Let's see what Rhonda and I can do about buying back the hotel. In the meantime, I'll do what I can to get that room for you."

Liz let out a sigh. "That's not all. With all the problems we've had trying to arrange the wedding, Chad and I have agreed to go ahead and just get married at the court house by a justice of the peace. We don't want to wait any longer. We've been together for two years. I love him, he loves me, and we both are ready to start a family. Nell and Clint have announced they're having a baby. Angela is trying for a second baby. And I'm not sure, but I think Ty and June are trying too. Where does that leave me?"

I reached over and squeezed Liz's hand. "You don't start a family because your best friend or a sibling might have one."

"Oh, Mom! I know that. But there are a lot of other things going on that lead me to want to go ahead with it. We've got Chad's computer business up and running along with his on-line store. Now it's time for us to do things as a family."

I studied her. She wasn't a foolish person—impatient maybe, but not foolish. I was heartsick that the people at The Beach House Hotel were ruining Liz's perfect wedding.

Liz rose and hugged me. "I think I'd feel differently if it weren't for all the complications trying to plan our wedding. It's made me think I don't even care if I do get married. Chad and I have already committed ourselves to one another."

Hiding my panic, I gazed into her eyes. "For many reasons, you need a wedding. What it's like and where it takes place doesn't matter as long as you are legally bound. But, Liz, we've both always wanted a nice ceremony for you."

"I'll hold off on doing a wedding elsewhere, but I'm not waiting for long." Liz leaned over and kissed me on the cheek. "Love you, Mom! I've gotta go. Chad and I are meeting up with Angela and Reggie."

I watched her go, so conflicted my hands knotted and loosened in a regular pattern. I couldn't blame everything on the management at the hotel, but I could damn well blame them for rocking my daughter's world. And mine.

When Vaughn and Robbie came into the kitchen, Vaughn took one look at me and said, "What's wrong?"

"Liz is being jerked around on the arrangements for her wedding at the hotel, and now she's decided that if she can't have the one she wants, she and Chad will forego a formal occasion and just get married at the courthouse. After all this planning, it breaks my heart. You know how it is with mothers and daughters and weddings. I'm sure Ellen was hoping to see her daughter married in a nice ceremony."

Vaughn's expression grew reflective. "Yes, that was a dream of hers. Cancer took that away."

"Nell's wedding to Clint was sweet, in part because of the tribute to Ellen," I said.

"And a tribute to you." Vaughn wrapped his arm around me and gazed down at me with such love my heart skipped a beat and then raced to catch up. Viewers of his television show weren't the only ones who thought he was sexy.

"Did you tell me that Robbie was going next door for a playdate?" he said, wiggling his eyebrows. "Maybe we could do ... something."

I laughed, knowing exactly what *something* meant. Playdates next door for Robbie were sometimes a very nice thing.

CHAPTER THREE

My time with Vaughn always sped by, and true to form, the weekend with him passed too quickly. After we dropped Robbie off at his preschool, I reluctantly drove Vaughn to the airport.

"It's hard to see you go back," I said, unable to hold back a sigh.

"Yes, but I'll make it up to you at Christmas when I'm taking a whole month off. If Liz decides not to have a wedding, perhaps we can do something different, go somewhere."

I smiled, but, inside, my heart was pounding. Holidays were busy times at the hotel. Surely, he understood that if Rhonda and I took back the hotel, I'd have almost no time to do all the things he wanted. Rather than bring it up, I let the subject drop, but my hands tightened on the steering wheel.

When I pulled up to the curb at the airport to drop Vaughn off, melancholy filled me. Our crazy life kept romance burning, but it made daily living hard. I turned to him, trying to hide my anguish.

Vaughn cupped my face in my hands and stared into my eyes. "I love you more than anything. And this business with Lily doesn't mean a thing. You know that, right?"

"Yes. I trust you to be faithful, just as you trust me. It's difficult at times because we both work in businesses that have many opportunities for us to stray."

A flicker of surprise crossed Vaughn's face and disappeared. "Yes, I guess you're right. You have opportunities in your business too."

As we smiled at each other, I closed my eyes, waiting for his warm lips to come down on mine.

With a tenderness I knew so well, Vaughn kissed me, deepening the kiss until I reached for him, wishing I'd never have to let go.

"Hurry along," said an officer, tapping on the window.

I reeled away from Vaughn and then laughed at the startled look on his face. "Guess you'd better go. Love you, honey."

He drew a deep breath. "Love you too."

He got out of the car, retrieved his suitcase from the trunk of the car, and gave me a little wave before he entered the airport terminal.

I drove away and headed for Rhonda's house. We were to meet there before going to Mike Torson's office for a strategy session. I couldn't wait to unload my story of Liz's frustration with the hotel and what it might mean for the future. We had to get control of the hotel soon. I wanted Christmas at The Beach House Hotel to be like it once was—with sparkling ornaments, warm candlelight, delicious food, and lots of love and laughter for our guests and us. And I wanted my daughter to be part of the Christmas excitement with the wedding she'd always planned.

Rhonda greeted me at the door holding Drew. At seventeen months, Andrew William Grayson was a darling, dark-haired, chubby little boy whose smile could bring you to your knees with adoration. A combination of Rhonda and Will, he was both easy-going and stubborn.

I held out my arms, and Drew happily came into them. I kissed his cheek and hugged him close. I'd missed the first two years of Robbie's life, but I wouldn't let time go by without giving Drew whatever attention I could.

Willow toddled over to us and clutched the edge of my skirt. Looking up at me with bright hazel eyes, she announced,

"Me want up. Not Drew."

Amused, I handed Drew back to Rhonda before lifting Willow into my embrace. She was a combination of both parents, but, with her light-brown hair and fine features, she looked more like Will than Rhonda. Her temperament, however, was definitely Rhonda's. I adored her.

"Come on in. Rita should be here shortly." Elena's sister, Rita Ramos, was as beloved a nanny in Rhonda's family as Elena was in mine.

"Have you spoken to Rita about our plans?" I asked, carrying Willow into the kitchen.

Rhonda shook her head. "Not yet. I didn't want to scare her off. If necessary, I can hire someone to help her. Two at this age is pretty tough on anyone."

Money, I knew, wasn't an issue for Rhonda. A few years before I met her, she'd won one hundred eighty-five million dollars in the state lottery. Most of it was tied up in trusts for family and some charitable trusts that Angela and Reggie were beginning to oversee under Will's tutelage.

We set the children down in the middle of the floor. I watched Willow give Drew a toy and then take it back.

Amid Drew's howls, Rhonda said, "Willow, let Drew have that toy. Then you can show Annie your new doll."

Willow dropped the toy onto Drew's head and turned to go. When Drew let out a cry, Willow turned back and, realizing what had happened, leaned over and gave him a kiss.

I couldn't help laughing. I understood why Rhonda sometimes called her life a circus.

After I oohed and aahed over the stuffed doll Willow showed me, Willow sat down and started playing with a couple of toys on the floor.

Rhonda poured me a cup of coffee. "What's up?"

I took a sip of the hot liquid and set the cup down on the

table. "You'll never believe what the hotel has done now. Bree has gone ahead and canceled Liz's reservation for the small dining room for her wedding because he wants to hold a private party there himself. When Liz couldn't work it out with the hotel, she even tried to book reservations at the Ritz."

"The Ritz?" Rhonda's eyes widened. "Oh my God! It's come to that?" She slammed a fist on the table. "How can they treat us and ours that way?"

Her shout scared Drew, who let out a howl and toddled to his mother. Willow ran over to them and tried to crawl into Rhonda's lap.

"Help!" said Rhonda.

I picked up Drew and hugged him to me. "It's all right," I crooned to him. "It's just those ... those ... jerks at the hotel who are making us mad. Not you."

At my quiet words, Drew stopped crying. I gazed over at Rhonda. She was holding Willow in her lap and singing softly to her.

My eyes widened. "Rhonda, I didn't know you could sing."

She smiled and shrugged. "Not that well, but Willow loves it and so do Drew and Evan. What a great, little grandson Evan is! He looks exactly like Reggie but, thank goodness, he has Angela's sweetness."

A laugh bubbled out of me. "Rhonda, who would have thought a few years ago that we'd end up with all these babies?"

"Yeah. I didn't think I'd ever get married again after Sal left me. But after you and I decided to turn my house into an exclusive, seaside hotel, and you introduced me to Will, my whole life changed. I still can't believe it sometimes, ya know?"

We exchanged affectionate smiles. We both were lucky, and we knew it.

Rita came bustling into the kitchen. "Sorry, Rhonda. Lots of traffic this morning."

Drew waved his arms with excitement and Willow jumped off her mother's lap and ran over to her. "Rita! Me!"

Rita laughed and picked her up for a kiss and turned to Drew, accepting him from me.

Rhonda checked the clock on the microwave. "We've got a few minutes before we have to leave for Mike's. Let's go upstairs so we can talk."

We climbed the stairs to the sitting room off the master bedroom. It was Rhonda's favorite room in the house. Overlooking the backyard and pool, the little balcony off the room reminded me of the rooms at The Beach House Hotel.

We sat facing each other. All the anger and frustration Rhonda had kept in control in front of the children burst out of her. "Those bastards are not going to get away with treating Liz that way. We'll fight them at every step. I'm sick of their nonsense."

My eyes grew moist. "All my life I've been dreaming of Liz's wedding. Ever since she was a little girl, we've talked about it. She's pretty resigned to giving up that dream, but I'm not. I want the wedding for her she's always dreamed of, with a pretty white dress, beautiful flowers, music, everything. You know?"

Rhonda nodded. "I finally got that with Angela, but I wasn't sure it was going to happen. And you have to admit that Reggie's parents didn't make it easy." A bright red color emerged from beneath Rhonda's tan. "Katherine Smythe and I will never get along—not after she had the nerve to think Angela was beneath Reggie."

I knew enough not to argue. Rhonda was one of the kindest, most generous people I knew. But if you crossed her or her family, she wasn't about to forget it.

"We'd better go," I said, checking my watch. "I don't want to be late for our appointment with Mike. We need to have him start on our project right away."

Rhonda gave me a steady look. "Annie, we're gonna work this out. We'll have our Christmas at The Beach House Hotel exactly like we want with Liz's wedding and everything. No one is going to stop us. Agreed?"

"Yes," I answered firmly, more determined than ever that the hotel would be ours again and would operate in a first-class manner as we'd always done.

Rhonda hefted herself to her feet. "Yeah, I can't believe we let ourselves think we couldn't run the hotel and have a family at the same time." Her expression grew troubled. "We can do it, can't we, Annie?"

"We can only try our best," I answered honestly. Other women had to juggle business and home. We could too.

Rhonda paced back and forth in a small conference room while we waited for Mike to appear. "The more I think about all the insults we've had to endure from the owners, the madder I get. I never want to be put in that position again," she grumbled.

"Me neither," I said, remembering the put-downs, the dismissal of our ideas. Now that I knew we had a chance to get the hotel back, I couldn't wait to run it again.

Mike entered the room. "Good morning, ladies. I have bad news."

"Bad news?" said Rhonda, looking aghast at him. "What are ya talkin' about?"

"You'd better sit down," Mike said, motioning us to seats at the conference table. Mike Torson was usually the picture of calm. Today he looked both hassled and furious.

My knees, which had turned to jelly, quickly folded as I collapsed in a chair. "Mike, what's wrong?"

"I just got off the phone with Aubrey Lowell. He made it clear he's taken over his father's position in the financial group for this project. He actually laughed when I informed him that we intend to go ahead and exercise our option to buy back the hotel. And then he told me he'd fight us all the way. Apparently, he's been working behind the scenes for some time on getting rid of the two of you. He says he's even started extensive research into both of your lives." Mike drew a deep breath. "I've never had to deal with someone as rude and vulgar in my life. And in this business, that's saying a lot."

"What do you mean 'extensive research into our lives'?" I asked, thinking of Vaughn and how Aubrey might try to harm his career. My stomach knotted so hard I could barely breathe. The whole story of Robbie might be told, destroying both my children. Feeling as if I might throw up, I covered my mouth with my hands.

"That little ..." said Rhonda. "He's nothing but a snot-nosed kid who thinks he has the right to treat us or anyone else this way."

"Can you talk to the others in the group?" I asked. "Maybe they will be more professional."

Mike looked at me and nodded. "I've got calls into the other two men. George Peabody and Samuel Logan will be reasonable, I'm sure, but this situation won't be easy. Among other things, Aubrey let it slip that they have big plans to make changes to the hotel by tearing down the garage and adding a two-story building to increase the number of available rooms. It seems they have made a friend of Brock Goodwin, who is the president of your Neighborhood Association."

Brock Goodwin? My jaw dropped.

Rhonda pounded the conference table with her fist. "That

bastard! I thought we'd gotten rid of him."

Mike's eyebrows rose. "You didn't know he was back on the board?"

"No, we didn't," I said in icy tones. "It can't be good. When we first opened the hotel, he tried everything to keep us from succeeding. We haven't heard from him in a long time. He had some financial problems, left the area, and rented his house out. I didn't realize he was back for good."

Rhonda leaned forward and spoke directly to Mike. "Are you willing to play hardball with him and the others?"

Mike, gentleman that he was, simply smiled. "Oh, yes. Dealing with people like Aubrey Lowell and Brock Goodwin is what gave me my nickname of 'Tyson.'"

I let out the breath I'd been holding. Now that Mike had introduced the idea of getting the hotel back, I wanted it more than ever.

"We agree then that you will go forward with your plan to buy back the hotel regardless of what it might take. Right?" Mike studied Rhonda and turned to me.

Rhonda and I exchanged looks of determination and then we both nodded.

"Let me be clear," said Mike. "You have the legal right to pursue this. No one can take that away from you, but they can make it difficult. I'll draw up papers today officially notifying them of your wish to proceed. We'll also lay out a timeline for the number of inspections we'll have to do on the property. These must be carried out in such a way as not to disturb the business. The owners may not make it easy, but I'll work with the more reasonable members of Peabody, Lowell, and Logan to make it happen."

"I think ya should know that Aubrey Lowell is also ruining Liz's wedding plans at the hotel," said Rhonda, her voice trembling with anger. "Liz booked the private dining room for

Christmas Eve, and now she's being told it's unavailable because Bree Lowell is hosting a private dinner there,"

"Yes." My voice caught. "Now, Liz thinks she might not even have a wedding."

"Sorry to hear that," said Mike, "but that's a separate issue—a painful one for sure. Can't you appeal to the hotel manager?"

"If Bernie were still there, it wouldn't be a problem," said Rhonda. "But after he was forced to leave, they brought in a friend of Bree's to run it. He's a Cornell grad, but still, he's young and influenced by his friend."

"Peabody, Lowell, and Logan is a well-respected company," said Mike. "I wonder what has happened with this particular property? I'll try to find out."

"What do we have to do?" I said, worried about Rhonda. She was trying to hold her temper in check, but I knew her well enough to understand she was ready to take action with or without Mike's advice.

"Give me time to get things set in motion and then we'll draw up a more-detailed plan. In the meantime, keep things on an even keel at the hotel." He gave Rhonda a steady look. "Can you do that?"

She looked at him and glanced away. "I ... I don't know."

"It will be to your benefit to do so," warned Mike. "Let's meet later this week. I'll have paperwork for you to sign."

He rose, indicating our meeting was over. "I'm sorry. This isn't what I envisioned at all."

Worried sick, I got to my feet. Taking back the hotel now seemed a risk I wasn't sure I wanted to take. Not if it hurt my family.

CHAPTER FOUR

Stonily quiet, Rhonda and I left Mike Torson's office.

I turned to her. "What are we going to do if they price us out of the market? I know we need to have more than one appraisal done, but, Rhonda, I can't ask Vaughn for money for our venture. Not when he doesn't want me to do this, and especially if something happens that hurts our family or Vaughn's career. And you know very well I won't accept money from you."

Rhonda put her hands on her ample hips and glared at me. "Annie, ya know I can handle whatever price we're forced to pay."

I shook my head. "We're not doing business that way. It's an equal partnership, remember?"

Rhonda clenched her hands into fists and stared up at the sky. "I'm so pissed about this whole thing. I swear, if that little pipsqueak tries to tangle with me, he won't forget it."

Just then, Rhonda's cell rang. She looked at caller ID and clicked on the call. Her whole tone changed. "Hi, sweetie! What's up?"

After listening for a few seconds, Rhonda's eyes widened. "Okay, Annie and I are on our way. Hold on. Stay calm." She ended the call and turned to me with a worried expression. "It's Angela. Evan has taken a tumble and is bleeding. She's crying like crazy, and so is he."

We rushed to my car and got in.

"Hurry, Annie!" said Rhonda, buckling herself into her seatbelt.

I quickly buckled my own, and we took off.

Angela and Reggie lived in a cute house in a nice, middle-class neighborhood full of families with children. Playmates for Evan and their future children was one reason they'd chosen it.

I had no sooner stopped the car in the driveway when Rhonda was out of the car and racing up the front walk. After parking, I hurried along after her.

Her face white, Angela met us at the door, holding her screaming toddler. Blood oozed from the kitchen towel she held to his head.

"Oh, honey. It's going to be all right," said Rhonda to Angela. "Let's go sit down, and Annie and I will take a look at it. He might need stitches."

In the kitchen, Angela, holding Evan, sank into a kitchen chair and carefully lifted the towel away from Evan's head. The wide gash indicated stitches would be required.

"How did it happen?" I asked.

"He was running away from me and fell on the corner of the coffee table in the living room. Is ... is he going to be all right?" Tears welled in Angela's eyes.

"He's going to be fine," said Rhonda, "but we'd better head to the hospital. I'll go with you, hon."

"Thanks, Mom. I don't know what I'd do without you. I try to be the best mother I can."

"All kids get hurt from time to time," Rhonda said in a soothing voice. "Grab your purse and let's go, honey."

"Do you want me to take you?" I asked.

"Better not," said Rhonda. "I know you have to pick up Robbie from school. You can't miss that."

I checked my watch and nodded. "Okay, call me, and let me know how you do with Evan."

Outside, I watched as Angela backed her SUV out of the

driveway with a roar of the engine.

After seeing them off, I slid behind the wheel of my car. I was a little early to pick up Robbie, but I didn't care; I was curious to know how his day had gone and didn't want to take a chance on being late.

By the time I arrived at the school, a stream of cars had already formed in the front circle. I pulled into the line and turned off the car's engine.

Sitting in the quiet interior of my car I thought about Angela's anguish at seeing her child hurt. Mothers hurt for their children, no matter the situation. I thought of Liz's disappointment about her wedding. It made me even more determined to do something about Aubrey Lowell.

I got out of the car and stood at the curb to wait for Robbie to appear. A teacher led a line of children outside and then stood by watching carefully as the children went to their mothers.

Robbie saw me, waved, and started toward me. My heart lifted, and I rushed to meet him.

"How was school?" I asked, kneeling to take him into my arms.

"Good. I liked snack time best."

I laughed. "Did you do your ABCs?"

"We did E's today," he said proudly.

I helped Robbie climb into the car onto his booster seat and buckle his seatbelt before settling behind the wheel. These short mornings would be the beginning of what I hoped would be good school years for him. Liz had always been a top, dedicated student. Robbie was bright and motivated at this age, but I'd heard all kinds of stories about girls and boys and how they reacted differently to school.

When we arrived home, Elena met us at the door. "Hello. How are you? How was school, Robbie?"

"Good. I'm hungry."

"Well, I've got lunch ready for you," Elena said, smiling. "Your favorite—a peanut butter and banana sandwich."

"Thanks, Elena," I said. "I'm going to eat lunch and then go to the hotel to check on a few things." I hadn't mentioned it to Rhonda, but I intended to talk to the manager about Liz's reservation for the private dining room.

After settling Robbie at the table, Elena and I hastily fixed ourselves small salads and ate in comfortable silence.

When I'd finished my meal, I rose, kissed Robbie goodbye, and left for the hotel to do battle for my daughter.

CHAPTER FIVE

As I drove through the gates of the hotel, I recalled how hard Rhonda and I had worked to convert the seaside estate into the small, exclusive hotel it became. We'd learned as we went—fighting Brock Goodwin and the Neighborhood Association, forcing Robert to make his required payments to me, and living life the best we could. Even now, I sometimes wondered how we'd done it. I gritted my teeth at the need to do it all over again, but we would. And this time, I vowed, we'd win big time.

I pulled up in front of the hotel and got out of the car as a young valet approached. I handed him the key fob. "I won't be long. Can you keep the car close by?"

He gave me a wide smile. "Sure, Ms. Sanders. For you, I'll do it." He leaned closer. "Mr. Lowell told me I could park only luxury cars like his Porsche in front, but not any others."

I didn't know if my Lexus SUV would meet Mr. Lowell's idea of luxury, but I was not having any of his nonsense. He'd been on site for only nine months, but ever since he'd come, acting as if he owned the hotel all by himself, things had gone wrong. "I'm not in favor of this new policy of his."

The valet looked away and then turned back to me with a worried look. "I shouldn't have said anything. Sorry."

"No, no, it's quite all right," I said, knowing it wasn't okay at all. Some of our nicest guests through the years did not drive luxury vehicles and never would.

Warning myself to rein in my irritation, I headed into the hotel. I had to make Stuart McPherson, the young manager

Bree had brought in to run the hotel under him, understand how important Liz's wedding was to me.

In the lobby, a couple was asking about the coupon they'd received in the mail. I stopped to listen.

"It says right here that we'd get a twenty-percent discount on the room if we stayed for three nights," said the man who looked to be in his early thirties.

The desk clerk looked at the piece of paper the man handed him. "I'm sorry, sir, but the date has expired on this. I can't accept it."

"But the manager said to come ahead, and he'd try to fix it for me," the man grumbled.

"I'm sorry, sir," the desk clerk repeated, glancing at me nervously. "You can go ahead and write to the manager to complain, but I'm not able to do anything about it."

"Maybe I can," I said, stepping forward. "Hello, I'm one of the owners here. I'm afraid there's been a misunderstanding. May I see the coupon?"

The man handed it to me. I stared at the colorful, printed card that appeared to be a personal invitation from Bree Lowell who'd also announced he owned and ran The Beach House Hotel. I'd never seen the coupon before and was quite certain the board would not approve of the wording on it. And, as the clerk stated, it was outdated. "Help me here. How did you get this card?"

The man smiled. "I'm a graduate of the hotel school at Cornell. Bree Lowell and I graduated together. I think he did this mailing to the entire class."

I felt my cheeks grow hot and drew a deep, calming breath. "We'll be glad to go ahead and honor this coupon," I said, forcing a pleasant smile at the same time my stomach knotted. "How was your stay?"

"Okay. I understand you're in transition, trying to making

it hipper, with a vibe like South Beach."

"Yes," said the woman with him. "It needs a little jazzing up with more rock music and that kind of thing."

Too appalled to answer her, I turned to the desk clerk. "Will you please take care of this?"

He nodded politely. "Yes, Ms. Sanders."

I quickly moved away before I blew my cool with angry words—words that would horrify the strict grandmother who'd raised me.

Outside the manager's office, I paused. Stuart McPherson was no Bernhard Bruner. Nice enough, he was relatively inexperienced and willing to follow every one of Bree's commands. After Bree came on board, Rhonda and I had tried to appeal to the other owners about having him here, but they were happy to have him "keep busy" at The Beach House Hotel so he wouldn't interrupt operations at the other properties in their group.

I knocked on the door, and hearing no answer, cracked the door open.

Stuart and Julie, one of our desk clerks, jumped apart, breaking up their passionate kiss.

"Sorry, I didn't know I'd interrupt something like this," I said, trying in vain to hold back my dismay at their breach of conduct.

Stuart straightened and gave me a sheepish look. "Yes, Ann? You needed to see me?"

I moved aside as Julie hurried out of the office, tucking in her Beach House Hotel blouse.

"Come on in," said Stuart. He took a seat behind his desk and gave me a frank stare as I sat down facing him.

"What can I help you with?" he asked, brushing his brown hair away from the face that looked an awful lot like Matt Damon.

"Some time ago, my daughter, Elizabeth, made wedding plans here at the hotel for Christmas Eve. It's a small, intimate wedding that was to take place in the garden with a reception in the private dining room. Now, she's being told she'll have to change her plans because Aubrey Lowell wants to use that room. You can understand my distress," I ended just as the door opened.

Bree came in. Tall, thin, blond, blue-eyed, and sure of himself, he walked with a swagger. Eying me with suspicion, he plopped down in the chair next to mine. "What are you distressed about now, Ann?" he asked in a tone that deserved a slap across the face.

"I understand you have canceled my daughter's use of the private dining room on Christmas Eve. That room reservation was made several months ago for her wedding reception. You can imagine how upset we all are about it."

Bree peered at me with a bored expression. "She can use the library. I told her that."

"You and I both know the settings are entirely different, that while the library might be suitable for a business dinner, it is not suitable for a wedding reception. I, as an owner of the hotel, am asking you both to honor that commitment."

Bree actually smirked at me. "You may be a minority owner of the hotel, but I'm part of a majority ownership. We'll have our wedding coordinator work with you on trying to make the library suitable for your daughter. Anything else?"

"As a matter of fact, there is. I was told you offered short-term parking at the circle only to owners of luxury cars."

Bree held up a hand to stop me. "All hotels do that."

"We're not like all hotels," I snapped. "We've treated each and every guest with respect. That's what has always made us so distinctive."

"It's also what has kept you from becoming the hippest

hotel on the Gulf Coast of Florida," Bree said. "We want a different kind of guest—a younger group."

I refused to give way to the sting of tears. It would only show Bree my weakness. Rising, I got to my feet.

"I can see that this conversation is going nowhere." I turned to Stuart. "Let it be on record that I requested the hotel to honor its commitment to my daughter."

He pulled at the collar of his shirt and nodded.

Neither man stood as I left the room.

I lay in bed reading a book when Vaughn called. "How's it going, hon?" he asked.

His low, sexy voice brought a momentary smile to my face, then it quickly disappeared.

"Not too well. Rhonda and I are going ahead with our decision to buy back the hotel, but Aubrey Lowell is a real problem. He wants to increase the size of the hotel, make it more suitable to a younger crowd, and has, in fact, already talked to Brock Goodwin about it."

"Brock Goodwin? That slime?"

"Yes, apparently, he's back in town and on the board of the Neighborhood Association once more. Bree wants to tear down the garage and make a new, bigger building with more guest rooms. He says Brock is agreeable to it. That, after all the B.S. he put Rhonda and me through."

"And does he mean to get rid of the other facilities as well as the apartments that Manny and Consuela and Troy once used?"

"Yes. But that's not the least of it. He wants the hotel to be hip like some of the hotels on South Beach in Miami. It makes me sick to think of it."

"Where are the other partners in all this?" Vaughn said.

"Mike is going to talk to them, but they dumped Bree here to keep him away from the other properties they own. I guess they already know how awful he is and don't want to have to deal with him. In the meantime, Mike told us Bree's been investigating Rhonda and me and our families to try to dissuade us from going ahead with our move to buy the hotel back. In fact, he did that to try to build a case to get us out of the business altogether. Sick, huh?"

"Very disturbing," Vaughn quickly agreed. "I would hate for his actions to hurt the kids, even though the three oldest have had to learn to handle bad publicity caused by rumors about me in my job." He paused. "Speaking of rumors, they've already started about Lily and me. With some of the acting we're required to do, I'm sure they won't go away anytime soon. Sorry about that, Ann, but you know that's all they are—rumors."

"Yes," I said, but I hated the false stories irresponsible newspapers and magazines published. I was a private person by nature.

"So, how is the filming going?" I asked.

"It's going. Lily wants to redo scene after scene, trying to get it better. I'm not happy about having to do it, but I've been cooperating."

"What kind of scenes?" I teased.

"Uh, the typical ones for this pair," Vaughn said, and I could tell he was uncomfortable.

I didn't dare complain. After all, I was about to become tied to the hotel once more. If, and it was a big IF, Rhonda and I could wrest the hotel away from the investment group.

"Ann?"

"Hmmm."

"What are you wearing?" His voice was soft, sexy.

I laughed, loving the games we sometimes played. The only

trouble was, I'd have to make up an answer. With him away, I was wearing a pair of comfy pajamas, not the kind of sexy nightgown he liked to see me in.

CHAPTER SIX

At the end of the week, Rhonda and I sat in Mike Torson's office trying to keep ourselves calm. Mike explained that the owners' management company overseeing The Beach House Hotel, which was currently being run by Bree, had come back to him with a list of requirements for us to follow when doing our due diligence for the takeover.

"How are we going to keep to the hours they want?" said Rhonda. "I can't be at the hotel at all times of night. I've got a family to take care of."

Mike gave her a sharp look. "That's the point. They're hoping you'd take that position and then use it against you."

"I assume these are points of negotiation, right?" I said, disgusted by the turn of events.

Mike nodded. "Of course, but I think we'd better plan our response carefully so that while we might lose a few battles, we'll win the war. We want to take control as quickly as possible, right?"

"Fuckin' right," murmured Rhonda, sitting back in her chair with a ferocious glare. "I'm tired of all their B. S."

I reached over and patted her shoulder. "Don't worry; we'll do this."

"Will told me we'd better get hold of the financials." She gave me a worried look. "He doesn't trust these people since Bree brought in his new manager."

"You get monthly reports, don't you?" Mike said.

"Yeah, but according to Will, we need more than that," said Rhonda. "Can you help us get them?"

"Yes," said Mike, letting out a long breath. "Let's give them pretty much what they wanted for inspections and add this request to our list. Unless something is wrong, they shouldn't be unwilling to give us complete access to the financials. As minority owners, you're due that anyway."

As we discussed other strategies, my thoughts returned to the dilemma with Liz's Christmas wedding.

"What is it, Ann?" Mike asked me.

I told him of my meeting with Stuart and Bree regarding the private dining room. "We had everything planned. It was going to be the sweet, small wedding Liz has always wanted. Now, its ruined. I know others may laugh, thinking one room is as good as another. But you don't know Liz. She's no bridezilla, but like every other bride, she wants her day to be perfect. And so do I."

"This is the kind of thing they don't care about," said Rhonda. "I could wring their frickin' necks for the way they talked to Annie. How can someone like Bree be allowed to act like this?"

Mike gave us a steady look. "I've not been able to get in touch with George Peabody, but Samuel Logan confessed to me that the idea of the investors was to send Bree to one of the smaller properties for training and to keep him out of the way. His father is the one who pushed Bree into the group, telling the others that Bree would be taking over for him. I gathered from Logan's tone that he wasn't altogether pleased about it."

"Can't he get Bree away from us?" Rhonda said. "The kid is nothing but a little brat!"

"I wish it were that easy," said Mike. "Let's go forward with our plan. Between the two of you, work out a schedule for the due diligence portion, and I'll work on getting a deep dive into the books."

"Okay," said Rhonda, "but if he gives us any more trouble,

he's going to be sorry. And for the record, I don't like the idea of Bree and Brock Goodwin working together on approvals for expanding the hotel."

Mike and I exchanged worried looks. We both knew that nobody crossed Rhonda and got away with it.

Rhonda and I spent the rest of the morning at my house laying out our plans for the takeover process.

I agreed to do a lot of inspections during the off-hours when Robbie would safely be asleep under Elena's supervision. It was the logical answer. Elena was easily able to spend the night whenever Vaughn was in New York, but her sister, Rita, was unable to stay nights with Rhonda because of commitments to her own family.

"We'd better call Bill Richardson and get him and his engineering company lined up to do the inspections," said Rhonda.

She lifted her cell phone and punched in his number.

As we waited for him to answer, she whispered, "He and Will have played golf together quite a bit recently. I'm sure he'll help us."

She straightened. "Hi, Bill? This is Rhonda Grayson. My business partner, Ann, and I have an important project for you. We need you to perform a series of inspections on our hotel."

I watched Rhonda's eyes widen and the way her lips narrowed. *Trouble.*

"And when did you get this message from Aubrey Lowell?" she asked in a deceptively calm voice. "Oh? Well then, since you haven't responded to his similar request, you can do the job for us. Right, Bill?"

Anyone with any sense would understand that choice

wasn't an option—not in this town where Rhonda was known and loved by all.

A smile crossed Rhonda's face. "I'm so glad you see it that way, Bill. This is an important case for us, personally, and for the town as a whole. Things have been quite different at the hotel since Annie and I left the daily operation."

As she listened to his response, Rhonda's expression grew grim. "I'll have Mike Torson email you a contract right away to avoid any confusion."

While she and Bill continued to talk, I quickly called Will. Reggie answered the call.

"Hi, Ann, how are you?"

"Fine," I answered automatically, knowing I wasn't fine at all. We needed to move fast to keep ahead of Bree and his cronies. "Can you put Will on the line? I'd like to talk to both of you."

"Sure, hold on." Moments later, Will came onto the conference call. "Hi, Ann. What's going on?"

"We need to have someone look over the financials for the hotel to check for irregularities."

"We can do that for you," said Reggie with an eagerness I found touching.

"Yes, but in addition to us, you'll need a neutral auditor to come in and make a thorough exam of the books," said Will. "Ann, are you sure you want to do this hotel thing? Buying back the hotel means a sacrifice to your family."

I kept my voice light. "Remember when I introduced you to Rhonda? You knew then how committed we were to the project. You even encouraged us."

In the following moment of silence, Reggie spoke up. "I'll hang up now. Talk to you later, Ann."

Grateful for the privacy, I again spoke to Will. "Rhonda loves you and the kids, but she deserves a chance to do something she loves, something we both love."

"I'll find an auditor for you," Will answered crisply. "Talk to you later, Ann."

"Goodbye, Will," I responded, ending the call.

Rhonda bit her lip, drew in a breath and then let out a long sigh. "Bet Will didn't like you talking to him like that."

"He was pretty quiet," I admitted.

"He and I got into it last night. I asked him to get a vasectomy, and he freaked."

"You did what?"

"You heard me. I've gone through all sorts of stuff with my body, why can't he take care of this? I don't want to get pregnant again." She shook her head. "Honest to God! You'd think I'd asked him to cut off his dick."

"Some men are sensitive about things like that," I said, trying to calm her.

But she was having none of it. Her cheeks turned a bright pink. "Since the birth of our kids, he's been strutting around like a rooster. All I'm asking is for him to stop being able to get me pregnant. He can crow all he wants about anything else, but I'm done having kids." Tears moistened her eyes. "I want my hotel baby back."

"Me too," I said, hoping I hadn't interfered in her battle with Will. "Will has agreed to go ahead and find a neutral auditor for us. That's a step in the right direction."

"Yeah? Well, if he thinks he's going to sweet-talk me into anything, he's got another think coming." She paused and her lips curved. "But he sure can be sweet sometimes. Honestly, you'd think we were teenagers the way we are in bed. He ..."

I held up my hand. "Stop! TMI!"

A sheepish grin creased her face. "Yeah, I guess you're right. Too much information."

I laughed. Rhonda and Will had always been adorable

together. She'd fallen for him the first time she met him when he'd come to The Beach House before we'd even opened it to the public.

She faced me with a look of concern. "How does Vaughn feel about all of this? I know you said he was okay with it, but is he, really?"

"He's worried about any repercussions to the family," I confessed, "but he knows it's unfair to hold me back, especially now that he's working with Lily Dorio."

Rhonda pulled a face. "I have to tell ya, I don't like the idea of him working with Lily on the show. She's such a whore, and I've always thought she was in love with him."

A shiver, like the imprint of a thousand spider legs, crossed my shoulder. Lily was everything I was not. Her bodacious body, her New York style, the way she constantly flattered Vaughn were all things I couldn't compete against.

Rhonda grabbed hold of my hand. "Oh, Annie, I'm sorry. I didn't mean to make you worry. Vaughn loves you. You know that."

I nodded, but inside, my old insecurities kicked up a cloud of doubt.

"Is Bill going to go ahead and handle the inspections on the hotel?" I asked.

Rhonda nodded. "But, Annie, we're going to have to watch Bree. He's trying hard to make things difficult for us already. I told Bill I'd have Mike send a contract right over, so there's no question about who he's working for." A sigh escaped Rhonda's lips. "I've got to get home. I'll call Mike and talk to you later."

After Rhonda left, I decided to phone Vaughn. I didn't call him often, but usually waited for him to call me when he was free. Now, I wanted to hear his reassuring voice.

After punching in his number, I waited for him to pick up.

After several rings, his voice message came on. "Hello, you've reached Vaughn Sanders. Please leave me a message, and I may or may not be able to get back to you." Those of us who knew him understood the message. We carefully guarded his cell number, but sometimes unwanted callers left messages that he had no intention of returning.

"Hi, darling. Just wanted to hear your voice," I said and hung up.

Moments later, Vaughn called. "I heard your distinctive ring on my phone. What's up?"

Feeling a little self-conscious, I stuttered, "I ... I just wanted to hear your voice. How are things going?"

"Not as well as I'd hoped. Not sure I can make it home this weekend," he answered with a hint of irritation in his voice.

I worked to hide my disappointment. With the way things were up in the air regarding the hotel and knowing he was working with Lily, I needed his presence. "I hope you can. You know how much we all love having you at home."

"Yeah, I do. Look, I've gotta go. Love you, Ann." He clicked off the call.

I lay the phone down on the granite kitchen counter and stared out at the inlet. Maybe, I thought, a stroll on the beach would help.

Checking the clock, I saw that I'd have time for a short walk before picking up Robbie at preschool. That was one task I was unwilling to share with Elena. Someday, I'd be forced to give it up, but for now, I wanted to be the one he saw when he got out of school.

Rather than go to the hotel where I might be caught up in emotions I wanted to avoid, I drove to a small, public access to the beach not far from the hotel and stepped out of the car.

The salty tang of the onshore breeze caressed my cheeks like a loving hand. I felt the muscles in my face relax. The ties between Vaughn and me were strong, and, surely, Rhonda and I would somehow be able to carry off the purchase of the hotel and keep things steady at home. We could have it all, couldn't we?

I slipped off my sandals and wiggled my toes in the sand, then lifted my face to the hot, bright sun and drew in a deep breath. Feeling better already, I headed down the beach.

Little sandpipers scurried across the sand at the edge of the water where frothy remnants from the waves made patterns on the hard-packed sand like magical spider webs. Watching the small flock of birds hurry into the world ahead of me, I told myself to be as trusting as they.

"Ann! Wait up!"

I turned and let out a long sigh as Brock Goodwin approached me.

A tall, striking man with gray hair and green eyes, he looked a little heavier than when I'd last seen him. As he drew near, I could see new lines creasing his forehead and suspected not all of his financial troubles were over.

His gaze traveled over me, settling on the curve of the T-shirt I wore with my shorts. He'd always been a slime.

He leaned down as if to give me a kiss.

I quickly stepped back. "Hello, Brock. How are you? It's been what? Two years?"

His leering smile evaporated. "Yes, but I'm back now. My new business is better than ever."

"Apparently, your new business includes trying to do some sort of deal with the owners and managers of The Beach House Hotel. Bree Lowell and you working together? What's going on?"

"I met him at one of the parties I'm always invited to, and

he and I got to talking. We've agreed on a number of things and have decided to work together on making some changes to the hotel." He gave me a challenging look. "Any problem with that?"

"As a matter of fact, I'm curious about the change in attitude. You did everything you could to keep Rhonda and me from going ahead with our hotel project. And even after it was underway, you tried your best to interfere."

"Ah, Ann, you're not going to continue to hold that against me, arc you?"

"Why the change, Brock?"

He gave me a condescending look that caused me to press my lips together. "Let's just say I like the idea of young, sharp businessmen running a place like The Beach House Hotel in my neighborhood. It gives me and others a sense of comfort that things will be done properly."

His words cut deep inside me. "I see you haven't changed a bit," I said in measured tones, moving away from him.

"Ann?" he called to me. "You haven't changed either. Be careful. Your pansy, soap-opera husband may not be able to control your actions, but I can and will."

I stopped and faced him, emitting a snort of disgust. I couldn't help myself. "That's ridiculous. He's more of a man than you'll ever be." Though I wanted to claw his face with my nails, I turned around and kept walking, determined not to show his effect on me.

With my time on the beach ruined, I headed back to my car.

In my car, I was still seething as I relayed the details of my meeting with Brock to Rhonda.

"What a fucking jerk," she muttered into the phone. "If he tries to interfere with us again, I'm going to make sure that that smooth-talking liar is going to suffer like he never has before. I still have a lot of friends who'd like to see him disappear for good. In fact, I'm going to call Dorothy now."

"Good idea," I said, checking the time. "We'll talk later. I have to pick up Robbie from school."

As I drove through town, I thought of Dorothy Stern. A woman in her sixties, bright and bored with retirement, she'd been our first office worker. Loyal to us and still very active, she was working part-time for Will. More importantly, she still had enough friends in the neighborhood to counter most of Brock Goodwin's attacks on us. No doubt about it, we needed her to help us.

I pulled into the line of cars waiting for school dismissal and got out. The woman in the car behind me climbed out of her car and walked over to me. Cyndi Brigham was my next-door neighbor and, more importantly to Robbie, Brett's mother. A redhead with pretty green eyes, Cyndi was young, full of energy, and unfazed by the fact that she was a quite a few pounds overweight. I loved her. Her honesty and her joy in life affected everyone around her. More than once, I'd received a dash of insight along with a nice cup of coffee.

"Hey, Ann! How are you doing?"

"Frankly, I'm still a bit irritated by my encounter with Brock Goodwin."

"Brock Goodwin would irritate anyone. But I notice that since he's back in town, he's back into his old routine of schmoozing everyone in our neighborhood and being the extra man every hostess likes to invite to her party."

"He's smooth all right ... until you get to know him. He's been nothing but a problem to Rhonda and me over the hotel."

Cyndi gave me a steady look. "I wasn't going to say anything to you, but I can't hold back. Charlie and I had dinner at The Beach House Hotel last night, and the service and food have gone down even more. I know you've been concerned about it, so I thought you should know."

I bit back one of Rhonda's favorite words. "Rhonda and I are working to make some changes." I wished I could tell her the whole story, but, of course, I couldn't. It might jeopardize the whole takeback.

We both looked up to see our boys waving at us.

I swung Robbie up into my arms and inhaled the scent of him, well aware I wouldn't have many opportunities to do so as he grew older. "How was school?"

"Good. I got a gold star. See?" Robbie held out his hand to me. A shiny gold sticker was placed on the back of it.

"Nice. How did you earn your star?"

"For cleaning up my cubby," Robbie said proudly.

"I got one too, Ms. Ann," said Brett, holding up his hand to show me.

"Good job. Maybe we should celebrate," I ventured, waiting to say more until receiving a nod of approval from Cyndi.

"Sure," said Cyndi. "Let's go to J.R.'s for lunch."

We smiled at each other. J.R.'s had great kids' meals and yummy salads. More than that, it would be a time for Cyndi and me to talk.

CHAPTER SEVEN

Following lunch with Cyndi and Brett, Robbie and I dropped into Liz's office down the street to say hello. Robbie loved his big sister, so, when he asked to see her, I quickly said yes.

Chad's small storefront on Palm Avenue displayed computers and a variety of computer games. Strategically placed between two of the busiest clothing stores on the street, it was a magnet to men waiting for their wives to shop.

When we entered the store, three men were browsing the various displays. Chad was demonstrating one of the games to another. Tall, with strawberry-blond hair and startling blue eyes, Chad would, I thought, make a marvelous poster boy for any Florida tourism campaign. His easy-going manner was as attractive as his looks. I'd always liked him. He was still managing the computers for the hotel.

Chad saw us enter the store, and out went his arms to Robbie, who sprinted toward him.

"Hi, where's Liz?" I asked.

A frown momentarily crossed Chad's face. "She's in the back room."

I found Liz sitting in the cubicle she used for office work, her back to me.

"Hi, sweetheart!" I said, approaching her.

When she swiveled around in her chair, I saw that her eyes were red-rimmed and teary.

"What's the matter?" I asked.

"Everything," she said, dabbing at her eyes with a tissue.

My heartbeat sputtered. I lowered myself into the chair next to her desk and patted her hand. "Better tell me."

"Chad's mother was furious when we told her we weren't sure about going ahead with a formal wedding. She's been working with the choir director at her church, writing a wedding song for us. She blamed this new idea all on me, though Chad was the one who suggested it."

Aware that Sadie Bowen was a well-respected talent in the community, I could well imagine how important this wedding and her song would be to her. I forced myself to maintain a neutral expression as I awaited more information.

Liz drew a deep breath and slowly let it out. "I thought Chad would defend me against his mother. Now I'm not even sure I want to marry him. And none of this would have happened if things hadn't gotten messed up with the hotel."

"But I thought you loved each other," I said, hiding my panic. *Was this a bridezilla thing or something far worse?*

"I want to come home and stay with you for a while to straighten out my head," said Liz, ignoring the tears that made silvery tracks down her cheeks.

I gave her a steady look. "I'm not sure that's such a good idea. You two need to stick together and work things out. If you can't do it now, you'll never be able to deal with life as a married couple and, later, as parents."

"But, Mom!" she wailed.

On legs gone wobbly, I rose and put my arms around her. "I love you, Liz, but I don't want you to come home. I want you to work this out with Chad and, if necessary, talk to a marriage counselor. Life is going to throw you more problems than the hotel has. Believe me, I'm furious with the way they've treated you, but let's take it one day at a time. And then, if that doesn't work, you can always come home. Okay?"

Liz nodded, her blue eyes shimmering with tears. "I do love

Chad, Mom; it's just that I've become so emotional over this whole wedding thing that I sometimes can't handle it."

"I understand, but I think you and Chad need to talk over the situation, including his defending you with his mother. He's a good guy, Liz, who's still learning. Don't give up on him or having the wedding you've always wanted at the hotel. Rhonda and I are quite a team, and we're determined to win."

A smile crept across Liz's face. "Yeah, you two are the best together."

"Mommy? Where are you?" came Robbie's voice.

Liz and I looked up as Robbie rushed into the room. When he saw Liz, he ran over to her. "Lizzie? Why are you crying?"

"It's okay. I'm better now." Liz drew him into her arms and hugged him tight.

Observing them, I wondered if some of Liz's rush to be married and have children was over guilt for not being able to take responsibility for Robbie when his parents died. A thread of annoyance wove through me when I thought of what my ex-husband had carelessly done without thinking it through. It had all worked out in the end, but the impossible situation had left Liz with so many doubts about herself.

Chad came into the back room and went over to Liz and Robbie. Robbie squirmed to get down. Chad placed a hand on Liz's shoulder and looked down at her with such tenderness that my doubts about him eased. He was a good man who was facing some heavy decisions with the daughter I treasured.

I took Robbie's hand. "C'mon, buddy. Let's go home."

As we walked out of the room, I heard murmuring behind me and prayed Liz and Chad would be able to work things out.

I'd just put Robbie down for the night when I heard a car drive up to the house. Concerned, I looked out the front window. Had Liz decided not to heed my advice?

At the sight of Vaughn getting out of a cab, my worries fled. I hurried to the front door to greet him. "Welcome home! What a nice surprise!"

A huge grin split his face as he strode up the front walk to meet me, small suitcase in hand. As I raced toward him, he dropped his suitcase on the ground and opened his arms.

I ran into them.

His lips came down on mine, creating a familiar tug of desire inside me. When we pulled apart, he studied my face a moment and then caressed my cheeks with his hands. "I love you, Ann. I always will."

His intensity sent a frisson of alarm through me. "What's going on?"

He sighed and picked up his suitcase. "Let's go inside."

I followed him into the house and into our bedroom. He set the suitcase down in his closet and turned to me. "Have you been watching the show?"

"No, I'm sorry. I've had to tape it because that's when I pick Robbie up from school."

His nostrils flared. "It's Lily. She's overacting her part, and there's little I can do about it when the camera is on us. The director loves it."

I frowned. "What aren't you telling me?"

He sank down on the bed and stared up at me with a troubled expression. "The studio is doing a whole advertising campaign around the theme of two real lovers back together again. I told them how opposed I was to it. I even called my agent and tried to get out of the contract, but advertising provisions are out of my hands."

I staggered back, so shaken I felt sick. "So, the whole world is now going to believe that lie about you and Lily and the baby?" Tears sprang to my eyes. "And everyone will believe that you and Lily are lovers again?" I clenched my fists. "Why would they do this? Surely, they know how hurtful this is to our family."

"It's not quite as simple as that. I had a shouting match with Roger, threatened to quit the show and everything, but the numbers for the show are way up, and that's what matters to them." Vaughn stood and took me into his arms. "I'm sorry, honey, I really am. I know how private you are, how difficult these things can be. And I'm not giving up the fight."

As I settled my head on his chest, my thoughts pulled back in time to when we were first dating. I'd been troubled by my being in the spotlight because of Vaughn's work. I'd loved him enough then to work through it. I could do it all over again, couldn't I?

Vaughn lifted my chin. "Sweetheart, have faith in me. I would never carry on an affair with anyone else. You know that."

Hearing the anguish in his voice, I nodded and straightened. "Yes, Vaughn, I do. We'll handle this together, though I suppose we'll both be questioned by the sleaziest publications."

Vaughn smiled down at me. "That's my girl."

At his words, Trudy trotted into the bedroom and greeted Vaughn with a welcoming yip, demanding to be petted.

Vaughn bent over and rubbed her ears. "You're my other girl, Trudy."

She gave him a doggy smile and rolled over for a tummy rub.

Vaughn laughed and did as she asked. When he straightened, the creases that had marred his brow had eased a bit. "I knew I was right to come home. This is where I want to be—with you and our family."

"C'mon, let's go into the kitchen. How about a cup of coffee or a glass of wine?"

"Wine sounds good," Vaughn said. "It's been a hell of a day."

I poured two glasses of wine, and we took them out by the pool.

Vaughn stretched out in one of the chaise lounges. "Anything new here?"

"Liz and Chad are going through a difficult time." I set down my glass of wine on a table and made myself comfortable in a chair beside him. "I'm not sure what's going on with Liz. She's not herself. She even wanted to come and stay here for a while. I told her I didn't think it was a good idea, not until she and Chad had resolved issues concerning the wedding. Chad's mother is furious that they might not have a formal wedding. She's been writing a wedding song for them."

Vaughn's look of concern was broken by a smile. "Sadie Bowen is a performer all right. No wonder she was upset. But, seriously, do you want me to talk with Liz? She's always been straight up with me."

"That would be wonderful," I said. "I think she needs to hear advice from someone other than her mother."

"Okay, I'll talk to her tomorrow."

I lay back and gazed up at the stars that shone in the ebony sky like little sparks of hope.

He turned to me with a lazy grin. "Feel better?"

I smiled. "Yes. It's good to have you home."

He reached out and wrapped his fingers around my hand. "Home is where I get my grounding. You give me that."

We gazed at each other with such compassion I knew that no matter what came our way, Vaughn and I would be all right.

The wind picked up. The rustling of palm fronds in the

palm trees edging our property seemed like a gentle song. When I turned to Vaughn, I saw the question in his eyes and smiled.

"Shall we go inside?" I said.

He jumped to his feet. "Good idea."

Naked, I lay beside Vaughn reveling in the way his lovemaking always made me feel—loved, pampered, fulfilled.

He pulled me up against him, spooning his body around mine. "Never can get enough of you. Don't know why you keep talking about being raised by a straight-laced grandmother. You're not that way at all, you little minx."

I laughed and rolled over to face him. Sex with Robert had never been this fulfilling. Vaughn had urged me to become a woman open to enjoying what we could do to make each other happy in bed. I'd always be grateful to him for it.

I felt his renewed arousal against my skin and welcomed the chance to play some more.

"Ahhh," he sighed. "Home is where I want to be—with you."

I smiled and lifted my lips to his.

I awoke and stretched like a lazy cat, feeling wonderfully alive. I turned to the pillow Vaughn had recently used and brought it to me for a hug. No doubt Vaughn was with Robbie. When he was home, Vaughn liked to get up before anyone else to share early morning time with his son. Thinking of them together, I smiled. Vaughn was such a sweet man—so eager to take in Robbie, my ex-husband's son. Not many men would be so generous. At first, I'd struggled with the idea myself.

I padded into the bathroom and took a long shower,

content that my family was together for at least another couple of days.

After dressing, I went into the kitchen to get a cup of coffee. I poured myself some and stood at the kitchen window staring out at Vaughn and Robbie. They were sitting on the edge of the pool talking. Robbie was a serious child who adored Vaughn. His expression as he looked up at Vaughn was filled with adoration. As I'd thought many times, our sweet little Robbie was a lucky little boy.

On a whim, I decided to invite Liz for breakfast. Though I didn't want her to come live with us because she wasn't willing to deal with issues in her relationship with Chad, I always wanted her to feel welcome here.

Liz answered on the second ring. "H-hello?"

"Hi, sweetheart! How are you? Vaughn's here, and I thought you might like to join us for breakfast."

"Vaughn's in town? Oh, yes. I need to talk to him."

"Great. Come right along." I hung up satisfied. Liz had always been able to have conversations with Vaughn without fearing judgment, and the timing couldn't be better.

I walked outside to check on the guys.

"Mommy, look what Daddy and I can do," said Robbie.

Vaughn got into the water and sunk down in it. Holding onto Robbie's hands, he helped Robbie stand on his shoulders. Then, wading to a deeper part of the pool, Vaughn let go of Robbie's hands so Robbie could jump in.

"Bravo!" I said to Robbie when he surfaced out of the water.

Robbie grinned and gave me a thumbs-up.

Vaughn swam over to the side of the pool where I stood. "Thought you might want to take a swim. Guess it's too late."

"Liz is coming over for breakfast. She's happy you're here and wants to talk to you. I have a feeling it's about the wedding thing. Hope you don't mind."

Vaughn hoisted himself out of the pool and got to his feet. "Not at all. I've been doing some thinking about what you said and will be glad to talk to her about the situation. She's a lot like my Nell, you know. And not just in appearance."

I smiled. Liz and Vaughn's daughter, Nell, looked so much alike I'd been startled when I first met her.

Vaughn went inside to get dressed, and I took Robbie to his room to get his clothes out for the day. It being a Saturday, there was no school, and Elena had the day off.

As I helped Robbie slip a T-shirt over his head, Trudy started barking, and I realized it must be Liz.

I hurried to greet her and stopped, astonished to find Rhonda entering the kitchen.

"Hi, there!" I said, unable to hold back my surprise. "Good to see you so early in the morning. What's up?"

An impish grin crossed Rhonda's face. "I have the best son-in-law in the world," she announced, waving a piece of paper in her hand.

"Oh?" Reggie Smythe hadn't been a favorite of Rhonda's in the beginning. She still didn't like his parents.

"Yeah. Will gave Reggie the job of looking over the financials for the hotel, and Reggie's pointed out a few things that add up to a lot of fudging of figures. He's just getting started, but he wanted me to know about it. And even though we're hiring auditors who are not connected to us in any way, Reggie is going to continue his own investigation."

"What has he found so far?" I asked, feeling a new sense of concern.

"He thinks those frickin' asses have been overpaying themselves for the management fee. And that might be just the beginning. He's going to look into everything." She shot me a triumphant look. "How do ya like them apples, huh?"

"I do, and I don't," I said. "If they're doing something like this, what else are we going to find when the inspections begin?"

"I'm not sure. But I've already signed the contract with the Richardson Company. Now I can't wait to get started. Even better, I can't wait to tell those guys to fuck off!" Rhonda let out a raucous laugh that was contagious.

"God! That will feel so good," I said, chuckling with her.

"What's going to feel good?" asked Vaughn coming into the kitchen.

"Telling those guys at the hotel to ..." Rhonda noticed Robbie quietly watching us. "... To go away. Right, Robbie?"

Robbie grinned. "Yeah, fuck off."

"Oh, honey," I said, ruffling Robbie's hair. "That's a grown-up word. Let's use a different word instead. How about take off?"

Robbie studied me, glanced at Rhonda, and then nodded solemnly. "Take off."

"I'm sorry," said Rhonda softly. "Please don't tell Will. I'm trying to be better. Honest!"

I hugged her. "Don't worry about it. The day will come when we'll both tell the men at the hotel exactly what to do."

"Can't wait," said Rhonda, and we laughed together. "Right now, I've got to get back home."

"Are you sure you can't stay for at least a cup of coffee?"

Rhonda shook her head. "I can't leave Will for too long with the kids, or else he freaks."

My eyebrows rose. "You do see the irony in this, don't you? He wants more kids, but he gets panicky if he's with them alone for any length of time."

"Yeah, poor guy doesn't know how to handle it." She laughed. "Sometimes I don't, either. Thank God for Rita. I'm giving her another raise."

I laughed. I knew how much Rita was paid and it was more

than the hotel manager made.

As Rhonda drove away, Liz pulled into the driveway.

CHAPTER EIGHT

I waited for Liz to get out of her car and then went to greet her.

"How are you doing, hon?" I asked her.

She shrugged, giving me a troubled look that concerned me.

"Are you and Chad going to be all right?" I asked, unable to hold back.

"I love him, Mom, I really do, but I have to sort some things out in my mind. Vaughn is the perfect one for me to talk to about it. I'm so glad he's here."

"Okay, let's go inside. Vaughn's cooking breakfast. After we eat, you and he can go find a private place to talk."

"Thanks, Mom." Liz threw an arm around my shoulder, and we headed into the house.

"Lizzie! Lizzie!" cried Robbie, running to greet her.

Liz picked him up and hugged him to her. When she glanced at me, tears swam in her eyes.

Robbie reached up and patted her cheek. "No crying."

Liz smiled at him. "It's okay. I'm just so happy to see you."

Vaughn came over to them and wrapped his arms around both of them. "Good to see you, Liz."

"Yeah, same here," Liz said through trembling lips.

Vaughn and I exchanged worried glances. This was not the daughter we knew.

Working together, Vaughn and I put together the breakfast. Soon, we all were seated at the kitchen table. Looking around at three of the people I loved most, I marveled at what precious gifts life had given me.

When we were through eating, Vaughn rose. "Hey, Liz, how about a sail?"

She smiled and jumped to her feet. "Thanks. I'd love it."

"Me too?" said Robbie.

Vaughn shook his head. "Not this time, buddy. I want some time alone with your sister. She's been feeling sad and needs to talk to me."

A pout formed on Robbie's lips.

"Shall we have Brett come over?" I asked as Robbie stared glumly at the figures of Vaughn and Liz walking down to the dock.

He nodded. "Okay, I want to play with Brett."

When I phoned Cyndi, she said, "I was just going to call you. We're about to take off for the day in Sarasota. Charlie is looking at boats. Brett doesn't want to go with us unless Robbie can come too. Would that be all right with you?"

"That would be wonderful," I gushed. "Liz is here, and I need to give her some attention. She's talking to Vaughn now."

"Oh, then, definitely, we'll take Robbie with us. I know how little time you have with Vaughn."

My lips curved. "Thanks, Cyndi. I owe you big time for this."

She laughed. "It all works out in the end. Don't worry about it."

I hung up and turned to Robbie. "Brett wants you to look at boats with him and his daddy. I'll pack a snack bag for both of you and then walk you over there."

"Boats?" Robbie's face lit up. "I like boats. Big boats."

"I think you're going to see a lot of them. Brett's daddy likes big boats too."

--ooo--

Later, I watched Liz and Vaughn head toward the house arm in arm. Vaughn was talking, and Liz was bobbing her head in agreement. Some of the tension that had tightened my shoulders eased from my body. Liz was usually calm and collected, not the frazzled, worried, weepy person she'd been lately. Liz and Vaughn hugged, and then Liz waved at me and hurried around the house to get to her car.

When Vaughn came into the house, I studied his face for a clue. A half-hearted smile spread across his face, bringing my heart to an abrupt stop.

"Is she all right?"

He nodded and drew me to him. "Just trying to figure a few things out. I hope we did the right thing by adopting Robbie."

I gazed up at him. "What do you mean?"

"Liz is conflicted about giving him to us. She wants to prove to herself and everyone else she can be a good mother."

"She understands she didn't have the ability to give Robbie a secure home when Robert and Kandie died, doesn't she?"

"Oh, yes. She's still a little angry at her father for leaving them both in such a bad situation, but she feels guilty that she didn't feel capable of doing as he wanted."

My lips thinned. "Robert should have provided for them both. I honestly don't understand what happened to him. Was it a mid-life crisis? He dumped me for Kandie and then went about making foolish financial decisions, losing his business, and eventually losing his house. There was a brief moment when I wanted to say to him, 'I told you so,' but I was sorry it happened."

Vaughn took my hand and led me to the sunroom couch. We both took seats on it, and then he faced me. "I suggested to Liz that she call Barbara Holmes, the therapist that Tina Marks used. I think it would do Liz good to get things settled in her mind."

"Did she mention Chad? How is he doing with all this?"

"Apparently, he wants to get married now, and he wants to have children, but not right away. She was angry about that, but she understands what pressure she's been putting on him. And I think she has a clearer idea of all the reasons we took Robbie. Not only for his sake but for hers as well. She likes the idea that we're one big family. She and Nell talk all the time, and Ty and June are in touch too."

Regret filled me. "She always wanted brothers and sisters. I just couldn't give them to her."

"Aw, Ann. Don't beat yourself up," said Vaughn, wrapping his arms around me. "I think it's probably a good thing that all these feelings came out before the wedding."

My eyebrows shot up. "There's going to be a wedding?"

"Yes, Liz and Chad have agreed on that. They're not sure where, but Liz has always wanted a Christmas Eve wedding, and Chad is fine with that. And before she left, Liz tried to call Barbara Holmes."

I let out a long sigh of relief. Barbara Holmes was a great therapist. Thinking of her and the work she did for Tina, I said, "Have you heard anything about Tina Marks recently? I haven't heard from her in a few months."

A smile lit Vaughn's face. "She's dating a really good guy—the director she and I worked under for that awful film we did together. His name is Nicholas Swain. He and I talked the other day. He wants me to see about doing another film with him. I haven't spoken to the producers of my show, but after the bullshit they pulled on the advertising campaign with Lily, I might."

"I'm happy for Tina," I said. She'd been such a mess a few years ago when she was sent to hide out at the hotel to lose weight. But, after going through difficult times together, she and I had become friends. And since that time, too, she'd become one of the best film actresses in the business.

"Yeah, with that mother of hers willing to use her daughter to get ahead, Tina deserves a nice break." Vaughn studied me. "We did the right thing with Robbie. Don't you agree?"

"Yes," I said with conviction. "He's happy and well-adjusted. I'm just sorry that Liz is going through this hard time. Do you think some of her worries are that Nell is pregnant, and Angela is trying for a second baby?"

Vaughn nodded. "We talked about it, and she admitted that's what got her started on the whole idea of needing to show everyone that she could be a mother too. By the time we docked the boat, she was a whole lot calmer, more like our Liz."

I reached over and caressed his cheek. "Where did you learn how to handle all these kinds of issues?"

"I'm on a soap opera, remember? Everything that could possibly go wrong for anyone goes wrong on the show."

A laugh escaped me. "You're so right. *The Sins of the Children* has it all."

Vaughn looked around. "Where's Robbie?"

"Cyndi and Charlie have taken him and Brett to some big boat show in Sarasota."

A sly grin crossed Vaughn's face. "Really?"

I returned his smile. "Really. C'mon, big boy! Let's go for a swim."

"Swim? I had something better in mind."

That afternoon, hot, humid air wrapped around me as I finally headed to the pool in the lime-green bikini that Vaughn loved on me. I decided to simply enjoy the afternoon. Later, I'd tell Vaughn about what Reggie had found in the financials at the hotel. For now, Vaughn was here, and he was mine.

I lowered myself step by step into the pool where Vaughn was waiting for me.

He skimmed a hand across the water's surface.

I jumped out of the way. "No splashing," I said, giving him a warning look.

"Aw, you're no fun," he grumbled, but his teasing smile grew wider.

I settled into the water and gazed at the plants and thick foliage edging our lawn. After buying the house, we'd done a lot of extra landscaping for privacy. We'd also put in an electric pet fence so Trudy wouldn't run off chasing a bird or looking for a snack that she shouldn't have.

Vaughn swam up behind me and wrapped his arms around me. He caressed my breasts and then unhooked the top to my bathing suit.

"You don't need that," he growled, turning me around to face him. Even in the relatively cool water, I felt how ready he was for what he liked to call "a little afternoon delight."

"Again?" I said, secretly pleased by his reaction to me. It was something that would help me through the weeks ahead when our relationship would likely be questioned by the disreputable newspapers and magazines ready to print anything but the real truth.

He sat down on the pool steps and pulled me onto his lap.

I wrapped my arms around him and pressed my lips against his. Tasting the peppermint of his toothpaste, I deepened my kiss and closed my eyes, enjoying the sensations rolling through me. The chemistry between us had always been good, but even after a thorough lovemaking in the morning, I was ready for more. Not only was Vaughn sexy, he was the best man I knew, and I was eager to please him.

When we finally pulled apart, he whispered, "You're so damn hot!" He slid off his trunks and gave me a wry look.

"Aren't you a little overdressed?"

"What? You don't like me in green?" I teased, playing along with him.

He gave me a roguish wink. "I like you in nude."

CHAPTER NINE

Too soon it came time for Vaughn to return to New York. Trudy sat by the kitchen door, her black and tan ears drooping, as she watched Vaughn, Robbie, and me leave the house.

"Don't worry, Robbie and I will be back," I said to her, and closed the door.

I helped Robbie buckle himself into his booster seat and slid behind the wheel. Vaughn loaded his suitcase into the trunk and settled into the passenger's seat.

As we took off for the airport, Robbie said, "Daddy, why are you always going away?"

Vaughn glanced at me and twisted around to face Robbie. "Daddy has a job in New York. That's how I earn my money."

"Oh," Robbie said. "I remember New York. So many big buildings."

"Yes, and even though I work there, I come home to you, Mommy, Lizzie, and our friends here."

Robbie nodded solemnly, and I wondered what, if any, memories he had of his parents' deaths. Sometimes he seemed so introspective for his age.

Vaughn turned to me. "I hope nothing more comes of the advertising campaign for the show, that it remains a New York thing, and you don't have to deal with it."

I tried to smile, but I hated that side of Vaughn's business. "As long as we're open with each other, things will be all right. But make sure Lily understands about us, okay?"

"She's used to getting any guy she wants, so I think it drives her crazy that I'm not interested. The producers know that, which is why I'm really PO'd about the way they're going ahead and promoting Lily and me as a couple."

My stomach clenched at the idea of losing Vaughn to someone like Lily. She was beautiful, voluptuous, flirty, and eager to please. I, on the other hand, was about to embark on a project that would make it even more difficult for Vaughn and me to have quality time alone. I knew it was silly to feel this insecure, but Robert had rocked my world when he abruptly left me. I knew if the same thing happened with Vaughn, it would destroy me.

I pulled up to the drop-off zone for the airline and turned to accept the kiss Vaughn was offering me. As his lips met mine, I closed my eyes and inhaled the spicy aftershave I associated with him, storing the smell of him in my mind for the lonely nights ahead.

"Me too, Daddy!" cried Robbie from the backseat.

Laughing, Vaughn and I pulled apart.

Vaughn got out of the car, opened the back door and leaned in to give Robbie what he called a growly kiss.

Robbie squealed with delight.

Vaughn grabbed his suitcase. "See you later, honey. I'll call as often as I can. Love you."

"Love you too," I said, aware of the looks of recognition he was already receiving.

"'Bye, Daddy!" Robbie waved to Vaughn as I pulled away from the curb.

I dropped Robbie off at his preschool and went to the grocery store to pick up several items that Robbie and I liked to eat when Vaughn was away.

It wasn't until I was in the check-out line that I noticed his picture on the front of a scandal magazine. In the photograph, he and Lily Dorio were gazing lovingly at each other. A small inset of my picture appeared in between them. A caption read: "Vaughn Sanders and Lily Dorio sharing their onscreen love for real?"

The woman behind me said to her friend, "That Vaughn Sanders is such a hottie! And Lily Dorio? They're perfect together."

When I turned to face them, the woman's friend gasped. "Oh! I'm so sorry. We didn't know it was you." She and I had worked on a community project together, but we'd never really socialized.

I forced a pleasant tone. "You can't always believe what you read in the news. Thank goodness."

After the women left, the man at the cash register gave me a sympathetic smile. "I don't know why we even carry magazines like that."

"Because people will buy them," I said, wanting to cry.

Moments later, I sat in my car, drawing deep breaths. I couldn't let lies ruin the magic Vaughn and I had between us. I'd almost let it happen once before, but we were much stronger together now.

Still, after I got home and had put the groceries away, I called Rhonda.

"Oh, hon! Sorry that trashy news is out. Okay if I come over? I want to talk to ya about something, and you have more privacy than I do."

"Everything okay?" I asked.

"It will be," she answered cryptically. "Is it too early for wine?"

I laughed softly. "I'm sticking to iced tea, but you can have wine."

"I guess I'd better wait until later for the wine," Rhonda said, emitting a sigh that told me things weren't okay after all.

I'd just finished putting together Consuela's recipe for

berry tea when Rhonda arrived.

She saw what I was doing and grinned. "Great! What a treat!" She happily accepted a frosty glass of the tea from me.

"What's going on?" I asked as we both settled into chairs in the sunroom.

"I'm wondering if I could borrow Elena for a few days. I've decided to go ahead and get my tubes tied. Will is still not committed to a vasectomy. Dr. Benson says it will take me a couple of days to recover from the procedure and a whole week before I can lift the kids. I can't leave Rita alone for that length of time. Don't worry. I'll pay Elena well."

"We'll ask her. I'm sure she'd be happy to help you out, and we can work out a schedule that suits everyone. But, Rhonda, is this really what you want to do?"

She nodded thoughtfully. "I love my kids. You know I do, but I don't want any more children. Neither does Will, though he's reluctant to go ahead with a vasectomy. It's a guy thing."

Rhonda and I exchanged knowing smiles. Men!

Holding up her glass of iced tea, Rhonda said, "This tea reminds me that, though we've talked about getting Consuela and Manny back with us, we haven't done so. Why don't we call them now?"

"Okay. And then we need to get hold of Bernie to see if he'd be willing to come back to The Beach House Hotel once we own it again."

I sat by and listened as Rhonda made the call to Consuela. Manny and Consuela were like family to us. Even though they didn't like the new owners, they'd stayed at the hotel out of loyalty to us. But after Bree came into his position, they left, telling us they could never work for anyone like that.

"Yes," Rhonda was now saying. "We want to keep this a secret. Once we buy back the property, we'll move you into the apartment again. We love you and Manny, Consuela, and want you back in the family." She paused and listened. "And some other members of our old staff? Really? That would be great, but tell them to keep it quiet."

After the call ended, Rhonda turned to me with a grin. "They'll do it for us, but not for anyone else. And, Annie, I think she was crying by the time we ended the call. She's going to get Maria and Ana and the others to help us, too."

"Wonderful. Manny knows every plant on the property, and Consuela? She's the glue that held the kitchen together for every breakfast and lunch. I wonder if we can get Jean-Luc back for dinners and special events?"

"And don't forget Sabine. You know she'll do a lovely job of arranging the wedding Liz wants."

Hope spiraled inside me. "Let's call them right now."

I punched in the number for our old chef and his wife and was forced to leave a message asking them to give us a call. Hearing Sabine's voice on the message machine brought a sting of tears to my eyes. She and Jean-Luc had been highly offended by their treatment at the hotel and angry with Rhonda and me because there was nothing we could do about it. They finally quit. If we ever got them to come back to work with us, it would be a miracle—a miracle we'd need.

CHAPTER TEN

The following week, inspections of the property began in earnest. Rhonda and I accompanied Bill Richardson or one of his employees in his engineering company as often as we could. I asked when I could see my house and was told I'd have to wait a bit, that Bree was living there. Then, one day when I called the hotel and found out Bree would be off-property, I immediately phoned Rhonda.

"Want to accompany me to inspect my house?"

"You bet!" said Rhonda. "I want to see why that little prick won't let you in. Is Bill or one of his people going to be there?"

I drew in a breath, wondering how I should answer.

"Oh my God! We're doing this on our own?" Rhonda's laugh was gleeful. "Serves him right."

"I hope it doesn't cause any problems, but they can't keep denying me entrance to my own house. It's made me sick with worry. It's in the rental contract that I'll have reasonable access."

"Okay, Annie, we won't call it an inspection. We'll just say we're doing a sneak preview, and to hell with any complaints."

"Good. I thought you'd see it my way. Meet me down the street, and we'll walk to the property from there."

"A real spying move? I love it!" said Rhonda. "Give me twenty minutes."

I was sitting in my car when Rhonda rolled up in her Cadillac behind me. When she stepped out of the car, a laugh burst out of me. She was wearing sunglasses, a dark tunic, and black tights.

She grinned as she approached me. "Thought I should wear my spying clothes."

I put my arm around her shoulders. "C'mon. Let's go!"

We walked down the street to a spot in the thick hedge that I'd once used to escape the press. I pulled apart the branches of one of the pink-flowered oleanders and held them while Rhonda squeezed through to the other side. Then, I followed.

Studying the house I so proudly owned, I noticed that though the landscaping was in fine shape due to the hotel landscapers, the patio and pool looked ... unkempt. There were beer bottles lying next to the pool steps, and newspapers had been just tossed on the patio furniture; several sheets were floating in the pool. The patio clearly had not been swept for several days.

"C'mon, Annie. Let's see inside."

We went around to the garage. Hoping Bree hadn't changed the code, I punched in the numbers for the door opener and stood back.

The garage door slowly opened, exposing the silver Porsche Bree loved to show off.

Rhonda and I edged past it and tried the kitchen door. Locked.

I pulled out my house key, inserted it into the lock, and turned it. The key twisted, stopped, and then clicked into place.

"Hurry," I whispered, "let's go in."

"Wait! Close the garage door," said Rhonda.

As soon as the garage door rolled down, Rhonda and I burst into the house.

The first thing I noticed was the stale smell of smoke—not from cigarettes but the sweeter smell of marijuana.

My nostrils flared. "He knows my no-smoking rules!" I looked around at the dirty dishes in the sink, the cooked-on food atop the stove and felt my eyes swim with tears.

"What a frickin' mess! I thought hotel staff was supposed to keep the house clean," said Rhonda.

"Me too." My voice was a whisper of pain.

Rhonda followed me into the living area, and we both stopped in shock. Two large holes gaped at us from the far wall of the room. One of the pictures on the wall was hanging at a tilt. Another had fallen to the floor.

The pillows on the couch were lined up on the floor as if someone had slept there. The sweet smell of marijuana mixed with cigarette smoke was stronger here. Beer and red wine had been spilled onto the carpet and one of the upholstered chairs.

Feeling numb, I entered the bedroom which held precious memories of Vaughn and me. The bed sheets were wadded into a ball and thrown on the floor. I could well imagine why.

On legs gone wooden, I entered the bathroom. The long mirror above the double sinks in the vanity was cracked. A woman's shoe rested on the marble surface of the vanity. Nauseated, I gripped the door frame. My home, my beautiful home was wrecked.

At the sound of someone opening the front door, Rhonda grabbed my hand and pulled me into the master closet among the shirts and other clothing that reeked of a pungent aftershave I knew I'd never forget.

We heard footsteps coming toward the room.

I squeezed Rhonda's hand, trying to decide what to do.

"Hey, Bill! Better look at this room," called someone.

Then I heard the familiar southern drawl of Bill Richardson. "Comin'. This place is ruint."

Rhonda and I hurried out of the closet. We were heading for the door when Bill emerged from what used to be Liz's bedroom. "Hey, there! Got my message, did ya?"

Rhonda and I stared at each other wide-eyed.

"Tried to get you on your cells when I found out that the guy who lives here had to leave town unexpectedly. Thought it would be a good time to take a look around and make our inspection of the property."

I couldn't stop the tears welling in my eyes from sliding down my face. Looking at the destruction of the house I'd so lovingly put together, I felt sick to my stomach.

Bill, a kind man in his sixties, shook his head soulfully. "Sorry, Miss Annie. So far, all I've seen is a mess, but I don't think it's going to go too much beyond that. The hotel staff normally cleans it, right?"

I nodded. "But it looks like he hasn't let them inside in a while."

"There must have been one hell of a party here," said Rhonda. "I could kill the little prick for what he's done."

Bill held up his hand. "Don't worry. We'll make a thorough inspection of the house, but our primary concerns are with the mechanicals, not the décor. That's a matter you and your lawyer will have to handle."

He placed a hand on my shoulder. "I'll get the report right over to you. Now, I'd suggest you take as many pictures as you can with your phones. You'll want to document everything."

I nodded numbly. "I'm calling our lawyer right now."

Rhonda and I went out to the lanai, so I could make my call. After telling Mike what had happened, he agreed to meet us at the house later that day.

I gave Rhonda the news and then we walked outside.

Back at our cars, Rhonda gave me a hug. "Don't worry, Annie. We'll get this all straightened out. But no matter what happens, I want Bree off the property right now. I don't think we'll have trouble making that happen. Not when the others in the group see what has happened."

I sniffed, still too upset to say much.

"Let's get out of our spy clothes and into our hotel owners' clothes. It's going to happen, Annie. Ya just gotta believe."

All the way home I thought of Rhonda's words. I knew it would take more than believing we'd be able to do all that we wanted. It would take planning and hard work. But then, that was nothing new for us. We'd done it once, and by damn, we'd do it again.

CHAPTER ELEVEN

When Mike met us at later that day, he was as shocked as we'd been by the condition of the house. He'd brought a camera and went around the house taking pictures of each piece of damage. When he was through, he gave me a grim look. "We'll sue for damages, of course, and demand that Aubrey Lowell be removed from the property." He checked his watch. "I've got another appointment in twenty minutes, but I'll put in a call to Boston before then."

"No one will ever appreciate what this house means to me," I said. "We can sue them for a lot of money, but I feel it will never be the same."

Mike studied me. "It's amazing what you can do to restore this, Ann. Think about the rooms at the hotel. Time and time again guests abused the rooms, but you always managed to restore them to their proper condition."

"Oh my God!" gasped Rhonda. "What if they haven't taken decent care of the rooms? It will cost us extra money and time to get them right. Can you make arrangements for us to tour the rooms right away?"

"I'll try," said Mike. "But, remember, we can't interfere with the running of the hotel. Maybe we can arrange to do a block of rooms at a time. Again, we'll want to document everything. In the meantime, draw up a detailed checklist of things to look at in the rooms."

"I can work on that," I said, happy for something to take my mind off my house.

"Okay, then. I'll talk to you later," said Mike, giving us a wave goodbye.

I cupped my face with my hands as another thought came to me.

"What's wrong, Annie?"

"After seeing the damage at my house, I'm worried about the cost of redoing the rooms. If they're in the shape I think they're in, then we're going to have to do a complete renovation of them. After Ana was fired as head housekeeper, things have not been the same."

Rhonda gave me a worried look. "We'd better do some work behind the scenes to figure out just what it's going to cost us to make our hotel right again."

"And don't forget to factor in the lost revenue while rooms are renovated," I said, aware of the sinking feeling in my stomach. I'd invested my share of the funds from the sale of the hotel, but I knew the game the financial group was playing, and I didn't know if I'd be able to contribute my fair share.

When Vaughn called me, I told him about the damage to the house, becoming angrier and angrier. Mike Torson had placed a call to the company in Boston demanding the removal of Bree from the property. They had agreed to keep him from living in the house, but he would now be staying in a room in the hotel until a settlement was reached.

"They don't care that he trashed the house?" said Vaughn, sounding incredulous.

"Mike emailed them photos of the house and told them we were suing them for the damage, but they aren't going to relieve Bree of duty until they complete an investigation. As Rhonda says, 'it sucks,' but that's where we are with him at the moment." My voice caught. "They can't destroy my memories of you and me there."

"No, they can't. I'm sorry this happened, honey. I hope it's resolved soon."

"I think they're just waiting for a place to put him," I said. "But if Bree isn't gone soon, everyone is going to be sorry, because Rhonda is out to get him."

Vaughn chuckled. "Poor kid won't know what hit him. Seriously, though, is someone doing a thorough evaluation of the damage?"

"Bill Richardson's team is handling all the mechanicals, but I'll have to go in and check everything else myself. I don't trust any other person to do it. I know every inch of that house."

"Just be sure he's not around when you do it," warned Vaughn. "I don't trust him."

"Neither do I. Once we got the owners' approval to get Bree out of the house, I had the hotel staff remove his clothes, and then I made them move his car out of the garage. He was furious about it when he returned, but it's parked by the front circle where he likes to see it."

"What about the locks on the doors?"

"They're scheduled to be changed tomorrow morning. A guard will keep an eye on the house tonight. He still can get into the pool area, but I don't think he'd dare do that, not with everything else he's facing."

"I wish I could come home this weekend, but I'm due to attend a ball for one of my favorite charities concerning kids in foster care."

"Are you going with Lily?" I asked, knowing from the resignation in his voice that he wasn't entirely pleased with this particular commitment.

"Yeah. It's another PR thing the producers set up. We compromised. I agreed to go if they made a large donation to the cause."

I didn't respond. Instead, I brought up Robbie's latest achievements in school.

"Ann? You could come up to New York and come to the ball with me," said Vaughn. "I'd love it if you would."

"Thanks, I wish I could, but I have to take care of the situation with the house. Things will soon get easier. Consuela and Manny and a lot of other staff members have agreed to come back. Rhonda and I are going to get things running smoothly and then step back and let our trusted staff do their thing with only occasional supervision from us."

"I hope so," said Vaughn.

"It'll work out. You'll see," I said with more confidence than I felt. We still hadn't heard back from Bernie, and Jean-Luc and Sabine were out of the country.

After dropping Robbie off at pre-school the next morning, I headed right over to my old house. The hotel housekeepers were standing by to clean the house, but I didn't want them to touch anything until I'd documented each piece of damage once more, making sure we got everything. The holes in the wall, the paintings, the mirror were all obvious damages, but I was looking for the things that might go unnoticed.

I pulled into the driveway, got out of the car and stood a moment studying the small house. Originally a caretaker's cottage on the seaside estate, I'd worked with architects to redesign the interior and add an extension to it. It was more than a house to me. It represented my rebirth. I'd watched its recreation with love and hope for a different future.

I unlocked the door and stepped inside, angered once more by the odor that still greeted me. The carpeting and soft goods throughout the house would have to be replaced. If Bernie would agree to come back to the hotel, he and his wife,

Annette, would not be willing to live in a house that smelled of smoke, among other things.

It must have been some party, I thought sourly, gazing at the spill of red wine on the light carpet in the living room. I went through the room and marked down every bit of damage. By the time I got to the master bedroom, I was shaking with emotion.

I plunked down into a chair. There was no way I could keep the furniture, the bedding, anything that reminded me of what might have gone on in here.

"Ann?"

I jumped to my feet and hurried to greet Rhonda.

She took one look at me and pulled me into a quick hug. "I just got off the phone with Mike. Bree's father is flying down to meet with us today."

"Good. He's got to get a good look at this mess," I said. "Come here. I want to show you something."

I led Rhonda to the master bathroom. Nothing had been moved. The high-heel shoe still lay on top of the vanity counter, a mystery. I picked it up. "This may be our only clue to a witness who can help us, if necessary."

Rhonda grinned. "Sorta like Cinderella, huh? All we have to do is find the owner of the shoe."

I returned her smile. "Only instead of searching for a princess, we're searching for a foolish party girl who can help us nab Bree if it comes to that."

"But, really, I don't think that will be necessary," said Rhonda. "We know damn well who's at fault here. Mike said Bree's father was very annoyed with the whole idea of our suing them. I have a feeling he's going to be as much a prick as his son."

The sigh that escaped me came from deep inside. I hated confrontation, but, if I had to, I'd fight him on this.

The locksmith worked on the locks while Rhonda and I looked over the kitchen one more time. We'd just finished our inspection when both of our cell phones rang at the same time.

We looked at each other with surprise and checked our phones.

As I picked up the call from the hotel, I heard Rhonda say, "Hi, Bree."

I clicked onto the call from Stuart. "Yes?"

"Bree's father is due to arrive any minute. Thought you'd want to know."

"Thanks. I appreciate it."

I ended the call and faced Rhonda.

"Bree's father?" she said.

I nodded. "He's due to arrive any minute."

"Let's go!" said Rhonda.

I glanced down at the pants I was wearing, brushed dirt from my shirt, and shook my head. "Not like this."

Rhonda grabbed my arm. "Yes, like this. I want him to see that you've been working hard in the house his son destroyed."

I drew in a long breath and let it out. "Okay, let's go."

Rhonda and I hurried over to the hotel. As we approached the front circle, a white limousine rushed past us. We paused and watched as a tall, silver-haired man exited the limo and handed a leather suitcase to the bellman.

The man looked up at the hotel and then focused his attention to Bree, who was rushing down the stairway to greet him.

I turned around and headed back to the house. The man had put an arm around his son, and they were climbing the stairs in step. No way was I going to meet him without looking professional. I knew his kind well from my work in Boston when I'd helped Robert run our consulting business.

"Where are you going?" said Rhonda.

"I'm going to lock up the house, and then I'm going home to change. I want to meet Bree's father on an equal footing. Otherwise, he's just the type to dismiss me."

Rhonda nodded. "He'd probably just call us housewives, huh?"

"Maybe, but I'm not taking any chances. I'm furious at what his son has done and how he's treated us."

Back at the house, I gathered my notes, my camera, and my purse, ready to do battle.

Mike agreed to meet us at the hotel in time for our conference with Bree's father. I wanted a witness to what I was sure was going to be a difficult scene.

The three of us walked into the hotel together and headed for the small conference area in what used to be Rhonda's and my office. Even with Rhonda and Mike by my side, my fingers grew frigid with dread.

The tall man Rhonda and I had earlier seen from a distance rose from a chair at the table. His stern, elegant appearance was intimidating. I was glad I hadn't tried to meet him earlier. He looked down his patrician nose at Rhonda and gave me a silent stare before offering his hand to Mike.

"You must be Mike Torson. I'm Austin Lowell, Aubrey's father."

They shook hands and then Mike introduced Rhonda and me to Austin while Bree stood aside, not saying a word.

After we all sat down, Austin looked around the table. "I'm afraid there's been some mistake. My son tells me he wasn't at the house the night of the party, that friends of his are responsible for the damage." He turned to Bree. "Isn't that right, son?"

Bree nodded, but I knew he was lying by the way he avoided looking at me.

"So," Austin continued, "to be fair, I'll go ahead and pay for the destruction because Aubrey should have known not to allow friends to use the house without clearing it with the hotel first."

"We have quite a list of items that need to be replaced or repaired," said Mike. "Regardless of who pays for it, they all must be made right." He handed Austin several sheets of paper. "Photographs will verify what I said."

Austin looked over the list and shook his head. "Preposterous! I'm not paying for new carpets and new furniture."

"The carpet has been heavily stained and has absorbed so much smoke from cigarettes and pot over a period of time that it will never be right anywhere in my small house," I said.

Austin shook his head. "Pot? Not from my boy." He turned to Bree. "Right, Aubrey?"

Bree nodded, but we both knew he was lying again.

"I'll pay for broken mirrors, ruined pictures and holes in the wall, but I'm not paying for anything else," said Austin.

"We'll see about that," said Mike. "We can go to court or make a fair settlement ourselves."

Austin shifted his feet. "Well, now, let's not be too hasty. I don't want my son's name mixed up in anything like this. He's to finish his hotel experience here before going on to a different business." He turned to me and then gazed steadily at Rhonda. "You do intend to buy back the hotel. Is that correct?"

Mike spoke up. "My clients have already notified the group of that intention."

"Well, then, it's just a matter of time until Aubrey leaves this property. So, let's not make it more difficult than it needs to be. Aubrey has, I hope, learned to choose better friends."

"Aubrey has a lot to learn about the hotel business," Rhonda began, drawing herself up in her chair.

Mike quickly cut her off. "We will not get into any discussions about Aubrey's work at the hotel, but we will need to have a better sense of cooperation from him if we're going to proceed with any agreement between us."

Rhonda sat back in her chair, but I knew she wanted to slap the smirk off Bree's face as much as I.

Austin once more looked over the list of estimated renovation expenses and pulled out his checkbook. "I think we can call this a draw." He wrote out the check for the amount we'd requested and handed it to Mike. "Are we settled now?"

Mike looked at the numbers on the check and nodded. "I believe we are."

He rose, and Rhonda and I followed suit.

Austin stood and shook hands with Mike and then turned to Rhonda and me. "I believe you're making a big mistake by buying back the hotel. Best to leave the running of it to those of us who understand the hospitality business."

I placed a hand on Rhonda's arm to keep her from charging him.

"We know very well how to please our guests," I said. "It's something that we hope to bring back to the property."

Austin's eyebrows shot up. "Our numbers are doing just fine."

"Numbers are just numbers," I said, "and that explains it all."

Squaring my shoulders, I followed Mike and Rhonda out of the room.

It was a moment before I realized I'd left my purse in the office. I hurried back to get it. Standing outside the door, I heard Austin say, "Do you realize what all your foolishness has cost me once more, Aubrey?"

My lips thinned. He knew all along that his son had lied. No wonder Bree was such a mess. When I knocked on the door, their conversation stopped.

Austin opened it. "Yes?"

"My purse," I said.

Without a word, he retrieved it for me and closed the door.

Moments later, when I caught up with Rhonda and Mike chatting together off to the side of the front circle, Rhonda was fuming.

"That little liar. I know damn well that Bree was at the house and smoking pot. Did you see that fake look of innocence that crossed Bree's face when his father asked him about it?"

"His father knows he's lying too. When I went back for my purse, he was shouting at Bree about what it had cost him to make things right. It's a bad scene."

"It's clear to me, Austin Lowell has had to bail his son out of sticky situations before," said Mike calmly. "Be glad he's willing to do so. Otherwise, it would be a long road of conflict between you and the company to restore the house to its proper condition again."

Rhonda studied him. "Did ya hear the snide remark Austin made implying we don't know about the hospitality business? And this? After he and his buddies were dying to buy The Beach House Hotel because of us?" She pounded a fist in her hand. "I can't wait to get rid of those guys!"

Mike gave Rhonda a worried look. "Remember, it was a subtle statement, but part of the deal of being paid completely and promptly is that Bree will be on site during the transition. So, regardless of how you feel about him, you're going to have to work with him."

Rhonda turned to me. "You'll have to keep me under

control, Annie, because all I want to do is slap that kid's face."

Knowing it wouldn't be easy, I sighed. I felt the same way.

Bree emerged from the hotel with his father and got into an old Jeep I'd seen around the hotel.

"Wonder why he's driving that thing?" said Rhonda.

"Or if Bree's father knows he usually drives a Porsche."

Rhonda turned to me with a devilish grin. "Bet he doesn't."

I decided I'd do a little investigation on my own. Something didn't seem right about it.

CHAPTER TWELVE

That afternoon, Rhonda and I decided to call the hotel's former head of housekeeping. Ana Peña was a hard worker who'd managed a good team of housekeepers. With Bernie's cooperation in allowing her to staff her team her own way, she'd made sure the hotel looked polished at all times. Now, after knowing through Consuela that she'd come back on staff after we bought the hotel back, we wanted her input on the room inspections we planned to do.

Bree, of course, didn't make it easy. He would open up only a few rooms at a time, claiming they were booked. Gritting our teeth, Rhonda and I agreed to his schedule.

A few days later, with Ana in tow, we entered the first room. At first glance, it did not look bad. Then I took a closer look. Something was off with the cushions on the settee. I walked over to it and realized the seat covers were brighter than the rest of the couch. I lifted them and recoiled at the stains on the other side.

Ana came over to me and fingered the material. "It's too stained to clean." She lifted her hand and slapped it against the cushion. Dust flew up into the air.

She quickly stepped back. "They should be vacuumed every day. But that is not happening."

"Look at this, Annie," said Rhonda, standing at the door to the bathroom.

Ana and I hurried to her side and stared into the room. The grout around the tub/shower was stained, and someone had spilled red nail polish on the marble countertop of the vanity.

I entered the bathroom and walked over to the vanity. "This should have been cleaned properly. A simple scraping, perhaps."

Ana's lip curled. "I told Stuart it wasn't a good idea to bring in someone from Miami to run housekeeping. I told him our local workers did an excellent job, but they needed to be able to have flexible schedules. That's why so many people have left housekeeping."

As we went through the allotted rooms, I tried to control my rising panic. If Rhonda and I were to become the new owners, neither of us would settle for rooms in this condition. Dollar signs did a dance in my mind, making my thoughts whirl and my stomach tighten. We faced a battle to get the purchase price adjusted.

We inspected the patio furniture on the balconies. On the less expensive pieces recently added, rust appeared here and there. Dealing with salt air could be a problem, but we'd kept a line in our budget for constant replacements. In a high-end property, it was important to have things as nice as guests expected which is why we'd originally used teak and high-quality vinyl.

Some of the damage was due to normal wear and tear by guests, but this, too, should have been addressed. Dings on walls; chips in counters; stained carpets; loose shower curtain rods—all were stark reminders that someone wasn't overseeing the housekeeping department, and the owners weren't spending money on repairs, maintenance, and replacement. Rhonda and I had questioned management about this before, but, as always, our concerns obviously had been ignored.

After completing that day's inspections, Rhonda and I thanked Ana and promised to get back to her to discuss her role with the hotel.

She left us, and I said to Rhonda, "C'mon, let's go down to the beach. I need fresh air and a moment to gather my thoughts."

"Okay. I'm feeling a little sick about the situation we're facing," said Rhonda. "I'd wanted to be able to take over the hotel and simply run it. But, Annie, I don't want our names as owners of The Beach House Hotel until it looks like it used to."

"I know," I said, trying to tell myself that we could do it. But, of course, the substandard condition of the hotel would have to be worked into the price as an adjustment to what the owners would try to get for the hotel. For us, it meant another hassle, more money, and more worries.

Rhonda and I walked slowly across the pool deck noting the condition of the furniture. Like the other public places in the hotel, better attention seemed to have been paid to this area, though I noted a few deck chairs that should be replaced. I'd have to remember to ask about replacement costs for the pool area. I didn't recall having any problems there when we had owned and operated the hotel.

After we removed our shoes and stepped onto the sand, Rhonda placed a hand on my shoulder. "I know you're upset about the cost of renovations, but we're not going to let that stop us from doing things right, are we? Ya know I can lend us the money, if necessary."

"But we need to make the owners accountable for not doing things to keep the property in decent shape, even after we complained about it. They ignored us just to save money."

"Agreed. But first things first," said Rhonda. "We're going to get control of the hotel and then get their sorry asses off our property."

"C'mon, let's take a walk. We'll both feel better if we do." I took Rhonda's arm, and we headed down the beach away from the hotel.

Amid the comfortable silence between us, I listened to the splashing of the waves against the shore, the squeals of delight from children running into and out of the water, and welcomed the sounds of beach life.

We walked a mile or so before turning around and heading back to the hotel. The quiet companionship and the tang of the fresh, salty air calmed me.

"Feel better?" Rhonda asked.

I smiled and nodded.

"Ann! Rhonda! Wait up!"

At the sound, our bodies stiffened. *Brock Goodwin.*

Rhonda whirled around and narrowed her eyes as Brock approached us.

He waved. "Hello, my friends. How nice to see you!"

"I heard you were back in town," Rhonda said. "What happened?"

His smile wavered and then strengthened into a self-satisfied expression. "I've got a new business. It's still dealing with imports, but now I'm in charge, not the guy I used to work for—a guy who knew nothing about dealing with native artwork." He puffed out his chest comically, like a rooster about to crow. "I'm doing well. Very well in fact."

"We'd appreciate it if you stayed out of the business of The Beach House Hotel," said Rhonda stiffly, and I knew the effort it was taking her to keep from yelling at him.

He gave her a sly smile. "As I told Ann, the Neighborhood Association feels much better about having real professionals run the hotel. Naturally, we're in favor of supporting them."

Rhonda put her hands on her hips. "In case ya haven't heard, Annie and I are buying back the hotel. So, don't frickin' mess with it or us. Got it?"

"What? Buying it back? You can't do that. The owners are going to expand the property, and I'm doing the interior decorating for them and maybe all their other hotels."

"Apparently, you haven't talked to them recently," I said. "Better not order too many pieces of artwork because we won't be using them."

Brock's face turned an angry red. "Bree and I had a deal. I'm going to see that he and the others follow through with it. I've already commissioned several large pieces."

"Too bad," said Rhonda. "Sometimes it pays to clear things with so-called friends."

"We'll see about that," said Brock. He turned around and walked away from us, his feet pounding the sand.

Rhonda and I looked at one another and shook our heads.

"I knew there had to be an angle to Brock's friendship with Bree," I said. "They deserve each other."

"Right." Rhonda's eyes gleamed with determination. "And it's up to us to see that their deal is exposed for what it is. If they don't cooperate, I have ways of doing just that."

I remembered the newspaper campaign Rhonda had once mounted against Brock and hoped he'd be smarter this time. We couldn't let him interfere with our plans.

When I got home, Robbie and Trudy greeted me with kisses and then went back to their game of tag. My heart expanded at the sight of them—boy and dog cavorting together. Observing Trudy's determination as her short legs raced to cover ground, I resolved that Rhonda and I shouldn't be intimidated by the more powerful owners of the hotel. Like Trudy, we'd display courage and will power, and like the tortoise in a race against a hare, we'd win.

Elena and I talked awhile, and then I went to my office to begin calling various purveyors. Though I'd been given money to refurbish my beloved house, I needed to carefully count every penny to achieve the look I wanted. I was totaling up numbers when my phone rang. When I saw the familiar name, my lips spread into a smile.

"Hi, Tina! How are you?" I trilled with happiness. Her acting career had become very successful after winning an Academy Award six months ago. And she deserved it. Knowing the more intimate details of Tina's life, I'd cried all the way through her movie about a young woman tormented by an evil mother. Tina's role had been spellbinding. And truer than most viewers knew.

"Hi, Ann! How are you? The rumors about Vaughn and Lily are just that, aren't they?"

"Yes," I said, "but that doesn't make it any easier to deal with them."

"I'm sure it doesn't. Lily is loving it. I ran into her in New York a couple of nights ago. I've never cared for her. Honestly, I wish she and Vaughn weren't working together. She has a thing for him."

I took a couple of deep calming breaths and turned my attention to Tina. "You sound a little down. Is everything all right?"

"I'm going through a terrible time. I don't know if you happened to see or hear the news, but my mother and brother were recently killed in a terrible house fire. I'm not doing well with it. You know how much I loved my brother and how I felt about my mother. To think she took away my brother's life, difficult as it was, because she carelessly left a cigarette burning in bed. It makes me furious! I hated her, you know."

"Yes," I said, concerned about the rising hysteria in Tina's voice. "Oh, honey, I'm so sorry that happened. I know how hard you've worked to see that your brother had a good life. And we both know how much he loved you. Is there anything I can do for you?"

"I was wondering if I could come stay at the hotel for a while after my film gets wrapped up, which should be in a few weeks. You're the closest thing I have to a real mother, and I need you. I also thought I'd make an appointment with Barbara Holmes to work out a few things with her. She's such a good therapist. Talking to her to resolve my anger and hurt will be helpful. I think Nicholas is going to ask me to marry him, and I want to have a happy heart, if you know what I mean."

"Indeed, I do. I'd love to have you here at the hotel with us. However, Rhonda and I are in the midst of a battle with the new owners. We're trying to buy back the hotel, and they're giving us a hard time."

"What about your house? Is that available?"

I hesitated, my mind racing. "When exactly would you come to Florida?"

"The week of Thanksgiving. I'm willing to pay a good rate for the use of it. You know I love that house."

"You wouldn't love it now," I said feeling angry all over again. "It's been trashed by one of the owners, a young, obnoxious brat. But I think we can have it ready for you in time for your visit. In fact, I'll make sure of it. And if there are any problems, I'm sure you'll understand." My anger felt trite compared to the painful emotions Tina was experiencing. And my house could be fixed, but Tina's brother couldn't.

"Ann, I'll understand. I promise. It would be awesome if I could stay there! I need to see you and have some healing time in Florida."

"I can't wait to see you, Tina. It's been too long. I'm just sorry it's under these circumstances." In the quiet that followed, I could hear her sobbing. Trying to pull her from painful memories, I blurted out. "It's true? Nicholas? Nicholas Swain?"

"Can you believe it?" responded Tina sniffing and giggling like a school girl. "He's such a nice guy, and he says he loves me, really loves me."

"I'm so happy for you. Didn't his wife die of cancer a couple of years ago?"

"Yes," said Tina. "It's still painful, but he's ready to move on. He took such good care of her and was heartbroken when she passed. It's another reason I love him. And though he's in the business, he's not a star. You know how they can be. Ugh."

Ann laughed. "All but Vaughn. He's not that egotistical."

"Oh, Ann, I didn't mean ..."

"Of course, I know. Vaughn knows Nicholas, and he says that Nicholas has a good reputation for being thoughtful and kind, even as he insists upon things being done professionally. Speaking of that, how is this latest movie going? I hear it's going to be another tearjerker."

"It is. I've cried buckets over this script. It's tender and sweet. I can't wait for you to see it. Maybe you'll be able to come to the premiere for this one."

"We'll see. It's a whole lot different with a little boy in the household," I said.

"How is that sweet little Robbie?" she cooed.

"He's doing well. He loves preschool, especially snack time."

Tina and I laughed together.

At the sound of voices in the background, Tina said, "Look, I've got to go. I'll let you know my exact date of arrival. I'm hoping Nicholas will be able to join me for Thanksgiving. And if he likes it, we might stay on for Christmas."

"That would be great," I said. Tina had become like another daughter to me, and I was happy to help her.

After I hung up, I called Rhonda to give her the news.

"What's up?" Rhonda asked above the wailing I heard in

the background.

I described my conversation with Tina and mentioned she wanted to come to the hotel for Thanksgiving along with Nicholas Swain.

"That could be good for us," said Rhonda. "It will be another way for us to restore the hotels' reputation as a place for celebrities and other well-known people to stay with the assurance of privacy. Some of the new guests the owners have brought in have blabbed things to the press that you and I would never have allowed to happen in the past. It's hurt not only the hotel's reputation but ours as well."

"And Tina and Nicholas will be able to spread the word among their friends," I said, feeling more confident about the future of the hotel under our management.

We hung up, and I sat and stared out at the water, trying to find some peace. Tina's worries about Lily bothered me. Tina would never have mentioned it if she wasn't concerned.

I knew I could trust Vaughn working with Lily, but I didn't think Lily would allow Vaughn to escape her attention for long. And that bothered the hell out of me.

CHAPTER THIRTEEN

Now that I knew Tina Marks was going to be staying in my house over the holidays, I decided to try to get in touch with Bernhard Bruner again. When we'd tried to reach him earlier, he and his wife were traveling. I didn't think it would be a problem if we were not able to offer them use of the house, but I wanted to make sure. If necessary, we'd put Tina in the Presidential Suite, though it wouldn't give her as much privacy.

When he'd first appeared for his interview to be our hotel manager, Bernie, as Rhonda had quickly dubbed him, was a surprise. Speaking formally, dressed in a white, starched shirt, navy-blue blazer, tie, and creased gray slacks unsuitable for the tropical weather, he seemed as stiff as he could be. His black and tan dachshund, Trudy, whom Vaughn and I now owned, had helped to soften his stern manner. After loosening up in the hotel's casual setting, Bernie had become a valued member of our staff, directing others with a competence neither Rhonda nor I had. And confessing he was unable to replace us in that way, he'd encouraged us to continue our involvement with the guests and public relations to retain the flavor of the hotel. It had turned out to be a perfect working relationship. We couldn't wait to get him back.

I mentally crossed my fingers as I placed the call. When Bernie's deep hello rang in my ear, hope rose in me.

"Hello, Bernie, it's Ann. Did you get our earlier message?"

"Ah, Ann, good to hear from you. I'm sorry I haven't returned your call, but Annette had a family issue to take care of, and I was traveling with her. So, tell me what's going on. Are those SOBs still giving you a hard time?"

"Yes, that's why we called. Rhonda and I have decided to buy back the hotel. We have an option to do so, and we're working on it now. Before Thanksgiving, it should be ours. And, Bernie, we want you to run it for us again. Please say you'll do it."

I clutched the fingers of my free hand as the silence between us grew.

"It would have to be under different circumstances," he said. "I would have to be able to clear the staff of those who were working so eagerly under Aubrey Lowell. And, of course, my salary would have to be adjusted."

"And the house?"

"Annette and I will have to talk about it, but I prefer to be off property."

I let out the breath I'd been holding. "Yes, that would be perfect. Tina Marks is going to be spending some time there after we renovate it. Bree has trashed the place."

"That scum ..."

"He's going to be the first to go. Rhonda and I can't wait. And, Bernie, Ana and others of our old staff are willing to come back ... with your permission, of course. You and they were the heart and soul of the hotel."

"No, Ann, you and Rhonda were always the ones who made the hotel what it was. We just helped."

Tears of gratitude sprang to my eyes. Over and over again, Rhonda and I had made suggestions to the new owners that were all but laughed at.

"Let me talk to Annette, and I'll get back to you. The idea, shall we say, is intriguing."

"Bernie, we need you, we want you. We want our team back together again with you as our leader."

"Thank you, Ann. That means a lot to me. I'll speak to you by the end of the week."

As I hung up, I thought I'd be willing to pay him almost anything to have him at The Beach House Hotel once more.

I immediately called Rhonda. Before she could say anything, I blurted out, "Good news, I think," and then relayed the conversation to her.

"Annie? How about I come over there and have a glass of wine to celebrate with ya? I need a break."

I grinned at the idea. "Great! Come along. I'll fix some light refreshments, and we can come up with a way to encourage Bernie to say yes."

"He's gotta do it, Annie, or we're sunk."

We both knew we could hire someone else to manage the hotel for us, but we also knew it wouldn't be the same without Bernie.

While I waited for Rhonda to arrive, I walked down to the dock to see what Elena and Robbie were doing.

"Hi, Mom! Look at this. I built a space station. See? And here are the spacemen floating in space."

"Nice," I said, wondering what had happened to sand castles. Maybe it was a girl thing, the fascination with castles and fairies and princesses. Having raised Liz, it always surprised me to see how different boys were from girls. I delighted in each of them.

I lowered myself onto the edge of the dock and listened as Robbie told me a story about his spaceship. He was a bright, little boy, thanks, no doubt, to some random genes. Kandie had been a looker but wasn't well endowed in the brains department. I thought of Robert and then of Vaughn, marveling at the differences between them. Vaughn had taken on the role of father to both Liz and Robbie so easily, so kindly. I loved him for that.

As if he knew I'd been thinking of him, my cell phone rang. *Vaughn.*

Smiling, I clicked onto the call. "I was just thinking of you."

"Good," he said, "because I need you to come to New York. This weekend I'm helping to host that charity event I mentioned the other day, and I need you to accompany me. The rumor mill is going wild about Lily and me, and I want to put an end to it. I don't give a damn what's going on there; I need you here. Send me your flight schedule. Gotta go."

Before I could respond, he hung up.

Shocked, I stared out at the water. I'd never heard him this upset.

"Everything all right?" Elena asked, giving me a worried look.

"I ... I don't know."

As I walked back to the house, I thought of Tina's reaction to Lily. Was Lily putting that much pressure on Vaughn?

Rhonda appeared as I placed a wedge of Brie and some crackers on a wooden plate. I put a bunch of frosty, green grapes next to them and turned to her. "Good to see you."

"Thanks for letting me invite myself over. I need a break. Rita is off today, and I'm about done in. How can two little humans make you so crazy? When one goes in one direction, the other takes off in another." She plopped down in a chair and took a deep breath.

I studied the circles under her eyes. "Are you okay?"

"It's just been one of those days, ya know? I'm actually looking forward to having that little operation of mine. A week where I have to take it easy sounds pretty good to me."

I nodded and handed her a glass of pinot noir. "Getting your tubes tied should be pretty simple. Let's sit on the lanai. It will be quiet there."

"Okay, I can't stay late. Will is watching the kids. He's

giving them their dinner and then a bath, which he loves to do, but he can handle them for only so long."

"Vaughn wants me to go to New York for one of those fancy charity events he's involved with. You know how I hate that kind of thing, but he was most insistent, and I have to be there for him. Even with all that's going on with you and your surgery, I'm planning to fly up there Saturday morning and come home Sunday afternoon."

"Oh, hon! That's more important than anything going on here. Besides, you'll only be gone a day or two. What could go wrong?"

Those words sent a chill racing through my veins. In the hotel business, anything could go wrong at any given moment.

Rhonda reached over and clasped my hand. "It's right for you to go, Annie. With all those rumors whirling around him, it's important for everyone to see that you two are really together. At the hairdressers, I looked at one of those cheesy magazines. It showed a picture of Vaughn and Lily kissing. I'm pretty sure it was taken from a scene on the show. I wasn't going to mention it to you, but now, I think you should know."

I lowered my head into my hands and then lifted it with fresh determination. Vaughn was my husband for now and forever. Lily Dorio was *not* going to pull him away from me.

"Annie, I know how much Vaughn loves you. We all do," said Rhonda.

"Maybe we can get our daughters to step in for us this weekend."

"Perfect," said Rhonda. "I'll talk to both of them and ask them to appear at the hotel from time to time."

Rhonda and I smiled at each other. We'd planned on bringing our daughters into the business at some point. They could start with this small project.

With that issue settled, Rhonda and I discussed ways in

which we could entice Bernie to join us. Ana, Consuela, Manny, and Dorothy Stern had already agreed to return.

"What about Tim McFarland? Do you think we could get him back from Marriott?"

I shook my head. "He's got a great job there. But what about Cliff Reynolds, our old night clerk and auditor?"

"I'll call him first thing tomorrow," Rhonda promised.

"And, Rhonda, I've been thinking. We've talked about setting up my house as a special place for VIP guests, and I think now is the time to do it. I'm also wondering how you'd feel if we offered the second apartment on the property to Troy again. He's about to propose to Elena, and they will need a place to stay while they save for a place of their own. After seeing what happened to my property, I'd feel better if someone we knew was keeping an eye on it. It would be a big break for them, and we'd have someone on site in addition to Manny and Consuela if we needed Troy during the night."

"Good idea. We could have used him to handle Bree and his group. And by not renting it out until after Tina leaves, she'll have the chance to stay there for as long as she needs." She shook her head. "Who knew she'd become such a big star."

"Do you remember how awful, how wounded she was when we first met her?"

We exchanged knowing glances. The hotel business drew in a lot of different people. Some guests were easy and pleasant. Others were not. Tina's reversal was one of our bigger successes.

That night as I read Robbie a story, I watched his eyelids flicker and finally close. Giving him a kiss, I pulled the light blanket up around him and tiptoed out of the room, eager to call Vaughn.

In the quiet of my bedroom, I punched in his number and waited for him to answer.

When he finally said, "Hello," I could barely hear him above the sound of voices in the background.

"Hi, it's me. I just wanted to give you my flight schedule. I'll arrive on Saturday morning and will have to leave Sunday afternoon. I'll text you the details. Vaughn, I can't wait to see you again."

In the silence that followed, a voice close to the phone said, "Vaughn, honey, who is that?"

I pressed my lips together to keep from saying anything while I waited for him to speak.

"It's Ann. She's coming up this weekend so she can accompany me to the event you wanted to attend with me."

"But, Vaughn," came Lily's cry. "I've already ordered a dress for it."

"Vaughn? Are you there?" I said, struggling to keep my dismay from making my voice shake.

"Hi, sweetheart. Yes, I'm here. I'm glad you're coming to New York. It will make things a lot easier for me. Text me the times, and I'll meet you. I'll call you later. I'm busy with the crew now."

Stung by his reaction, I pushed the button to end the call and sank onto the bed.

After tossing and turning all night, I dragged myself out of bed to get Robbie up for school. In those horrible moments between small periods of sleep, I'd imagined everything that could go wrong between Vaughn and me. Perhaps, I'd been too naïve about Vaughn's being able to work in New York while I stayed in Florida, but we'd both agreed to the idea.

I slipped on a robe and headed into Robbie's room.

He lay in bed like a dark-haired cherub, his cheeks flushed from sleep. Beside him was the giraffe I'd bought him at the

Naples Zoo a few years ago. I bent over and kissed his cheek.

His eyes fluttered open, and then a smile crossed his face. "Hi, Mommy."

I sat on the edge of his bed and hugged him to me. I loved this part of the day, even on those mornings when he frowned at me grumpily, unwilling to come fully awake.

"It's another beautiful day," I said. "You should have a good one. After school, you're going to play with Brett while Mommy goes to the hotel for a while."

"I like school. Brett is my best friend."

I ruffled his hair. "Better get up then. I'll go make one of your favorite breakfasts."

His eyes lit up. "Pancakes?"

"Yup."

Feeling better, I headed into the kitchen trying to conjure up a list of what I would need to take to New York.

As I was sipping coffee and mixing the pancake batter, the phone rang. I switched it to speaker and listened as Vaughn said, "Hi, honey. Sorry, I couldn't call you last night, but we were all celebrating Roger Sloan's birthday."

I was quiet. After pushing the promotion of Vaughn and Lily being together again, Roger Sloan was not someone I much admired.

"You there?" Vaughn said.

"Yes," I responded.

"I'll pick you up Saturday, and we'll have the whole day together before the event."

"I'm looking forward to it. Can you send me the details? Is it some kind of ball or something a little less formal?"

"Don't worry about it. I've planned a surprise for you."

At the excitement in his voice, I smiled. The weekend promised to be a good one.

CHAPTER FOURTEEN

When I saw the smile on Vaughn's face as he greeted me at LaGuardia Airport, the tension that had been my constant companion for the last few days eased. Vaughn was my husband, and I loved him. More importantly, he loved me.

"At last," he cried, ignoring the gasps of recognition around us and sweeping me up into his arms.

I nestled my face against his broad chest, resting it on the soft, blue sweater that brought out the chocolate color in his eyes.

"I'm so glad you're here," he murmured. "It seems like such a long time."

In truth, it hadn't been that long, but I knew exactly how he felt. With his arms around me, hugging me close, I felt as if I had come home.

I lifted my face to his, and suddenly aware of the crowd that had gathered around us, I let out a sigh even as I smiled at him.

He grabbed my hand. "C'mon. I've got a limo waiting for us. The driver can get your bag. I can't wait to welcome you home more properly."

I kept pace with his anxious footsteps, and we exited the terminal. At a signal from Vaughn, a man got out of a black limousine and hurried toward us.

Vaughn introduced me and described my luggage to him. Then, Vaughn and I slipped into the backseat of the limousine. With the darkened windows blocking views of us from the outside, we embraced. The hungry kiss Vaughn gave me let me know how much he'd missed me, and I wondered how long we could keep up the routine of living apart for much of the time.

He pulled away and stared down at me. "I'm really glad you came. Things have been ... uh ... difficult with Lily working with me."

I raised my eyebrows. "Something we need to talk about?"

He nodded. "Probably. But for the moment, why don't we just enjoy one another's company. We have the afternoon to ourselves. I promised we'd appear at The Plaza by six o'clock. Before then, I'm taking you shopping. And I've already made an appointment for you at Paris. I know Pierre's your favorite stylist."

My jaw dropped. "This is your surprise? How fabulous! You certainly know how to pamper a woman." I'd used Pierre at his salon, Paris, to do my hair and makeup in the past. Not as well-known as some in the city, Pierre was as clever as anyone the regulars in the New York social scene used. And not nearly as expensive.

He grinned and gave me a kiss. "We'll start at Barney's."

After the driver returned to the car with my bag, Vaughn spoke to him, and we headed to my favorite store. Along the way, I was startled to see the sides of two buses covered with a picture of Vaughn and Lily kissing. The caption read: "Together again!"

My stomach turned. I gazed away, but not before Vaughn noticed my reaction.

"I'm sorry, Ann. I know all this publicity bothers you, but that's all it is." Vaughn smiled and gave my hand a gentle squeeze.

At Barney's, I found the perfect dress. Long and strapless and in a shimmering gold that clung subtly to my curves, the silky, smooth fabric felt fantastic on my body. As I twirled in happy circles in front of him, Vaughn stared wide-eyed at me and all but licked his lips. Feeling good about myself, I went with Vaughn to the top floor to the shoe department and found the perfect strappy sandals to go with the dress.

Later, as we stood in the purse department, Vaughn turned to me. "Have I told you lately how much I love you?"

I smiled. "Yes, but I never tire of hearing it."

He cupped my cheek and gazed at me. "You're going to look beautiful tonight, but one thing is missing. I'm going to help you find the perfect pair of earrings for the dress."

"Really?"

"Oh, yes," he said, giving me a devilish grin.

I couldn't help returning his smile. He was doing everything he could to make this a special event for us.

Later, leaving Cartier with a pair of amulette earrings in gold, made with inlaid mother of pearl and diamonds, I felt as pampered as any princess. The earrings were stunning and yet simple enough to wear in Sabal for the few dressier occasions I attended.

Outside the hair salon, Vaughn kissed me. "This is where I leave you. Go ahead and have a good time. I'll meet you at the apartment."

I watched Vaughn get into the limo and stood a moment as the car pulled away from the curb and headed down the avenue. Grateful Pierre had agreed to meet me, I headed inside to what I hoped would be the final touch to my preparation for the evening ahead.

I stood in front of the full-length mirror in the master bedroom of Vaughn's apartment and gazed at myself in the mirror, hardly believing the image that stared back at me. Pierre had styled my dark hair so that it was pulled away from my face and swept up in a small gathering of soft curls in the back of my head. Staring at the changes, I held a nervous giggle inside. I looked like a high school girl about to go to the senior prom. But the dress, wrapped around my body in gossamer gold, made it clear that I was no innocent girl, but a sophisticated woman of means. And as Vaughn had hoped, the earrings confirmed that appearance.

When I stepped out of the bedroom and into the living room where Vaughn was waiting, I was surprised to see his eyes moisten at the sight of me.

"My God! You look stunning, Ann. No one will believe I'd ever choose Lily Dorio over you." He walked over to me and lightly kissed my cheek so he wouldn't mess my makeup.

I grabbed the light wrap the sales clerk had suggested, and we headed out to the limo.

Although Vaughn's apartment overlooking Central Park was close enough to The Plaza Hotel that we might have been able to walk, we were, Vaughn informed me, supposed to arrive in style.

At the hotel, after we got out of the limousine under the porte cochere, I stood a moment. Seeing the familiar landmark up close, I couldn't help thinking of Eloise, the character in one of my favorite books about the city. The façade of the property was as dramatic as any castle. My feeling of being a princess was suddenly intimidating, and as we entered the hotel, my pulse pounded in nervous beats.

Carrying the small evening purse we'd purchased, and draping the lightweight wrap over my arm, I accepted Vaughn's hand. We made our way to the Grand Ballroom. It too was like a scene in a fairy tale. Crystal chandeliers sparkled, and reflections of them in the wall mirrors sent rainbows in every direction. Large arches rose high above us, making me feel even smaller. Gold touches warmed the room everywhere, even in the details on the dozens and dozens of chairs standing by the rounds of tables dressed in crisp, white tablecloths. Crystal glasses repeated the colors of the assorted pink flowers displayed in crystal vases in the middle of each table.

As Vaughn and I descended a stairway to greet others in the assembled group, I drew a deep breath and told myself that for one night I was not a mother of a young woman in her twenties and a son of four, but a princess used to this lifestyle.

Vaughn smiled down at me and drew me over to where Roger and Darlene Sloan were standing.

"Ann, my dear, you look ravishing tonight," Roger said, bowing to kiss my hand.

Darlene and I exchanged an amused look before kissing each other on the cheek.

"Ann, I love you in that dress," said Darlene. "I'm sorry it's not one of mine, but I forgive you. It's perfect."

I smiled at her. Though I loathed her husband, I was and always had been an admirer of Darlene. She was a smart, savvy businesswoman who had a successful line of clothing. She'd had to endure Lily Dorio having Roger's child. Even four years later, the fact that Darlene and Roger were still together was a topic of much gossip because Lily had finally agreed to allow Darlene and Roger to adopt the little girl. For a lot of money, I was sure. But as the mother of a little boy Vaughn and I had adopted, I knew Roger and Lily's little girl was lucky to be part of their family. She, no doubt, held them together and gave Roger a reason to satisfy Lily's desire to be part of the show.

"I'm glad you called me, Vaughn," said Roger. "I made arrangements to have the seating changed so that Ann is sitting next to you as you requested."

I turned to Vaughn with surprise.

He shook his head. "Lily has been moved to another table. It's good for her to mingle with others. Part of the show and all that." Vaughn's voice held a sarcastic ring that was unlike him, but I understood his underlying frustration.

Darlene caught my attention and pulled me aside. "How are you doing with all this business of Vaughn and Lily?" she asked quietly.

I shook my head. "Neither Vaughn nor I like it. I don't understand why something can't be done about it."

Darlene's eyebrows rose. "Is that what you've been told?"

"That's what Vaughn has been told."

Darlene's lips formed a narrow line as she glanced at Roger, who was continuing to talk to Vaughn. "We'll see about that. I'll try to talk to Roger about it." She put a hand on my arm. "Please don't mention this to Vaughn or anyone else."

"I won't," I said, unwilling to get into any personal business of theirs.

"Ready, Ann?" Vaughn said, coming over to me and taking my arm. "Guess we should make the rounds."

We left Darlene and Roger and moved into the crowd.

"Sorry about that," said Vaughn. "I had a feeling I should check on a few arrangements here."

Vaughn introduced me to a couple of people he knew. While I chatted with them, I gazed around the room. I didn't know most of the people, but it seemed that others were well acquainted. The buzz of conversation rose to a congenial, high pitch.

A woman I recognized from a television news station that loved to report on celebrities approached us.

"Vaughn Sanders, how are you? Handsome as ever, I'd say. And where is Lily?" she said, eying me curiously.

"Hello, Marcy. You obviously haven't met my beautiful wife, Ann." He put an arm around my shoulders and drew me close. "She's not always able to be in New York, which is why I go home to Florida as often as I can."

He smiled down at me. "Ann, this is Marcy Winters."

With effort, my lips curved. "Nice to meet you, Marcy."

As she shook my hand, her gaze slid from my earrings down to my strappy sandals and up again. "What a lovely surprise to meet you." She glanced at Vaughn. "You should show her off more often, Vaughn."

From behind me, someone drew close. "Vaughnie, there's been some sort of mix-up. My seat has been changed. You have to make it right."

Vaughnie? Was she kidding? I turned around to face Lily.

Her eyes widened when she saw me. "Oh, Ann ... I didn't recognize you. You look ... different ... lovely, I mean." She stopped talking and gave Vaughn an apologetic look. "I forgot Ann finally agreed to come to New York. Of course, you two will have to sit together." The look she gave me was as cold as her voice.

Lily turned back to Vaughn. Gazing up at him with fluttering eyelashes, she beamed at him. "We'll have other opportunities. Won't we, darling?"

Vaughn stood stiffly as Lily gave him a kiss on the cheek.

Turning to Marcie, Lily smiled. "We'll talk later."

As Lily moved to the group standing next to us, I took a moment to study her from a distance. With her plunging neckline and expensive implants, she was all female. The see-through panels in her dress, strategically placed, were designed to capture interest. I understood why most male eyes in the crowd eventually landed on her. She was as sexy as the famous sisters on television.

Vaughn squeezed my hand for attention. "You're the most

beautiful woman in the room. Trust me."

I smiled up at him and pushed away my insecurity, determined to be the perfect partner for Vaughn. Heaven knew, others would be willing to take my place.

Once I'd decided to relax and just enjoy the evening with him, I became intrigued by all the beautiful people and the elegant surroundings as rich in décor as any castle anywhere in the world. Seated beside Vaughn on the dais, I had a good view of it all.

And later, as I listened to Vaughn speak about the importance of art in everyone's lives and its role in the upbringing of children, my heart swelled with pride. He was a good man, a generous man who sincerely loved his field of work, notwithstanding the recent troubles over public relations.

Amid the applause that followed his speech, he sat down. I leaned over and whispered, "I'm so proud of you."

A flush of pleasure colored his cheeks. "And I of you, my darling."

I glanced down at Lily seated at a table below us and froze at the angry glare she sent my way. I knew then that Lily would continue to play her game.

Later, after we'd been delivered to Vaughn's apartment and were sitting in the living room, he took off his tie and the jacket to his tuxedo and patted the space next to him on the couch.

"Come here, beautiful lady."

I kicked off my sandals and joined him.

He cupped my face in his hands and gave me a deep kiss.

As I responded, lust surged through me, making me long for something more.

He pulled away. "Whew! Let's not wait any longer. Let's go to bed."

I laughed at the leering look he gave me.

He grabbed hold of my hand and pulled me to my feet. He stood and studied me with appreciation. "That dress is perfect for you. I almost hate to have you take it off. Almost."

We hurried into the bedroom, where we both removed our clothes in a remarkably short period of time.

Standing beside the bed, the sexual chemistry between Vaughn and me thrummed like a guitar wire stretched too thin.

Eagerly, we climbed on top of the king-size bed that soon became a playground of sorts as we teased and taunted and finally satisfied each other.

Later, sighing with contentment, I leaned back against my pillow and nestled Vaughn's head on my chest.

"I love you, Ann," he murmured.

"And I love you," I replied. "But make no mistake, Lily is a determined woman, and she wants you. Vaughnie? Where in the world did that come from?"

He lifted his head. "Ridiculous, huh?"

I nodded. But ridiculous or not, I was going to keep an eye on things.

In the morning, I lounged in bed, reveling in the quiet. Vaughn lay beside me, snoring softly.

Carefully, so as not to wake him, I rose out of bed, slipped on Vaughn's pajama top, and tiptoed into the living room. The late October day was bright with promise. Unusually warm, the weekend was predicted to be a good precursor, weather-wise, for Halloween. Robbie had chosen to dress up as a race car driver. At the thought, a smile crossed my face. I gazed out the window at the fading colors on the trees in Central Park, loving the scene. I understood this was just one of the reasons why Vaughn enjoyed New York City, but I hoped he'd continue to understand how important Sabal was to me.

A step behind me caused me to swivel around in time to receive Vaughn's embrace.

He lowered his face and nuzzled my neck. "Ah, Ann, too many times I wake up and wish you were here like this."

I stared up at him. "I know because I miss your being in Sabal with Robbie and me."

His expression grew serious. "I'm trying to work on a new arrangement for more time together, but it's meeting with some resistance from the producers. I'm willing to work on some weekends if it means I can have more time in Florida. As much as I like it here, I prefer being in Florida with you and our family. It was different for Ellen and me. Back then, I could commute from our home in Connecticut to the studio by car. This flying back and forth to Florida can be a real pain. And with you and Rhonda back in the hotel business, it will become even more difficult."

"Yes, but I'm pretty sure Bernie is going to come back to work for us at the hotel. And if he does, we're going to turn the daily management of it over to him to a far greater extent than ever before. We have to."

"And if he doesn't?" Vaughn's gaze penetrated mine.

"I'm not going there yet," I said, shaking my head in protest. The truth was, I'd do most anything to get Bernie back because I needed and wanted more time with Vaughn.

"Well, then we'll take it one day at a time." Vaughn's lips curved as he wrapped his arms around me. "And on this day, we're going to have fun for as long as we can."

He gave me one of the sexy grins his audience loved.

I loved it too.

CHAPTER FIFTEEN

Too soon, it became time for me to head for the airport. As before, Vaughn hired a limo to take us. Snuggled up against him, I hid the tears that stung my eyes and threatened to spill over. I'd come to hate living this way.

At the airport, while the driver of the limo waited, Vaughn and I gave each other a last hug, and then I walked away from him into the terminal as conflicted as I'd ever been. If necessary, Robbie and I could move to New York, but was it the right answer?

Thankfully, after all the lovemaking with Vaughn and the challenge of the charity ball, I slept during most of the flight to Florida.

There, at the sight of Liz and Robbie standing in the baggage-claim area, my troubled spirits lifted. This is where I wanted to be, needed to be. If only Vaughn could be with us.

"Mommy!" cried Robbie. He sprinted toward me, running as fast as his legs could carry him.

I swept him up into my arms and hugged him close, smiling as Liz approached me.

She leaned over and kissed me on the cheek. "I'm so glad you're home, Mom. Rhonda and I didn't want to ruin your weekend by calling you, but there's been a fire at the hotel."

Shocked, I almost dropped Robbie. He slid from my embrace and landed on his feet, looking up at me with concern.

"Fire? Where?" I said, forcing words out through a throat clogged with worry.

"The beach hut burned to the ground last night."

"What happened?"

"We think the fire was set. We have no way to prove it, but I think I know who did it. One of the bellmen mentioned to Rhonda that Bree was drunk last night and vowed to get even with the two of you. I'm scared for you, Mom. He's such a creep."

I placed a hand on her shoulder. "We're going to be fine, Liz. But if it will make you feel any better, I'll talk to Rhonda about hiring an extra security guard to patrol the hotel. Aubrey Lowell is a spoiled jerk."

Robbie frowned. "Jerk?"

I ruffled his hair. "Not you, buddy." I took hold of his hand, and we went to the conveyor belt to get my suitcase.

As we stood together, Liz said softly, "Angela and I have already agreed to make appearances at the hotel whenever possible while Rhonda is recovering from her surgery. She's home, but is going to take it easy for the next few days."

"Things will be all right," I said in a soothing tone to her, but I thought their plan was something Rhonda and I should follow too.

The ringing of the alarm clock jolted me out of a dream of Vaughn and me cavorting on the beach. I blinked and looked around the room, trying to deal with reality. My bedroom door opened, and Robbie and Trudy burst into the room. Robbie lifted Trudy up onto the bed and quickly followed her for his routine, morning hug. Pushing away my romantic thoughts of Vaughn, I embraced Robbie. Trudy's nose pushed into the slit of space between Robbie and me. Laughing, Robbie and I gave her enough space to squeeze in between us so she could kiss both of us.

"Okay, time to get going," I said, putting Trudy down onto the floor. Robbie jumped, landing with both feet beside her before heading for his room.

I led Trudy to the kitchen door and ushered her outside. The humid air that swirled around me was so different from the warmth of the night I'd spent in New York. I looked up at the gray clouds boiling in the sky above me. Seasonal changes in Florida weren't so much about colors as they were about weather patterns.

When Trudy and I went inside, Robbie was in the kitchen wearing the goggles and driving gloves that were part of his Halloween costume.

"You're coming to my party today, right?" Robbie asked. "We're having Halloween cupcakes and apple juice."

"Yes, I told your teacher I would help her today." It was one reason I'd been unable to stay longer with Vaughn.

While I was on my way to school with Robbie, Rhonda phoned to tell me that, as we'd discussed, she'd called the security company we had used before at the hotel. The extra guard would be on duty for the evening shift and early morning hours. "Mike Torson called me back and said that at this point, he wasn't willing to go to the owners of the hotel with a mere suspicion that Bree was behind the fire. He said to be watchful, and to try to work with him and others on the staff to make this a smooth transition." Rhonda let out a snort of disgust. "How do ya like that? Huh?"

"He's right. The more trouble we give them, the more difficult they'll make it for us. After Robbie is down for a rest, I'll talk to Bill Richardson to see if we can speed up the inspections at the hotel. I'd like to move as quickly as we can, so we can get Bree and the owners out of there."

"Good idea. By the way, I talked to Cliff. He's dying to come back and work for us as our night auditor again. And I tried

Jean-Luc and Sabine's number again, but they must still be out of town. I'll just die if we can't get them back on staff."

"I certainly hope we can. Consuela can make our famous cinnamon breakfast rolls, but we need Jean-Luc to bring back the kind of cuisine our guests loved."

"Right. I miss that old French frog like crazy. Anything else I need to do before our board meeting tomorrow?"

"I can't think of anything at the moment. I'll see you this evening when I bring Robbie over for our trick or treat visit."

"Tell Robbie I can't wait to see him."

From the back seat, Robbie said, "Aunt Rhonda is going to love my driver costume."

I smiled at him in the rearview mirror. "Yes, I think so too."

I parked the car in the parking lot of the school and walked inside with Robbie. Seeing all the kids in his class dressed up, I was overwhelmed with their cuteness. But by the time Robbie and I were ready to go home, I was exhausted. Even though we'd tried to limit sugar intake, the kids were wired with excitement.

I hugged his teacher. "No matter what they pay you, it isn't enough."

She laughed. "Believe me, I know, but I love my job."

As Robbie and I left the school, I mentally changed gears, listing in my mind all I needed to do before the hotel board meeting the following day.

After Robbie went down for a nap, I called Bill Richardson and got a brief update on the inspections for the hotel. All seemed to be in order. While the owners had skimped on replacements of furniture, fixtures, and equipment, they apparently had maintained all the heating, ventilating, and air conditioning systems.

Hearing that, I let out a sigh of relief. Though we'd be forced to upgrade the interiors of the rooms, the basic bones of the building and the mechanical, electrical, and plumbing systems were intact.

My next call was to Reggie Smythe. Even though we'd hired an auditor to review the books, Angela's husband was thrilled to be working on his own, personal audit of the hotel's finances.

He picked up after two rings. "Hi, Ann! Glad you called. Something funny is going on with the management company, but I haven't been able to put all the pieces together yet."

My pulse skipped a beat. Bree was head of the management company for our hotel. "Rhonda and I have a meeting with the owners tomorrow. Any way I can help you?"

"Not yet, but maybe by the beginning of next week. I have an idea I want to follow through on. In the meantime, any new financial information you can give me will be helpful."

"Reggie, are we talking about the management company taking too much money?" My blood turned to ice. I had an idea or two of my own.

"Yes, that's it. But I can't come up with how they're doing it."

"Thanks," I said. "We'll talk tomorrow." I hung up the phone and called Elena to make sure she could spend the night. I'd be busy.

That evening, after the excitement of Halloween trick-or-treating had passed and Robbie was safely tucked in bed, I headed to the hotel. Rhonda had agreed to meet me there.

I was sitting in the lobby having a glass of wine when Rhonda hurried inside and sat on a small settee next to me.

"Okay, Annie, what's going on?" Rhonda whispered. Her eyes sparkled. "You said it was a top-secret mission."

"It is," I said, enjoying the private moment with her. "I talked to Reggie earlier today. He said something's wrong with the management contract numbers, but he hasn't quite figured it out. However, I think I have."

Rhonda moved closer and grabbed my hand. "Okay, spill."

I looked around the room to make sure no one could hear us above the conversations of others and the tinkling piano music in the background. Leaning close to her ear, I said, "Remember how odd it was that Bree took his father to the airport in that ratty old Jeep?"

Rhonda nodded.

"I talked to the bellman who'd mentioned Bree's car to me earlier. When I asked him about the Jeep, he told me that the Jeep was his, that Bree didn't want his father to know about his new Porsche."

"What a brat," muttered Rhonda.

"I think he didn't want his father to know about the new car because his father would know that something was up. Bree's salary is based at least partly on sales, and those aren't good enough to support buying a luxury car like that. Even if he spent his personal money, it seems like a high-priced vehicle for someone like him."

"Yeah, so?"

"So, I think he's fudging the figures somehow and getting paid more than he should for his role of running the management contract for this property. And I think I know who else might be involved."

Rhonda rubbed her hands together. "I hope you're right. I can't wait to destroy that twerp. What he did to Bernie and the others on our old staff is unforgivable. And firing a few of them without any notice? Awful. I just hope Bernie and some of the other staff members will return."

"Me, too. So, here's what we're going to do. When Julie comes on duty, we're going to ask to see the night auditor's books. They're locked away, but she should know where the key is."

"Julie? Why her? Because that red shoe belonged to her?"

"Because she and Stuart have a thing going on, and Stuart is willing to do anything for Bree. If I'm not mistaken, she, Stuart, and the night auditor are all taking part in a scheme to keep some rooms revenues off the books by selling rooms for cash, giving Bree and his cronies the chance to skim some of the funds. Remember how quick Bree was to fire Cliff Reynolds, our old night auditor?"

"Yeah, that caught us off guard. But the little prick wouldn't change his mind, and there was nothing we could do about it."

"I know it's just a theory of mine, but I want to test it. When I spoke to Bree about the impropriety of Stuart and Julie being romantically involved, Bree, as usual, brushed aside my concern. He tried to tell me it wasn't my business. I let it go, but it has never seemed right to me."

Rhonda ordered a glass of wine from the waitress who circled the room, and we sat quietly, observing the activity around us.

"They'd also need the head housekeeper to be part of their scheme, to fudge the daily occupancy reports," said Rhonda, giving me a worried look. "No wonder they fired Ana. She's as honest as they come."

My thoughts whirled. "I wonder how big this is."

"We're going to find out." She started to rise.

I tugged her back. "We have to act as if nothing is the matter, that we're just curious, not angry."

"Yeah, you're right." She sighed. "How could things have gotten so out of hand?"

"From now on, we trust but verify," I said grimly.

Brock Goodwin walked into the lobby. Seeing us, he headed right over to where Rhonda and I were sitting.

I didn't like the sly smile that crossed his face and braced for bad news.

"Understand there was a fire here over the weekend. If you think you can rebuild that ... that shack on the beach think again. I'll make sure the Neighborhood Association fights it all the way." He glared at Rhonda. "As a friend, of course."

Rhonda's eyes bulged. She opened her mouth to speak, but before she could, Brock all but sprinted away.

"That, that ..."

"Relax," I whispered. "Guests are looking at us."

Rhonda released a puff of air and sat back against the cushions on the couch, but her fists knotted. I understood. Brock Goodwin was enough to make anyone furious.

I noticed Julie taking her position behind the front desk and waited to point it out to Rhonda, who was staring in Brock's direction.

"Okay, let's go," I said, getting to my feet.

Rhonda gave me a quizzical look, then saw Julie and quickly rose.

"You do the talking, Annie before I say something I shouldn't."

We approached the front desk. "Good evening, Julie. How are you?"

She clasped her hands together and gave us an imploring look. "Ann, I'm so sorry. I knew Stu and I shouldn't have been fooling around in his office like that. Not on the job."

"I'm sorry too. The hotel policy clearly states that as well," I said coolly, aware that Rhonda and I couldn't fire her. At least not yet.

Julie nodded. "What can I do to help you?"

"We need to check something on the auditor's report," I said as smoothly as possible. "So, if you don't mind, we'll check the computer he uses in his room behind the front desk. I've got the password."

"Okay." Julie opened the door that was a discreet part of

the paneled wall behind her.

We stepped inside, and I sat at the small desk there. I typed in the usual password. Nothing. I tried it again, and once more the computer remained locked.

"Julie, do you know the password? Mine isn't working," I asked, exchanging knowing looks with Rhonda.

Julie came to the doorway. "Bree and Stuart set up a whole new series of passwords shortly after Bree hired Stuart. It's some kind of secret project of theirs."

Telling myself to remain calm I got to my feet. "Okay, no problem. We'll check it tomorrow."

Rhonda and I exited the office and walked out of the hotel. "Annie ..." Rhonda began.

I cut her off. "Let's go to your house. We'll talk there." As soon as the valet brought my car around, I climbed in and waited for Rhonda's car to be delivered to her. Then I followed her to her house.

Will greeted us at the door. "What's up?"

"A helluva lot," Rhonda said. "You tell him, Annie."

"Come inside into the kitchen. We can talk there."

At the kitchen table, Rhonda nudged me. "Go on. Tell 'em."

I drew a deep breath and began. "Reggie suspected something was wrong with the management fees being charged to the hotel. I've done some investigation on my own. Rhonda and I are pretty sure money is being skimmed from the hotel books. We're supposed to close on the hotel on November 7th, but we can't do that now. Not unless we find out exactly what is going on and then making them adjust the price we've agreed on." Tears came to my eyes. "It's a mess."

Rhonda nodded. "Yeah, a frickin' mess."

"It's a little late to call Mike," I said. "But he needs to be aware of this."

"With all the money we're paying him, we'll call him now,"

Rhonda said with determination. "He's our lawyer, and, like you said, he should know."

"I'm really sorry this is happening," said Will. "We'll have to move quickly. I'll set up a meeting tomorrow morning with Reggie and the auditors you've hired. You're right. If we can prove the skimming, the purchase price will have to be adjusted. That's only fair."

Rhonda punched in the number of Mike Torson. I listened as she explained what was going on. "Okay, tomorrow morning at nine," she said and hung up. "We'll meet with him tomorrow. He says this is a pretty serious accusation, so we need to gather all the proof we can. He's calling the forensic auditors first thing tomorrow morning."

Feeling waves of nausea wash over me, I bowed my head.

"You okay, Annie?"

I lifted my face and shook my head. "It's more than the money. It's the fact that people we trusted would willingly deceive us. If word ever got out, it might ruin the reputation of the hotel."

"As if it's not bad enough already," grumbled Rhonda.

"I'm sure the majority owners will want to keep this quiet too. That could work in your favor," said Will. "I'll help in any way I can."

Rhonda got up, walked over to Will, and hugged him to her. "That's so sweet. I know you haven't been one hundred percent behind me buying back the hotel. I love ya, Will Grayson."

A flush of pleasure crept up his cheeks. "Love you too, baby doll."

Watching them exchange such loving looks, I missed Vaughn so much it hurt.

CHAPTER SIXTEEN

The next morning, Rhonda and I sat in Mike Torson's office listening to him describe how best to address the situation with Peabody, Lowell, and Logan, the majority owners of the hotel.

"The auditors concur that there's enough evidence to present to them," said Mike, giving us a grim look. "While you're here, we'll call George Peabody. As the eldest of the group, he seems the best choice for reasonable talk. I happen to know he doesn't much like Aubrey Lowell, even though he and Aubrey's father, Austin, have been doing business together for years. Obviously, Austin will resist such news, and Sam Logan seems to be more or less merely an investor, not so actively involved."

I leaned forward. "I believe the Porsche that Bree recently purchased has been kept a secret from his father. And I suspect that it was partially paid for, or least the down payment was made, through the funds he skimmed. I don't know what benefits, if any, Stuart or Maria, the head housekeeper might have received from being involved. Maybe, just their jobs."

"Yeah, maybe they threatened Maria. I hope to talk to her this morning," said Rhonda.

"Okay, but be careful what you say," said Mike. "We want to undress this group in an orderly way, making careful notes along the way. The auditors are meeting with Reggie Smythe this morning?"

"Yes," said Rhonda. "Reggie's done a fantastic job going

through the financials. He's turning out to be a great son-in-law."

Mike and I exchanged smiles, well aware how opposed Rhonda was to having him marry her sweet Angela.

"The contract you signed allows you to extend the closing date," said Mike, reviewing the papers he held in his hands. "I would suggest you extend it to the Monday before Thanksgiving. That will give you enough time to complete your audits and come to a reasonable settlement with the sellers."

Rhonda looked as dismayed as I felt. We'd wanted to have all the rooms renovated by then.

"It could conceivably be settled sooner, but this will give you some wiggle room." Mike gave each of us a long look. "Okay, if we proceed with this?"

Rhonda shrugged, and I nodded, wishing things were different.

Mike rose to his feet. "All right. Why don't you relax here while I make my call to George Peabody? Rest assured, I'll give you all the details."

After Mike left the office, Rhonda and I turned to each other.

"You don't mind speaking to Maria alone?" I asked her. "I have a meeting with our favorite hotel supplier to discuss refurbishing my house. We're also talking about the guest rooms at the hotel. I'll gather the samples, and then you and I can decide what we want to order after we meet with Laura Bakeley to confirm our choices."

"I'll be fine with Maria. Besides, we don't want to scare her by making it seem that we both are attacking her."

Mike returned to the office. "By the time we finished our conversation, George Peabody was one unhappy man. It turns out that Bree Lowell has been nothing but a problem for them.

This time, George is done with trying to deal with Bree and his father peacefully. He's agreed that should our allegations be true, he, himself, will oust Bree from the group. Above all, he doesn't want the management company's reputation tainted. He's going to see that the board meeting scheduled for today is canceled."

"He's going to be agreeable to reducing the price of the hotel?" I asked.

"We'll have to do a complete audit proving it, of course, but he isn't going to fight us on this as long as we can show him the proof. I've called Reggie's office and have agreed to go meet with them now. Rhonda, you're set to meet with Maria this morning?"

Rhonda nodded. "She's scheduled to be at the hotel. I have a feeling Maria has been bullied into this, and I want to protect her from Bree."

"Good. We want to move as quickly as possible, before Bree gets wind of our intentions."

After leaving Mike's office, I hurried over to my house on the hotel property. I did a final walk-through, making notes on the spreadsheet I'd set up to track what I'd need for the renovation. Hotel Suppliers, Inc. out of Miami was a company we'd used in the past. They had a wide range of carpets, soft goods, and furniture. Though it was all nice quality, I'd been proud of the way I'd put together furniture from my old house in Boston with things I'd bought at estate sales. Now the look would be more commercial in nature but still nice for Tina.

When I thought of her, my heart filled with affection. It would be good to see her—not the gorgeous woman on a movie screen, but the young woman whose vulnerabilities I knew well.

I left the hotel and drove to Robbie's school to pick him up.

As usual, he left the building with a whoop of joy. "Mommy, look!" He held out a piece of artwork.

I smiled at the picture he'd drawn. "Great job! Your pumpkin is smiling."

Robbie looked up at me with shining eyes. "His trick-or-treat bag is full of candy, like mine."

I laughed. Robbie had a sweet tooth.

Later, while Elena was watching Robbie, I met with Harold Drayton, the salesman from Hotel Suppliers, at my house on the hotel property. Short, bald, and round-bellied, Harold was an honest man who understood my distress at what had happened to my home.

"We can take care of this, Ann. We'll keep your same sense of color and comfort. Then Laura can add some fun touches. We at Hotel Suppliers like to work with her on our projects."

"Good, because after we choose things for this house, we need to talk about the guest rooms at the hotel. They've been neglected by people who have no idea how to take proper care of things." I couldn't hide my frustration. Bree and his friends were accustomed to leaving messes for someone else to clean up.

"Okay, great. We'll choose excellent, commercial-quality items that have a residential feel," Harold said in a soothing voice that made me feel better.

Later that afternoon, I met Rhonda at her house. Upstairs in the privacy of her sitting room, we exchanged stories of our day.

"Annie, it was a good thing I went alone to see Maria. She became almost hysterical when I asked her about the daily housekeeping reports she's been making. It turns out she's not entering the daily, occupied-room numbers. Bree is doing that from his computer. He rigged up a system to make it look like it came from her computer."

"So why didn't she say anything?" I asked.

"It's like I thought. Bree threatened her."

"With what?" I asked, feeling my body turn cold.

"It seems her husband's father is an undocumented immigrant from Mexico. Bree found out somehow and threatened to expose them all." Rhonda let out a blast of angry breath. "I can't wait to get rid of him."

"Me too, but we can't let Bree know that we're building a case against him," I warned her.

We talked for a while longer, and then I left to go home.

Pulling into the driveway of Vaughn's and my house, I couldn't help wondering how things were going with him in New York. I hadn't talked to him in a couple of days, which was unusual. I hoped it didn't mean trouble.

I got out of the car and went inside. At the sound of Trudy's barking and Robbie's shouts from the pool area, I hurried to find them.

Robbie saw me and waved. Trudy rushed over on her short, crooked legs to greet me and, after receiving a few ear rubs and scratches, ran back to Robbie. These two always made my days brighter, better. I'd wanted lots of children after having Liz, but that hadn't happened. Now, this little boy seemed like a miracle.

Elena got to her feet. "How are ideas for your house coming along?" As she walked toward me, the diamond ring that Troy had finally presented to her sparkled on her left hand.

"It's going to be nice. I hope to have it finished in time for Tina Marks to use at Thanksgiving." I smiled at her. "There's something I need to talk to you about."

Her eyebrows rose. "Everything all right?"

"With you? Of course." I looked into her face. It was beautiful—full of kindness.

"I know you and Troy are looking for house rentals. Would you consider living in the second apartment at the hotel?"

"At the hotel?" Elena shook her head. "I don't think we can afford that."

I smiled at her. "What if we made sure you could by letting you have it rent-free? Part of the deal would be that you'd keep an eye on things at the hotel. Just knowing we have loyal friends there would make a world of difference to Rhonda and me."

The light that had filled her eyes dimmed. "What about Liz and Chad? Would they be upset?"

"No, because they're looking to rent a home in Angela's neighborhood."

Elena's face lit with excitement. "Really? Troy and me living at the hotel? That would be wonderful! Simply wonderful! Of course, I have to talk to him about it, but it would be an answer to our prayers."

"Okay, Rhonda and I will discuss it with him too."

Elena gave me a hug. "Thanks, Ann. That would be a perfect solution for us."

As I headed inside to change into a swim suit, I decided to give Bernie a call. He'd asked for time in making the decision, and though I knew he was busy, I couldn't wait to begin negotiations with him.

Bernie picked up after the first ring. "Hi, Ann! I was just about to call you."

My pulse sprinted. "And?"

"And I've drawn up a list of my requirements. There shouldn't be any problem finding common ground on most of them, but I need to have reassurance from you and Rhonda that my term as general manager will be based on my performance, not on some other group coming in and pushing me out."

"Believe me, Bernie, Rhonda and I have learned our lesson. The hotel will stay in our families."

"Okay, then, I'll email you the information I've put together, and you and Rhonda can get back to me. Under the right conditions, Annette and I would both like to return to Sabal."

"Thanks, Bernie. I can't tell you what this means to me ... to us. Once we agree on things, we'll have Mike draw up a contract."

"Good enough. Talk to you later, Ann."

Bernie hung up the phone, and I quickly called Rhonda.

"Great news!" she cried. "Getting Bernie back is a huge plus for us. Wonder what those requirements of his are."

"No matter what they are, we'll work it out. Agreed?"

"Yeah, no way we're letting him go."

I'd just slipped on my bathing suit when my cell rang. I checked Caller ID and smiled. *Nell.* I'd felt close to Nell since I'd first met her a few years ago when she came to The Beach House Hotel to visit her father during the filming of the soap opera. And though Vaughn and I didn't see much of his son, Ty, and his wife, June, we had a pleasant relationship with them, too.

"Hi, Nell! How are you?" I chirped with happiness. "The baby still scheduled to arrive in late winter?"

"Looks that way. We just had the sonogram done and, Ann, it's a girl! We're going to name her after my mother, whose maiden name was Bailey."

"Oh, how cute!" I said. "Your father will be so pleased."

"Actually, that's why I called, Ann. I just got off the phone with him, and I'm worried. He seems so unhappy. Is everything all right between the two of you?"

My heart bumped to a stop and raced ahead in breath-catching beats. "Why do you ask? Is it the hotel? Rhonda and I are buying back The Beach House Hotel. Your father wasn't thrilled about my doing it, but we both agreed for me to go ahead with it."

"No, I don't think it's that. I believe it has to do with Lily and all the fake publicity. It's always been difficult for him to be judged as the man he plays on the show, but now his personal reputation is being marred by how the producers portray him outside the show—a role that's not true. I think it's pretty rotten of them to make it seem as if he and Lily are together in real life just to boost ratings for the show."

"You can imagine how I feel about that," I said, unable to hide the bitterness in my voice.

"Well, I don't mean to worry you but thought you'd want to know. As far as the hotel is concerned, people are going to be ecstatic that you and Rhonda will be running it again. And Liz told me that she and Angela might become more involved with it in time."

"It's just a thought," I said, careful not to make Nell feel left out. And then I thought of all her skills and quickly added, "It might be something you'd be interested in too."

"Thanks, I might love to do that someday," Nell replied. "In the meantime, you and Rhonda have fun with it. I've got to go. Talk to you later. Love you."

"Love you," I said, still stunned by Nell's comment. *Have fun with the hotel? Didn't she realize what hard work it was? But The Beach House Hotel was our baby, and we'd do right by it.*

CHAPTER SEVENTEEN

After ending the call with Nell, I phoned Vaughn, hoping to be able at least to leave him a message.

He picked up the call on the first ring. "Hi, honey. I was about to call you. I'm coming home this weekend and hope you can arrange for us to have time away together. I really need it. I'm done with my life in New York."

"Have you quit the show?" I asked, alarmed by the resignation in his voice.

"No, I can't do that. Not with all the legal problems that would entail and the possible damage it would do to me professionally. I just need to get away from here."

"I have the perfect idea in mind. When will you arrive?"

"Friday afternoon. I'll send you the details. Ann? Gotta go. See you then."

We hung up, and I sank down onto the bed. Life was full of challenges, but being married to Vaughn Sanders was one I was willing to meet.

I made another phone call, and satisfied with the reservations I'd made, I headed out to the join Robbie at the pool.

Friday afternoon, I waited impatiently for Vaughn's plane to land. I'd done a lot of thinking in the last couple of days and had decided that now, and in the future, Vaughn and I would need to set aside time in our busy schedules for us, that it wouldn't otherwise happen.

A group of passengers descended on the escalator. My gaze swept over them, searching for Vaughn. A tall figure stood in the midst of them. When he turned and smiled, I realized that beneath the NY Yankees baseball cap and behind the yellow-lensed sunglasses was the man I loved.

Vaughn stepped off the escalator carrying his suitcase and walked toward me with long strides. "Hi, there!" He gave me a quick kiss on the cheek. "Let's get out of here."

He started for the elevator leading to the parking garage.

I held him back. "I've got a limo waiting for us."

He turned to me with a grin. "Going fancy, are we?"

"Uh, maybe not. Come with me. I've packed a bag for you. We're taking off for the weekend."

I led him to the limo waiting outside. After greeting the driver, Vaughn climbed in beside me and slung an arm around my shoulder.

"Where are we going?" he asked, smiling.

"Remember our trip to The Palm Island Club?"

"I remember everything about that trip," he said, giving me a squeeze. He tapped on the window between the driver and us. "The dock for The Palm Island Club as fast as you can."

Chuckling, I leaned back against the cushions of the seat, relieved my plan was being so well-received.

Vaughn took off his sunglasses, turned to me and, cupping my cheeks in his hands, lowered his lips to mine. I closed my eyes and savored the touch and taste of him. Our reunion in New York seemed months ago as his kiss intensified, sending surges of anticipation through me. My idea was a good one already.

After being dropped off at the dock, we waited with another couple for the Club's boat to arrive to pick us up and carry us across the water to their exclusive island site.

Vaughn pulled his baseball cap down on his head, doing his

best to hide his face as the other couple greeted us.

"Is this your first time here?" the woman asked.

"No, we've been here a couple of times. It's very nice," I said pleasantly.

"It's our twenty-fifth anniversary," she said. "We're here to get away from the rest of the world."

"Yes, you'll be able to do that here," I commented.

"We were going to stay at The Beach House Hotel," the woman's husband said. "But we were told there were no rooms available."

"Really?" I knew very well we weren't booked solid for the weekend.

"Yeah, and the guy wasn't all that nice about it," he continued.

"I happen to know the owners. If you give me your business card, I'll make sure you get a discount for a future visit." It was pure fate that I'd met up with them, but I'd put it to good use.

The woman held out her hand. "Thanks for doing that. By the way, I'm Heather Delaney, and this is my husband, Bud."

"Hello, my name is Ann Sanders, and this is my husband, Vaughn."

I waited uneasily for a squeal of recognition to be emitted from Heather's mouth, but she merely said, "Nice to meet you."

Vaughn and I exchanged smiles. Now I knew why so many celebrities loved coming to The Beach House Hotel, where the staff and others would treat them like any other guest.

Conversation ended with the arrival of the boatman in the Club's launch.

The boatman helped us aboard and stowed our luggage before we headed across the bay to what I hoped would be a restful, restorative break from our normal routines. When Vaughn had removed his sunglasses to kiss me, I'd noticed dark smudges below his eyes and could tell how distressed he must be.

I knew from my earlier visits that The Palm Island Club was deceptively rugged in appearance. But behind the walls of the main, wooden structure and the limited number of rustic cabins hidden among tropical growth lining the beach were hedonistic pleasures—silky sheets, private spas, gourmet items to order and eat.

Two bellmen met the boat, picked up the luggage, and led Vaughn and me and the Delaneys to our respective cabins. I'd reserved the same cabin we'd used a few years ago. Our time together then had been, well ... delicious.

We followed the bellman into our cabin, and I gazed around at our surroundings. A vase containing pink roses sat on the coffee table in front of the plush, tan couch. On the small dining table in a nearby nook, a welcoming bottle of champagne rested in a bucket of ice beside two tulip glasses. Soft, tropical music flowed through the rooms.

I opened the drapes to view our private patio and small splash pool, whose surface bubbled as water was pumped through it.

"I feel better already," sighed Vaughn, coming up beside me.

We waited for the bellman to place our suitcases on luggage racks inside the bedroom and then, after Vaughn gave him a tip, he left and shut the door behind him. Alone, Vaughn pulled me into his arms. "I love that you thought of this."

"I packed shorts, golf shirts, and bathing suits for you. Nothing fancy this weekend. We're simply going to relax."

"Good," Vaughn said. "This is exactly what I need. Do you mind if I lie down for a bit?"

"Not at all. Go ahead and take a nap. I've got a good book to read."

Vaughn nodded and yawned. "Think I will."

He went into the bedroom, and, while I hung up my clothes in the closet and settled my things in the bathroom, he changed into a bathing suit and turned back the bedspread.

From the corner of my eye, I studied his trim figure.

When he turned around and smiled at me, a rush of heat filled my body.

"Come here," he said, his voice a husky whisper of the loving promise that lay ahead.

I grinned. This was the Vaughn I knew and loved. Not the stressed-out, unhappy man who'd arrived at the airport. I hurried to him.

Vaughn caught me up in his arms and gently lowered me onto the bed. Tossing aside his bathing suit, Vaughn climbed onto the smooth sheets and drew me into his embrace.

The color of Vaughn's eyes deepened. "God! It's been too long," he murmured, helping me to undress.

When Vaughn began to explore and touch and taste, deep satisfaction filled me. He was the man who'd taught me what making true love was all about. I reached for him, and he groaned with pleasure when I began to demonstrate how much I'd learned from him.

Later, after we had stilled in each other's arms, I emitted a long sigh of contentment. As important as it was for us to talk—sharing ideas and thoughts—it was equally important that we communicate in this way.

Vaughn trailed a finger down the side of my face. "Any idea how beautiful you are?"

I smiled. He was a man who worked with women men drooled over, and I knew I was no match for them.

He raised his head and lifted his body up on one elbow. "You have no idea, do you?" A burst of laughter escaped him, and he hugged me to him. "My God! You're so perfect for me!

I sometimes can't believe you're mine."

He stroked my back with the palm of his hand. "You can't imagine what it's like working with someone like Lily. She and others like her are shallow and spoiled, determined to have their own way. I'm sick of it, sick of her, sick of the show."

I kept quiet, letting him vent his frustration. Vaughn was normally a man willing to put up with a lot to perform the job he loved. But, while I didn't know all that Lily was doing, I understood that it was ruining Vaughn's work.

"Is there any way the producers will get rid of her?" I asked. I didn't dare mention my conversation with Darlene.

"Not a chance as long as Roger Sloan has a say," he said, rolling onto his back and staring up at the ceiling. "The thing is, it's becoming harder and harder to hide my distaste of Lily. It's starting to affect the show. The director took me aside and told me I had to do a better job of acting." He nostrils flared. "Do you know how many years I've been on that show? How professional I've always tried to be? It's killing me that this has become such a problem."

I put a hand on his arm. "Look, Vaughn, you *are* a professional. You can do this. But, may I suggest that we work on getting you home on a more regular basis? I know you have friends and commitments in New York, but maybe it's time to step away from some of them."

He stared silently at the ceiling. "I wish you could come to New York more often."

"I'll try. I promise. Rhonda and I both know we can't run the hotel like we used to. And, Vaughn, we're going to see if we can have our daughters help us. I even mentioned it this week to Nell."

"You talked to her?"

I rolled onto my side and faced him. "She called me, worried about you."

"Guess I shouldn't have sounded off about my work."

"I want you to be open with her, with me, with all of us. People think your job is so glamorous that they forget the effort that goes into it. We're all here for you, Vaughn."

He nodded and exuded a long breath. "Thanks. I needed to hear that. Now, I'll stop whining and turn into the sex-hungry guy I really am."

As he yawned, I laughed. "Is that a promise?"

CHAPTER EIGHTEEN

The next morning, I awoke to an empty bed. I rose, put on one of the Club's robes, and wandered out to the living room to look for Vaughn. He wasn't there, so I opened the door to the cabin and peered out. Vaughn was sitting in a beach chair, his face lifted to the sun.

I walked out to him as quietly as possible and planted a kiss on top of his head.

He looked up at me and smiled. "The angel awakens."

"Don't know about the angel part, but I'm ready for a nice day with you. Looks like it's going to be a good one."

"It's a peaceful morning. Almost can't get used to the quiet after being in New York."

I sat next to his chair, settling into the soft, warm sand. Waves splashed gently against the shore with shy kisses and pulled away in a rhythm as old as time. Seagulls and terns swooped and dived in the air making less than their usual noise as if the Club had made a private deal with them to keep quiet. Some distance down the shore a couple was walking hand in hand.

I rose. "I'll be right back. I'm going to get in my bathing suit and grab a cup of coffee. Want some?"

His lips stretched into a broad smile. "Like I said, you're an angel."

I shook my head and left him to go inside to brew us some coffee. My cell rang. I checked Caller ID. *Rhonda*.

I quickly picked up the call. "Hi! What's going on?"

"Sorry to disturb your romantic weekend, but thought

you'd want to know Jean-Luc finally returned our calls. He told me he doesn't want to come back to the hotel. When I pushed him, he finally agreed to meet us on Monday. He refused to get together at the hotel, so he'll meet us at my house Monday morning."

"Great. He didn't say why he doesn't want to come back?"

"No. He said he'd explain everything when he sees us."

"Somehow, we've got to convince him to re-join the staff," I said, wondering how we could get somebody else of his caliber to work with us on our terms.

"How's it going?" Rhonda said with a smile in her voice.

I looked down at the robe hiding my nakedness and gazed out at Vaughn in only a swim suit that showed off his body. "Mmm. Very well, thank you. Gotta go."

"Have fun!" said Rhonda, cackling.

I grinned at her wacky humor and ended the call. She knew how worried I'd become about Vaughn's and my living apart.

Later, sipping coffee out on the beach with Vaughn, I thought about our talk and vowed to keep things interesting and fresh for him at home. Being with Robbie would be good for Vaughn too. Then, as usual, my thoughts returned to the hotel. Somehow, after the sale went through, Rhonda and I would have to pull things together as quickly as we could. I was making a mental list of things to do when Vaughn said, "Want to go for a sail? The Club has a couple of small sailboats for guests to use."

"Sure, that sounds like fun."

We went inside to get shirts, hats, and more sunscreen and then headed to the main lodge. We were standing by the concierge desk when Heather and Bud Delaney walked up.

"What are you two doing?" Heather asked.

"Signing up for one of the sailboats," I said. "Vaughn's a good sailor."

"Sounds like fun," Heather said. "We're going deep sea fishing. Want to come?"

I made a face. "I don't do well with that kind of thing. Sea sickness."

She turned to Vaughn. "How about you, Vaughn?"

He shook his head. "No, thanks. After we go for a sail, I'm just going to be a beach bum."

"Okay. Well, it was good seeing you. Perhaps we'll run into you later."

I waved goodbye. "Have a great trip on the water, and catch a lot of fish. The chef will cook what you bring in."

Bud grinned. "We'll probably catch nothing but too much sun, but it's my favorite way to relax."

They went on their way, and I made a mental note to send them a letter inviting them to the hotel after Rhonda and I took ownership.

After Vaughn made arrangements for us to use a sailboat, we walked down to the dock hand in hand. We were standing there when the Club's launch arrived with new guests. I stared in shock at a familiar face among them. Bree Lowell saw me and frowned. With him was a voluptuous blonde who wore such a short skirt I could almost see her crotch.

I waited for them to disembark and stood aside.

Bree stopped in front of me. "What are you doing here?"

"Hello, Bree. I could ask you the same," I said coolly. "Who's handling the hotel?"

"Stuart is on this weekend. I deserve some time off, especially during these last few weeks while my company is managing it. Is that a problem for you?"

"Not at all," I replied, working to keep my voice neutral at the sneer he'd given me. I clenched my hands, telling myself I wouldn't resort to slapping his face, though that's exactly what I wanted to do.

Vaughn glared at Bree. "Hold on, buddy! That's no way to treat my wife. You'd better show a little respect for your co-owner. Get it?"

"Eff off," mumbled Bree, backing away from Vaughn. Giving us a last look, Bree and his date followed the other newly arrived guests up the incline from the dock to the resort's main building.

"Is that the kind of treatment that asshole gives you and Rhonda?" said Vaughn. "I had no idea that little twerp was that bad. No wonder you want him off the property."

"Give me a moment. I'm going to call Reggie and tell him that Bree is here. This may be our chance to get more information from the night auditor."

"Okay. I'll get the boat ready."

I walked off the dock and found a private spot several yards away where nobody could hear me. Reggie wasn't available, but Angela promised to have him call me. I phoned Rhonda, quickly gave her the news, and hung up.

"All set?" Vaughn asked as I hurried up to him.

I crossed my fingers. "I hope so."

As we set off under sail from the dock, I told myself to forget hotel business, that Vaughn needed my attention. But my mind spun in circles. Surely, Reggie and Rhonda could take care of things.

"Are you okay?" Vaughn asked.

"Yes," I declared, determined to brush away my worries.

He smiled, and I leaned back against the gunwale and let the wind blow through my hair. The balance between work and home was something I'd have to learn to handle all over again.

By the time we returned to the dock a couple of hours later, my body felt liquid from the hot sun, the fresh salty air, and the utter relaxation from the gentle movements of sailing as we skimmed the water's surface. I sensed from the curve of Vaughn's lips that he felt as relaxed as I.

We turned the boat over to one of the staff at the dock and walked back to our cabin.

"Shall I order lunch?" I asked as we each grabbed a bottle of beer.

Vaughn nodded. "But tell them to hurry. I'm ready to take a nap."

By the look of him, sleep would come soon.

After a leisurely late lunch and a long nap, Vaughn and I decided to walk the beach. The sun was lowering in the sky. Pink edged the white clouds above us, promising a sunset within the hour. It was usually one of my favorite times of day. Today, however, the sight of Bree and his girlfriend lying nude beside him on the beach ahead of us made me stop and turn around.

"What's wrong?" Vaughn asked.

"It's been such a lovely day, I don't want to spoil the evening with another confrontation with Bree," I said quietly.

"I don't blame you. I don't like your having to deal with him. He's such an asshole." Vaughn checked his watch. "Let's go back to the cabin. I've planned something special."

"Oh?" I loved that Vaughn liked surprises.

"Yes, you're going to be pleased, I think ... I hope." He frowned. "Maybe not."

"What's going on?"

"I've invited some people for dinner," he said, looking pleased with himself.

I gave him a puzzled look. "But you said you wanted to be alone with me. Why the change in plans?"

"Our guests will be here only for dinner. You're mine after

they leave, and tomorrow morning too." He grinned like the mayor he played on the soap. "That's time with you I intend to enjoy."

My curiosity was on high alert. "Okay, who is it?"

"You'll see," he said cryptically as we returned to the cabin. Even when I asked again, he refused to answer, while I conjured up all kinds of possible and impossible situations in my mind.

"Guess I'd better take a shower," I said, resigned to wait.

"Good idea," said Vaughn, leering at me. "I'll join you."

"No fooling around," I said. "We have guests coming."

"Not until after our shower," said Vaughn, laughing.

I pushed at him playfully. "So, I guess it was a promise after all, this idea of being a sex-driven guy."

"I've missed you," Vaughn said, drawing me into his arms.

I melted against him. Maybe other couples quickly tired of each other, but I couldn't imagine that happening to us. We'd been married going on three years, but it sometimes seemed as if we were still on our honeymoon.

In the shower, warm water was like a waterfall as we played beneath it.

Later, as I was drying my hair, Vaughn came up behind me and cupped my breasts. Leaning down, he whispered into my ear, "I love you!"

Gazing at him in the mirror, I saw the satisfaction in his smile, the way his body folded around me and hoped times like this would always exist between us. "Love you too."

Vaughn smiled. "Better hurry. Our guests are due to arrive any minute."

"What shall I wear? Something fancy?"

He shook his head. "No need to. Shorts are fine."

I turned to him, hands on hips. "What aren't you telling me?"

At the sound of voices at the door to the cabin, I felt a huge smile spreading across my face. "Really? How wonderful!"

I slid on a T-shirt and a pair of shorts and hurried into the living room.

"Hi, Mommy!" cried Robbie, jumping up and down with excitement. "We got here in a boat!"

"I know." I wrapped my arms around him and smiled up at Liz and Chad. "I'm so glad you're here. Now it's like a real family adventure."

I released Robbie, hugged Liz, then turned to Chad. "Thanks for coming. I gather this was short notice."

He nodded. "Had to close the store early, but it's well worth it. This place is beautiful, and it's good to get away."

Liz looped her hand around his arm and smiled up at him. "It gives us time together out of the store."

I noticed the way Chad's eyes lit up at her smile and told myself to stop worrying about their wedding. They were fine, and with Sabine hopefully back at the hotel, Liz's plans for it would go forward.

A knock sounded at the door.

"Ah, it's here," said Vaughn. He opened the door, and a waiter pushed a rolling cart inside. On top of the cart was a silver bucket holding a bottle of champagne in ice, four tulip glasses, and a glass of orange juice with a plastic crazy straw. The waiter brought out two trays of hot hors d'oeuvres from the heated cabinet below. Cheese sticks for Robbie and clams casino, a favorite of mine, for the rest of us.

The waiter slid the cork out of the bottle of *Dom Perignon*, poured some champagne into the four glasses, and turned to Vaughn. "Anything else, Mr. Sanders?"

"I don't believe so," Vaughn responded, tipping the waiter. "We'll place our order for dinner shortly. Thank you."

After the waiter left, Vaughn passed out the glasses of

champagne and raised his glass. "Here's to my Florida family! I realized my time here wouldn't be complete without seeing you."

Touched by this thoughtful gesture, my eyes filled. It was the perfect thing to say. I noticed the moisture in Liz's eyes and knew she felt the same way. She'd formed a sweet relationship with Vaughn.

After a moment, Chad said, "I'd like to make a toast to Ann and Vaughn. You're showing me what a true marriage is like. My father left my mother and me when I was small, and I'm learning a lot from you, Vaughn." He gave Liz a teasing smile. "I might not be able to serve champagne for a while, but we'll celebrate however we can."

Liz's mouth quivered with emotion. Unable to speak, she nodded.

Relief swept through me. They were definitely back on track.

"Can I have toast too?" said Robbie, and the sentimental moment was splintered by laughter.

"That's my boy!" said Vaughn, setting down his glass and sweeping his son up into the air, laughing at the shrieks of joy coming from him.

At that moment, I knew I was the luckiest woman in the world.

Later, after seeing the kids off at the dock, Vaughn and I walked back to the cabin hand in hand.

"Putting together this evening was such a thoughtful thing to do," I commented. "The kids loved it, and so did I."

Vaughn squeezed my hand. "I meant what I said. I realized I needed my family together. And when Nell and Ty join us for the holidays, it will be even better."

"Yes," I quickly agreed. "It will be the best Christmas of all."

Vaughn looked down at me, searching my face with those intriguing dark eyes of his. "I'm going back to New York a new man. Thanks, Ann."

"And Lily?"

"I'm not letting someone like her ruin my career. It's only a few weeks until I'm back home for the holidays for a whole month. And then I won't have to deal with her for a while."

I smiled, but I wasn't so sure his trials with Lily were over. She thrived on salacious rumors.

CHAPTER NINETEEN

Monday, after dropping Robbie off at school and Vaughn at the airport, I headed for Rhonda's. Before we met with Jean-Luc, I wanted to talk to her about something that had been bothering me. After my weekend with Vaughn, I knew I couldn't commit to the hotel to the same degree I had when we were trying to get the hotel established. I needed to know our staff well and to trust them. My experience with Bree and his group had taught me that.

Rhonda greeted me at the door with a broad smile. "How'd the whole weekend go?"

"Great," I said, "but we need to talk."

Rhonda's eyes widened. She grabbed hold of my arm. "Uh, oh. Is something wrong, Annie?"

"It's not anything we can't handle," I said, "but I need to be honest with you about going forward with the hotel."

She tugged me into the house. "Grab a cup of coffee, and come with me."

Rita and the children were in the kitchen when I entered. I greeted Rita, gave Willow and Drew quick hugs, poured myself some coffee, and left the room, trying to put my thoughts together. When Rhonda and I were running the hotel, I'd ended up putting in more hours than she on many occasions because of my work with the financials. With the commitments I had to Vaughn and Robbie, I couldn't do that anymore. In addition to hiring Bernie as general manager, I thought it might be time to hire an onsite comptroller—someone recommended by Will.

Rhonda led me to her sitting room and pointed to one of the overstuffed chairs. "Sit. Spill. You have me worried. You're not backing out, are ya?"

"Good heavens! No! But, Rhonda, I can't handle all the financials as I did in the past, even with an auditor. We're going to need to hire a full-time comptroller with his own office on site. Will must know of someone we can trust."

"Whew! That's all? Sure, we'll take care of it."

"And another thing, we might have to increase room rates after we get things going. Bree's company kept running so many discounts, guests have expected to pay less and less, and we're going to have to convince them the higher, rack rates are well worth it."

The doorbell rang.

Rhonda jumped to her feet. "That must be Jean-Luc."

I followed her down the stairs as eager as she to see him again.

Rhonda swung open the door and cried, "Jean-Luc! We've missed you!" She flung her arms around him.

Standing aside, I saw a smile creep across his face and a light enter the eyes that had seemed almost dull a moment ago.

Rhonda stepped away from him so I could greet him.

"Jean-Luc, so good to see you," I said, giving him a kiss on each cheek. "Where's Sabine? She didn't come with you?"

He shook his head, and I watched in alarm as his eyes filled.

"She cannot," he said.

"Come inside and talk to us," Rhonda said gently, taking his arm.

She led him to the living room and offered him a seat on the couch.

Following behind, I noticed Jean-Luc's hesitant steps, the

way his shoulders bowed forward and realized he was a defeated man.

I sat next to him on the couch and placed my hand on his arm. "Jean-Luc, what's happened?"

"Sabine and I were driving on the *Autobahn* in Germany, and there was an accident. A terrible accident. I survived, but Sabine did not." He looked away as if he could not face us. "I was driving. It wasn't my fault, but I cannot forgive myself."

Rhonda and I exchanged looks of horror and moved to give him hugs.

"I'm so sorry," I said, unable to stop tears from filling my eyes and overflowing. "Sabine was such a lovely person." "Oh, Jean-Luc, that's awful! Simply awful! What can we do to help you?" Rhonda dabbed at her eyes with a tissue she pulled from a pocket. "We loved Sabine."

"I can't imagine how distraught you must be," I added. "We're here for you. Please, if we can do anything for you, you know we will."

"*Merci, merci,*" he murmured, sandwiched between us. He bowed his head.

"How long has she been ... gone?" I asked.

"It's six weeks now," Jean-Luc answered. "I haven't been able to talk about it." He raised his head, giving each of us a look of such sadness that my heart squeezed with sympathy.

Rhonda studied him. "What are you doing to keep busy? Anything?"

Jean-Luc's shrug was listless.

"We need you, Jean-Luc. Why don't you think about coming back to work with us?" I said. "Wouldn't Sabine like to see you busy? Productive?"

"Those *bâtards* in the new company will be gone?" said Jean-Luc with fresh energy. "I would never work for somebody like that again."

Rhonda leaned forward. "You would be working for us, Jean-Luc. We want you back in our family. We're going to make it like it was with you and Bernie and a lot of other old staff members running the hotel."

"Yes, it will be very much as it was when we were in charge. Believe me, we don't want Bree and his team at The Beach House Hotel ever again," I said emphatically. "That's why Rhonda and I are doing this. And we want you to be a part of it."

Jean-Luc leaned back against the cushions and stared up at the ceiling for so long I didn't know if he was praying. When he turned his attention back to us, he gave a little nod. "I will see how it goes. As you say, I need to keep busy, and Sabine ... she wants me to do this. I feel it."

Rhonda gave him another hug. "Thank you, Jean-Luc! Now, let's celebrate by having some refreshments, and then we'll talk about details. I'll be right back."

After Rhonda left the room, I turned to Jean-Luc. "You have no other family here?"

He shook his head. "Sabine was my family."

I patted his back. "You're not alone. You have all of us now."

Tears slid down his cheeks. He scrubbed a hand over his face to wipe them away. "*Merci.*"

My vision blurred with grateful tears for my extended family and the way he would be welcomed.

Rhonda returned with a tray on which she'd placed a plate of her famous cinnamon rolls, three coffee cups, and a pot of coffee.

"It's too early to celebrate with wine, but I thought you, Jean-Luc, might have missed having my sweet rolls."

He smiled at the wink Rhonda gave him. "Yes, they're very much a part of The Beach House Hotel." Jean-Luc and

Rhonda had had their fights in the past, but this was one thing they both agreed on.

"Are you still living in the same place?" I asked Jean-Luc.

"Yes, I like living by the water. Even though it's lonely, I will stay there."

"Good," said Rhonda. "It's nice to have you close by."

Jean-Luc's response was a listless shrug.

After talking about his hours and his pay, we discussed his going to the hotel to make a complete inventory of the kitchen utensils, supplies, and food.

"As before, the kitchen will be your domain," I assured him. He nodded. "Of course, that is how I want it."

By the time we finished our discussion, Jean-Luc's shoulders sat a little straighter on his body.

"It will be good to have you back," I said, giving him an encouraging hug before stepping back.

This time, his smile reached his eyes.

Rhonda and I showed him out and stood together on the front porch watching him get into his car and drive away.

"I feel so bad about Sabine," Rhonda said, turning to me. "Poor Jean-Luc. He seemed so lost. It will be good for him to keep busy working for us. And the guests are going to appreciate it."

"I liked his idea of bringing back Carl Lamond. I wonder if Jean-Luc can entice him away from La Mer." Since leaving the hotel, Carl had been working at a small, seafood restaurant on Marco Island.

"I hope he can. Carl and Jean-Luc make a great team, and working with someone of Jean-Luc's caliber would be a plus for Carl."

My sigh was full of the sadness I felt. "What are we going to do about someone taking Sabine's place? She was so good at working on weddings."

"How about Lorraine Grace at Wedding Perfection? She's helped us out before."

"Good idea," I said. "I'll go see her on my way home. Maybe she's ready for a change."

"And I'll talk to Will about bringing a comptroller on board," said Rhonda.

We embraced, and I left for Wedding Perfection's office downtown. Lorraine was an older woman who'd moved from her home up north to accommodate her husband's illness. She'd set up her wedding business in Sabal and was very good at her job. Alone now after her husband's death, I thought she might like the camaraderie of working with us. I was anxious to talk to her not only about the opportunity at the hotel but to get her suggestions about how best to transition out the wedding planner Bree had hired.

The downtown area was always a parking challenge, but on this early November day I found a place on the street within a block of her office, situated on the second floor above an art gallery.

I climbed the interior stairs and entered a space that was decorated to look like a tropical garden.

Sitting at a small, white desk, wearing a black sheath, Lorraine Grace smiled at me.

"How are you, Ann? It's been a while." She stood, walked over to me, and held out her hand. "I've heard a rumor around town. Is it true that you and Rhonda are buying back The Beach House Hotel?"

"Yes, it is. We are more than ready to restore the hotel's former reputation."

Lorraine beamed at me. "I can't tell you how happy that makes me. It's become difficult to make arrangements for my brides there. The young person running the wedding planning department is, I'm sure, fine for planning a beach party, but all the intricacies of handling a destination, society wedding are lost on her. I've had to do battle to get certain agreements from them for all that I require."

For a moment, she sounded so like Sabine, minus the French accent, that I blinked with surprise.

"Can we talk?" I asked.

"Sure, have a seat. I'm just going over my billings."

"Rhonda and I spoke with Jean-Luc Rodin this morning. He told us that Sabine was killed in an auto accident about six weeks ago. He's devastated."

Lorraine's mouth formed an oval of shock. "Oh, my! I'm so sorry to hear that. She was a lovely woman, and I enjoyed working with her."

Sorrow made me pause. After drawing a deep breath, I said, "I'm here to ask you if you would consider coming to work full-time at the hotel. In the past, you've planned many weddings there, and we thought ..."

Lorraine held up her hand to stop me. "I'm booked nine months in advance. I can't disappoint those brides." She held up a check. "I'm just drawing up a final agreement on this one."

Discouragement coursed through me. Then I straightened with fresh determination. "How about if we give your brides the opportunity to use The Beach House Hotel at a discounted rate? When we're through renovating the rooms, our hotel will be equal to the Ritz or any other upscale hotel in Florida. And if you'd like to have a hand in making certain settings on the property more suitable for their weddings, we can talk about it."

Lorraine sat back in her chair and studied me thoughtfully. A striking woman with silver-gray hair, fine features, and erect posture, she was the epitome of good taste.

"Put together a package for me to consider, and I'll take a

look at it. The rent on this space is going up and, frankly, I'm tired of doing everything on my own. If I can use hotel staff to help me, that might be a big plus."

I let out the breath I'd been holding. "I'll talk to Rhonda and get back to you."

After leaving Lorraine, I hurried to Robbie's school to pick him up.

At the sight of Robbie hurrying to greet me, I pushed aside my worries about the hotel and hugged him to me, loving the feel of him in my arms, aware it wouldn't last forever. He was growing fast, and the day would come when he wouldn't be willing to share hugs and kisses in front of his friends.

At home, I phoned Rhonda to tell her about my meeting with Lorraine.

"Good news, I hope," said Rhonda. "And maybe more good news. Will knows of someone who might be the perfect comptroller for us. He recently moved to Sabal from Miami, where he worked for a big hotel. He's looking for a less-demanding position so he can improve his golf game."

"Great. If he's interested, we'll have him talk to Bernie."

As we ended the call, I thought about the staff we were assembling, thrilled that so many of our original staff members were returning to replace Bree's people.

After lunch, I left Robbie with Elena and headed to my house on the hotel property. A cleaning crew had done a good job of eliminating the mess Bree had left behind, but the furniture I intended to get rid of was still there. I had to decide what to do with it. Laura Bakeley, the interior designer we used for the hotel, was going to meet me to talk about finishing touches.

Liz phoned as I was pulling into the driveway.

"Where are you?"

"At my house at the hotel," I answered. "What's up?"

"Chad and I are going ahead and renting the house we were looking at. We want to be all settled before the wedding. Any chance we could take you up on your offer to give us the furniture you're not going to use? You told me you were going to get rid of most of it."

"You can have all of it if you'll load it up and take it away. I'm going to make a fresh start with this house so we can rent it out to VIPs."

"Great! I'll tell Chad. I'm sure he can get Reggie to help him load it up. We've already signed the lease, so we can move in anytime."

"Nice. The furniture I've ordered won't be here for a couple of weeks, but I can use that time to re-paint and re-carpet the house, so everything is ready for Tina's visit toward the end of the month."

"Yeah, can't wait to see her. She was terrific in her latest movie."

"It will be good for her to be here, so our family can support her while she seeks help. She's feeling fragile after her brother's death."

"Sure, I understand. Thanks, Mom! Love you!"

A shadow came up behind the car. Startled, I let out a cry.

"Mom? Are you all right?" Liz's voice rang out from my cell phone.

Turning, I discovered Bree standing outside the car. "Yes, it's just Bree. Talk to you later."

I climbed out of my car and faced him. "What are you doing here?"

He kicked at the ground with an Italian loafer. "I wanted to ask if I could store my Porsche in your garage. I don't like parking it at the hotel."

I shook my head. "After all that's gone on, I don't think that would be a wise decision."

Bree's cheeks reddened. "Look, I'm sorry I fucked up, but my father is paying you a lot of money. Why can't you let me use the garage?"

"You're really asking me this? As I said, it's not a good idea. You've abused my property and, frankly, I don't want you, let alone your possessions, on it. You continue to be disrespectful." I raised my hand to stop another tirade. "And no fires here. Get it?"

His eyes rounded. "What? You think I started the fire at that beach hut?"

"I have no way of knowing if it's true or not, but that's the rumor."

Bree shook his finger at me. "If anything happens to my car, I'm blaming you, and then you'll be the one to pay."

He turned on his heel and walked away.

I was still stewing about our encounter when Laura showed up. She got out of the car and pointed to Bree in the distance. "Who was that gentleman I saw walking out of your property? I almost hit him with my car. It was an accident, but I must say that he was rude about it."

"That is Aubrey Lowell, the soon-to-be-ex manager of the property," I said with disgust.

"Oh, well, I can see why you would want to get rid of him," Laura said. "Honestly, it will be so good to have you and Rhonda running the place again. It's never been the same since you sold it. And I know I'm not the only one who feels that way."

"Thanks. We can't wait to take it over." I led Laura inside the house, to the kitchen, where I'd left fabric samples to show her.

We spent the next hour studying the samples, talking about the placement of new furniture, and selecting an overall theme to the house's décor. From there, she promised to come up with ideas for pillows, accent pieces, and choices of drapery fabric for the bedrooms.

"The painters start next week, and then new carpeting will be put down in the bedrooms. I need you to help me choose a rug for the living room. Liz is going to take the furniture that's here and will use what she can. The Oriental rug I'd brought from Boston is something she's always liked, and that will go to her as well."

"I have a good idea what you like, Ann, and I think we can have some fun with this, Laura said. "Might as well turn a bad situation into a good one."

The anger I felt as I looked around lessened. Laura was right. I might have grown to detest Bree, but I couldn't let him ruin my outlook on life. I had too many other things to be thankful for.

We embraced, and before leaving the house, I double-checked all the locks and then left the house with Laura, who was as eager as I to get rid of the last traces of Bree Lowell.

CHAPTER TWENTY

I'd no sooner walked into the house when Rhonda called.

"Annie? Ya won't believe this! Dorothy Stern just phoned to warn me that the Neighborhood Association has turned down our request to support rebuilding the beach hut. They said the fact that it burned right to the ground indicated it was a fire hazard, especially with guests smoking nearby. How do ya like them apples?"

"It's Brock Goodwin and his sidekicks all over again," I said feeling a headache coming on. "What about a grandfather clause? We're merely rebuilding a facility on a site that was approved earlier. I would think that would make it clear that this is nothing new. We're just getting a standard building permit to restore what once was there."

"We'd better call Mike. I bet he has a few strings of his own that he can pull," said Rhonda. "I'm sick of Brock trying to interfere."

"He was angry when we told him he could forget decorating the hotel. This is his way of paying us back," I reminded her.

"Well, we'll have to attend the next Association meeting to protest. Dorothy said she'd pass a petition to support us around the neighborhood like she's done before. Several people who live nearby like to join us at the hut for sunset events out by the beach."

"Maybe that will help. We'll see," I said without my usual optimism. It was one of those days when everything seemed monumental.

I ended the call and turned to Robbie, standing beside me.

Judith Keim

"Mommy? I don't feel so good."

"What's wrong?" I asked, leaning down to feel his forehead.

He groaned and threw up all over me.

Yup, one of those days.

That night, after I'd tucked Robbie in bed, I wandered through the house. It was a beautiful home, but without Vaughn, it seemed lonely. I sat in my bedroom, staring at the bed Vaughn and I shared, feeling sorry for myself.

My cell phone rang. *Rhonda.*

"Annie? Guess what? Reggie and Angela are having another baby! Isn't that great? I'm going to be a grandmother again."

My spirits lifted. "Nice, Grandma! Congratulations!"

"And that's not all. My brother and his family are going to join us for Thanksgiving. It's going to be a full house. I can't wait!"

"That'll be a lot of fun. I like Richie and Margaret and their kids. It'll be great to have them here." Richie was a male version of Rhonda—outgoing, dramatic, and full of life. Two peas in a pod I'd once called them as they'd elbowed each other, emitting identical, raucous laughs. They also shared big, generous hearts.

"Ready for the owner's meeting tomorrow?" I asked her.

"I guess so. I don't even want to sit in the same room with Bree, Stu, and the other slime balls. The auditors are finding all kinds of weird stuff."

"Remember, we can't give anything away until Mike is ready to take it to George Peabody."

"I know, I know, but while we're still investigating, the skimming is going on."

"Patience, my dear friend," I said, as restless as she.

The crying of children in the background prompted Rhonda to say, "Better go. See ya tomorrow."

I hung up and changed into my nightgown.

Trudy trotted into the room and sat by the bed, waiting for me to lift her up.

"Okay, girl. Guess you're going to have to be my companion tonight. I gathered her in my arms, placed her beside me on the bed, and turned on the television. The screen showed a building on fire.

The announcer said, "The fire fighters in New York City have been battling this fire at an apartment building for hours. The nearby Plaza Hotel, and, in fact, the entire area has been affected by smoke and streets filled with equipment—blocking traffic and causing a general uproar. No news on fatalities. We'll keep you posted."

Aware that Vaughn's apartment was in that area, I quickly punched in his number.

After several rings, he picked up. "Hello?"

"Vaughn, it's Ann. I just heard about the fire. Are you all right?"

"Yes, it's a mess around here, but my building isn't affected. Lily is here until she can get into her friend's apartment a couple of floors down from mine. It's her building that's on fire. She's pretty hysterical because the flames were coming from her side of the building and on the same floor."

"Oh, that's awful. I'm so sorry to hear that. Please tell her for me."

"I'll call you later," Vaughn said. "It's pretty hectic here."

After hanging up, I leaned back against my soft pillow.

Trudy sensed my unhappiness and laid her head in my lap, gazing up at me with brown eyes full of concern.

I stroked her smooth head. Sometimes, having her with me was a blessing.

--OOO--

The next morning, Rhonda and I sat in the hotel library, set up like a boardroom, waiting for the other members of the board to show up.

"Don't know why they can't show up on time," grumbled Rhonda.

I nodded but remained silent. Bree liked to play games by keeping us waiting. He was just that kind of guy.

Bree and Stuart arrived together.

"Let's make this quick," said Bree. "There's little to report. Things are pretty much the same."

"Do you have your usual weekly report ready for us?" I asked Stu.

He shook his head. "I should have it ready sometime this afternoon."

"Well, then," I said as evenly as possible. "Why don't we plan on meeting tomorrow?" Something was wrong, and I knew it.

Bree and Stuart stood.

"Sounds good," said Stuart. "Sorry for the delay. I'll email you the report, and then, as you said, we can have a quick meeting tomorrow."

After they left the room, Rhonda turned to me. Beneath her tan, her cheeks were becoming redder and redder. "They could have called us and saved our time. What's with those two, anyway? They acted guilty of something."

I rose to my feet. "I think it's time to do a little investigation on our own. Care to follow me to the reservations department? The numbers are falling, and though it's a shoulder season, we usually have more reservations than these."

Rhonda and I bypassed the kitchen and went to our old

office. A cute, young girl by the name of Amanda Collins was handling our reservations information behind one of the desks. I'd always liked her openness.

"Hi, Amanda," I said. "Thought we'd check some of the upcoming reservations. The weekly report is behind schedule."

"Sure," she said, smiling at us. "Bree is really happy with our new program."

I sent a warning look to Rhonda to keep quiet. "Yes, how does that work again?"

"Let me show you," said Amanda. "I'll print out a report for you."

"So, tell us about it," said Rhonda in a voice that I knew held fake cheeriness.

"Well, when someone calls in for reservations after Thanksgiving, we explain that there will be new management, and if there's any hesitation, we offer them a deal at our hotel in California. That way, the company's numbers remain strong. As Bree explained, it helps everyone. Bree hopes to run the California property, and I can earn a bonus for crediting him with those reservations."

I accepted the sheet of paper she gave me, quickly folded it up, and tucked it in my purse. "Thanks for your help."

I all but sprinted out of the office, Rhonda behind me.

"Annie ..."

I held up a finger to my lips and hurried for the front door. We had Bree where we wanted him, and we had to work fast.

As we neared the lobby, I slowed, not wanting to bring attention to myself.

"Whew! Wait for me," said Rhonda. "What are ya doing?"

"Follow me to my car," I said quietly.

I stretched my legs, moving as quickly as I could without running. Rhonda's huffs of breath followed me.

We'd just crossed the lobby when I saw Bree step outside of Stuart's office. Unaware of us, they stood talking. Bree was still engaged when we slipped past the hallway and through the front entrance.

At the sight of us, the bellman ran to get my car. He pulled the Lexus into the front circle and then handed me the fob.

Rhonda and I scrambled inside. As soon as we'd buckled in, I drove away.

"Where are we going?"

"Mike's office. Call him now, and tell them we have an emergency."

Moments later, I pulled into the parking lot next to Mike's office.

"What is going on, Annie?" Rhonda asked, following me out of the car.

"If we do it right, we have enough proof of things going on that we can get rid of Bree. That's why we need to talk to Mike right away."

Inside the office, Mike's receptionist smiled pleasantly. "I got your message, but Mike's with a client."

"Have you been able to tell him we were on our way to see him?"

The receptionist shook her head. "Not yet."

"Please let him know we're here and that it's an emergency," I said.

The receptionist's eyes rounded. "A real emergency?"

I nodded. "He'll want to know what we are about to tell him."

She rose and hurried down the hallway to his office.

Mike emerged from his office, took a look at our faces, and waved us into a small conference room nearby.

As soon as he closed the door, I pulled out the sheet of paper Amanda had given me. "Here's proof of another irregularity at the hotel. Mike, we can't wait for the sale to get rid of Bree. We need to get him out of the hotel tonight."

Mike studied the paper. "This is the number of reservations taken away from The Beach House Hotel and sent to their hotel in California?"

"Yeah, the pricks are ruining our business. They're telling people they don't want to stay at The Beach House Hotel, that there's new management. And Will told me the auditors are finding all kinds of stuff." Tears came to Rhonda's eyes. "They're ruining us!"

I fought to control my own emotions. "It's going to take us a long time to recover from the destruction of our business and our reputations. I don't care what anyone thinks; we have to get rid of them now."

Mike nodded. "You're right. I'm going to call George Peabody. We'll stage a hostile takeover. I've been through this only one time before. Back then, we handled it at midnight, so most guests would be unaware of what was happening. I'm with another client, but hang around, and we'll make a plan. We'll have to bring in cops and others to help us manage it."

I sank down into one of the chairs, my knees too weak to stand. Rhonda collapsed in a chair opposite me.

"It sounds pretty exciting until ya have to go through it," Rhonda said. "Cops? Hostile takeover? This is big-time, Annie."

"Yes, but it's the only thing we can do. I'll ask Elena to spend the night. Do you think you can get Rita to do the same?"

"I'll call her right now," said Rhonda.

While she made the call, I left the room to get a cup of coffee from the office kitchen we'd used before.

As I waited for the coffee to drip, I quickly phoned Elena and made arrangements for her to spend the next couple of nights. A takeover like this was serious business.

I fixed my coffee and made some for Rhonda before returning to the conference room.

"Thanks," said Rhonda when I handed her a cup. "I have to tell ya, I'm really upset about this whole thing. Even after we get rid of the little bastard, who knows what else he'll try to do?"

"As far as I'm concerned, he should be arrested."

Mike entered the room as I spoke. "It's a possibility, but no one is going to be arrested unless he overreacts to what we're doing. I've talked to George. He's agreed to cooperate in a takeover and will appear at the hotel sometime tomorrow to make sure things go well at their end."

So, if he agreed to this, it's no longer a hostile takeover, right?" said Rhonda.

"Bree is certainly going to consider it a hostile move," said Mike. "Now let's talk about how this is done. First of all, we need to know what help we can bring in to pull this off. We're going to need to secure the cash on site and make sure the computers are protected. It must all be coordinated, so it's done quickly and completely."

"I can ask Liz and Chad to help."

"Chad is your computer guy, right?" said Mike.

Rhonda and I both nodded.

"All right, we'll have him set up new passwords at every machine and back up all information."

"He can pretend that it's his normal, scheduled time to do it," I said. "I'm sure he'll play along."

"And someone will need to be at the front desk, protecting all property management systems from any of the staffers. Someone other than you two."

"Liz or Angela can do that," said Rhonda.

"The reservations system needs heightened protection. If

that gets messed up it can make chaos for many months to come."

"Let's put Reggie on that," I said.

"Okay, now let's set up a time schedule," said Mike. "We can have Chad come in at ten and quietly do his work. At midnight, the rest of the family members need to arrive promptly and quietly to do the things we're asking. It's essential that everything happens at once."

"What are Annie and I supposed to do?" asked Rhonda.

Mike's smile was almost evil. "You're going to have the pleasure of ordering Bree away from the hotel. I'll have a policeman accompany you. Bree will be escorted out of his room and off the property."

"What about his things?" I asked.

"He'll have to make an appointment to come back to pack them up. And that will also be done under guard."

Rhonda and I looked at each other with rounded eyes, and then we both chuckled.

"I'm so relieved," I said. "But what if he gets mad and decides to do something awful to us or the property, something like the fire?"

"George Peabody has assured me that Bree will leave the state. As to Stuart and the others who collaborated with him, they will have a little chat with me the next morning. I'll advise them that to avoid any legal issues, it would be best to cooperate with us until they're told to leave." He gave each of us a steady look. "Now, let's make a few phone calls."

All afternoon I felt as if I were in a movie coordinating a heist of sorts. Only, in this case, it involved a smart-aleck, self-entitled, greedy guy, not something of value.

When Rhonda and I contacted Ana to ask her to take over

housekeeping first thing in the morning, she eagerly agreed. "I will bring Rose and Anita, too."

Jean-Luc was less excited about being asked to work even briefly with the chef who'd forced him out of his job.

"That ... that man was no chef. He was a glorified cook," Jean-Luc growled. His French accent made the word "cook" sound worse than one of Rhonda's favorite words.

"That's why we need you, Jean-Luc," I quickly said. "We need to restore your reputation as well as the hotel's."

"*Ah, oui!* I will be there at six o'clock in the morning, as you want."

Rhonda and I let out similar, long breaths when we ended the call.

"Okay, now Bernie," said Rhonda. "You make the call, Annie. I'm too nervous to do it."

With fingers grown cold, I punched in Bernie's number and put him on speaker. In order for him to help us, he'd have to cut short his time with his present owner, at least for a day or two, until we got things in order here. And Bernie was one who followed the rules.

"Hello?" Bernie said in his precise, clipped way.

I explained the situation to him. "I know you were not scheduled to leave your present job just yet, but we need you. Can you help us with the transition?"

"To get rid of Aubrey Lowell? Of course, I can. I'll be there at midnight. Annette and I have bought a condo in Sabal, and this will give me a chance to check on the renovations she's making to it."

"Way to go, Bernie!" Rhonda said into the phone. "We want you here on the team."

"As the head of the team," I amended, knowing how crushed he'd been by the treatment given him by Bree and the young recruits he'd brought in.

"Yes, I will head the team," Bernie said, his voice crisp, his manner formal.

"Thank you, Bernie. We really appreciate it," I said, just as my phone beeped with another call.

I checked Caller ID and picked up the call. *Mike.*

"Hello?"

"Hi, Ann. Just a heads-up. George Peabody is flying down here today. He'll arrive this evening but won't check into the hotel until later. His visit will be a big surprise for Aubrey and his team. When George saw the information the auditors have put together, he went ballistic! I certainly wouldn't want to be in Aubrey's position. It won't be pleasant."

"It's not going to be violent, is it?" I'd hate to put anyone in danger.

"No," said Mike. "But to be sure, we'll have several undercover policemen on the property. And I'll be there too, making sure that things are going as we planned. I've got to go. I have other client business to attend to."

"Oh, yes! Mike, we're so grateful for all you're doing for us."

"I've always thought the two of you made a great team and are a big benefit to our community. It's just a shame that this has happened to you and the hotel."

After the call ended, I turned to Rhonda, who was tugging on my arm.

"What's going on, Annie? Is this going to get nasty?"

I shook my head. "Mike says it won't. But, Rhonda, I'll be glad when this is over. I don't trust Bree."

"Neither do I." She slung an arm around me. "But we've faced bad guys before and won, right?"

We grinned at each other. "Right."

Later, after I'd talked to Liz and Chad about their roles, Liz said, "I'm a little worried about Bree trying to get back at you and Rhonda."

"I think this is one time Bree will be outsmarted. However, why don't you and Chad come for dinner? It might ease the stress of waiting for the operation to begin." My nerves were firing like the spark plugs of an engine about to start.

CHAPTER TWENTY-ONE

I'd just finished serving Liz's favorite lemon chicken recipe and taken a seat at the kitchen table when I heard a car pull into the driveway. Frowning, I went to a window and looked out. Vaughn was getting out of a taxi.

Joy danced through me and then stumbled to a stop. Vaughn would not like the idea of us being in a situation that might be dangerous. Especially if it involved the hotel.

Robbie came up beside me. "Is it Daddy?"

"Yes, it is!" I said, trying to keep my concern out of my voice.

"Yay!" Robbie ran to the kitchen door and shrieked, "Daddy!" as Vaughn walked into the room.

Trudy barked a welcome of her own, and Liz and Chad jumped to their feet.

"Hi, everyone!"

Vaughn swept Robbie up into his arms and turned to me for a kiss. Our lips met, and my worries increased.

"You're just in time for dinner," I said, pulling away.

"Nice to have everyone together. What's the occasion?" he said, giving Robbie another hug before setting him down.

"We're doing a hostile takeover of the hotel," Liz said with a note of pride.

"Yeah, I have to be at the hotel by ten," said Chad, "to take care of protecting all the computer information."

Vaughn turned to me. "What's this all about?"

I sighed. "It's a long story. First, how about some dinner? There's plenty for you."

He looked at our plates. "Lemon chicken? Okay, sounds good. I didn't eat on the plane."

While I served him a plate of food, I heard Liz say, "Good to see you, Vaughn. What brings you here?"

"Lily's apartment was destroyed by a fire. While she's coping with that, I decided to take advantage of the free time and come home. There've been more rumors because she's staying at a friend's apartment in the same building as mine, and some people think she's staying with me."

Liz glowered at him. "I hate that woman."

As I carried Vaughn's plate to him, I sent Liz a warning look. "You might not like Lily, but surely you trust Vaughn."

"Sorry, Vaughn," Liz said. "I know I can trust you, but her? Not for a minute."

"It's okay. I know how you and others feel about her." He smiled up at me. "Thanks, hon. This food looks delicious."

Silence reigned as we dug into our meals.

"Why does a chicken say 'cluck, cluck'?" said Robbie.

"Because he can't say 'quack, quack'," said Liz, and we all laughed, bringing a sense of normality to the table.

"Tell me what's going on," said Vaughn. He looked around the table and turned back to me.

"As Liz said, we're doing a hostile takeover of the hotel. Bree is being escorted off the property at midnight. And by tomorrow morning, our staff will be in place, including Bernie, Jean-Luc, and Ana. We'll fill in as quickly as we can."

"I hope this time Bree doesn't pull any more stunts like starting a fire," said Liz, ignoring my silent plea to stop talking. "That was quite scary."

Vaughn's brow wrinkled. "Does this hostile takeover involve any danger?"

"No," I quickly assured him. "George Peabody from the investor group will be there, as well as a couple of policemen."

"Then you and Rhonda will be taking over the hotel earlier than we thought," said Vaughn. "I was hoping you'd come back to New York with me."

I shook my head. "I'm sorry. It'll have to be another time."

"Do you want me to go with you to the hotel?" said Vaughn.

"I'm not sure," I said. "But we'll definitely need you over the next couple of days. Are you going to be here in Sabal for a while?"

"Yes," he answered, and I knew his ego was a little bruised by my response. But, truthfully, I was a nervous wreck thinking about the takeover, and I didn't want to have to worry about Vaughn.

"I want Daddy to read me a book," said Robbie, jumping off his chair and running over to Vaughn.

I silently blessed Robbie for the smile that spread across Vaughn's face.

After Chad left to go to the hotel, Liz approached Vaughn and me sitting in the den. "I'm going to Angela's. She and Reggie are going to drop me off at the hotel just before midnight, and I'll ride home with Chad." She smiled. "And this will give you two some privacy."

I rose from the couch, "All right. I'll see you there."

We hugged, and then Liz turned to Vaughn. "Glad you're home. See you tomorrow."

He stood and gave her a quick hug. "Be careful."

After Liz left, Vaughn and I returned to the couch. I studied him. "You look tired, honey."

"I'm sick of leading a double life. The guy who's supposed to be having a thing with Lily and the guy who loves you and our family. I'm thinking of getting out of my contract, taking up Nicholas Swain's offer to do a movie, and going on with a different life. With you and the kids here, it's becoming harder and harder to stay in New York."

Touched by his words, I leaned over and kissed his cheek. "We miss you terribly, but I know it's your job, and I'm not about to pressure you on anything because you might then resent me."

"You're right. I need to think this through on my own. But, Ann, you and the family come first."

"Thanks. That's how I feel about you and my job at the hotel." I checked my watch. "Elena should be here any moment. I think I'd better get ready to go."

"Ann, what can I do to help?" It was more a plea than a question, and I knew it.

"Why don't you work the lobby to make sure no guests are aware of what is going on?" I said, suddenly inspired. "If they recognize you, you'll be able to keep them out of the way."

Vaughn's face lit with satisfaction. "I can do that. I know how important this is to you, and I want to be a part of it."

We arrived at the hotel just after eleven thirty under the pretense of having a celebratory drink to welcome Vaughn back home.

After placing an order with the bartender, Vaughn sat down beside me on a couch that gave me a clear view of the front hall.

As soon as I saw Rhonda enter, I rose to greet her.

"Come join the party to celebrate Vaughn's being home," I said loud enough for others to hear.

Rhonda blinked in confusion and then, seeing Vaughn, she smiled. "Sure thing."

We turned as Liz, Angela, and Reggie walked into the hotel.

"Just in time," I said brightly. "Come join the welcome

home party for Vaughn."

"Yeah," said Rhonda. "We have a few minutes before ... ouch!" She looked down at the foot I'd stepped on and gave me a sheepish smile.

Angela took her mother's arm. "This way."

Vaughn, gentleman that he is, stood and gathered chairs around the couch so everyone could have a seat.

"Shall I order drinks for everyone?" he asked.

Angela smiled at him. "Not for me. Reggie and I are expecting again."

"Nice," he said. "What can I get you?"

"Just bubbling water with lime."

As they exchanged words, I noticed the envious look on Liz's face and knew it wouldn't be long after the wedding when she hoped to make such an announcement. My heart went out to her. After seeing her with Robbie, I knew she'd be a good mother, even if she didn't yet believe it.

The bartender came out from behind the walnut-wood bar to serve us our drinks. The rest of the lobby area was quiet. A couple sat at a table near a window gazing at each other with such lust that I guessed they were on their honeymoon.

"Thanks," I said to the young man serving us. "Are we the last of the night?"

The bartender nodded. "Midnight is closing time."

"Go ahead and start closing," Rhonda said. "It doesn't look like anyone else is around."

He grinned his thanks and hurried back to the bar.

"I saw the apartment fire in New York on the news," said Angela. "We were worried about Reggie's parents' penthouse, but their place wasn't affected. How about yours, Vaughn?"

I tried not to fidget while Vaughn talked, but I couldn't stop worrying about the coup that was about to take place. Rhonda and I exchanged a worried glance, and then I rose.

"Excuse me. I'm going to check on something."

"I'll join you," said Rhonda, rising to her feet so fast I almost laughed.

We headed to the back offices. Chad was still there working in the computer room.

"How's it going?" Rhonda asked him.

"Okay, the backup is almost done, and all the computers are blocked."

Startled by a knock on the door, we turned as a tall, gray-haired man and Mike Torson entered the room.

Mike indicated the man to his right. "This is George Peabody. And, George, I believe you might recognize Ann and Rhonda."

He nodded gravely and turned to Chad. "And who is this?"

"Chad Bowen, who handles all the IT stuff for the hotel," I said, proud of the work he was doing.

"Ah, yes. Things in order here?" George said.

"Yes, sir," said Chad, standing and offering his hand.

George shook it and faced the rest of us. "Sorry things have come to this, but as I promised Mike earlier, we want to cooperate with you so that neither your reputation nor ours is compromised. I understand Aubrey is presently in his room. Shall we go?"

Rhonda and I looked at each other and nodded.

My heart pounded as we followed Mike and George out of the room.

Next door, in the reservations office, Reggie was at the computer, printing off material.

As we crossed the lobby bar, the only two people in the room were Vaughn and the bartender. Vaughn gave me a surreptitious wink and turned back to the bartender who was telling some kind of story.

At the front desk, Liz and Angela huddled by the computer

protectively as the night auditor demanded to talk to Bree.

Mike gave us a knowing look and stepped away to talk to him.

"This way. Hurry!" I whispered and led George and Rhonda down the hallway to one of the end rooms, where Bree was staying.

I stared in confusion at the man standing outside the doorway. "Aren't you one of the people who were just in the bar?" There was no moony expression on his face now.

He pulled a silver badge out of his pocket. "Off-duty cop. Here at your request."

"Wow. Thanks," said Rhonda. "Where's your wife?"

He grinned. "Gone home. I just used her to keep suspicion away from me." He stepped away from the door so George could come forward.

George rang the bell and knocked at the door.

"Go away!" came a voice from inside that I recognized as Bree's.

George's lips thinned. He knocked louder. "Open up."

"What the fuck?" came the cry from behind the door.

Then the door opened.

Wearing only undershorts, Bree gaped at us glassy-eyed. "What's going on?" He stepped back in shock when he recognized George. "What are you doing here?"

"I'm here to tell you to get dressed immediately so we can escort you off the property."

Bree's gaze traveled to Rhonda and me. His eyes narrowed. "Are you two behind this?"

"Actually, your behavior is." George's voice shook with anger. "Now get moving."

"Bree, baby! What is it?" A young woman approached us wearing a towel. Her tousled, blond hair and smudged lipstick were clear evidence of what we'd interrupted.

George let out a disgusted snort. "Don't know who you are and don't care. Get dressed immediately and get out of here."

She blinked with surprise and staggered back. "I don't know who you are either, but you don't need to talk to me that way. Bree invited me to his hotel."

"It's not *his* hotel, it's *ours*," said Rhonda, clenching her hands.

"Better do as the man says," I warned the girl, knowing how close Rhonda was to exploding.

Taking baby steps in an attempt at modesty, the woman hurried away.

"What's this about the hotel being yours," Bree snarled at Rhonda. "It's part of The Sapphire Resort Collection. Right, George?"

George shook his head. "Not anymore. Thanks, in part, to you. Now, if you want to save your ass from further damage, get dressed, so we can escort you out of here."

"What about my clothes? My car?"

George pulled a set of keys from his pocket and dangled them in the air. "Your father and I agreed that your brand-new Porsche isn't rightfully yours. We'll take care of that issue for you."

Bree's eyes widened in disbelief. "What? You've got to be kidding me."

"I'm not," said George firmly.

Bree's body slumped. He lowered his head. When he looked up, his eyes blazed with fury. "These ... these ... women have been nothing but trouble to me."

Rhonda stiffened. "Look, ya little punk. You should be sent to prison for all you've done. You've hurt a lot of people along the way, good people who were loyal to us and the hotel. If I weren't such a lady, I'd wring your fucking neck."

Bree opened his mouth and then closed it.

George and I stared at each other wide-eyed, and then George, his lips quivering from the effort of holding back laughter, spoke. "Well said, Rhonda. Now, move, Bree, before we escort you out of here in your underwear."

As Bree moved away from the door, Rhonda turned to George. "People like that make me crazy, ya know?"

He nodded. "It was a mistake from the beginning. My apologies to both of you."

"We want to make this as smooth a transition as possible," I said. "The people who have been marked will be met at the front door tomorrow morning. I imagine Mike has taken care of the night auditor already."

"I agree to everything," George said. He looked over at the policeman standing by. "Will you see that both the girl and Bree are removed quickly. I'm going to make sure that he takes nothing out of the room that he shouldn't have, including his computer. After your IT guy scans it for proprietary information regarding the hotel, he can have it back."

"Thank you for everything," I said, offering my hand to George.

He shook my hand and then Rhonda's. "Thank you."

As I walked with Rhonda down the hallway, I knew our troubles were far from over. The hotel wouldn't become ours until our people were in place, and the hotel was again the upscale property it once was, welcoming all who were willing to respect it and others.

CHAPTER TWENTY-TWO

When we returned to the front desk, our families had gathered there. Bernie and Mike walked toward us, wearing smiles.

I hurried over to Bernie and hugged him. "You made it! So nice to see you here!"

"Yeah," said Rhonda, "you belong here, not some big hotel in Miami."

He chuckled. "I'd rather work here than any other place."

"Everything seems to be in order," said Mike. "We're just waiting for Bree to be escorted out."

At the sound of noise, we turned to see Bree and his girlfriend shuffling toward us, their faces downcast. George and the policeman walked behind them, prodding them along.

We stepped aside to let them pass.

No one said a word until they were outside and descending the front steps. Then Mike spoke up. "Well done, guys!"

Liz started clapping, and then we all joined it, the sound of it like rippling waves of optimism.

"Well, partner! We did it," said Rhonda, giving me a quick hug. "The Beach House Hotel is ours!"

I grinned. Our baby was back.

"I need to speak to you," said Bernie. "I've brought someone with me—someone I can trust. He's willing to spend the night here, so we can get a few hours of sleep before the staff comes in. May I introduce him to you?"

"Sure," I said. "Is this the man you hoped to be able to hire as the manager under you?"

"Yes. His name is Juan Santiago."

"Great, let's go back to the office. We can talk to him there."

"Need me to stay?" asked Vaughn. "I can sit at the front desk and, if anyone needs anything, I'll come find you."

"Perfect!" I said, realizing how little I'd see of him over the next few days.

Rhonda and I headed back to the office we'd once practically lived in.

Opening the door to it, I paused. The rearrangement of furniture, the way it had been turned into a reservations office, and the clutter of too many people using the space made it seem too small, too unprofessional.

"What a mess," grumbled Rhonda.

I turned my attention to the young man sitting at the small, round table we normally used as a conference table. Books and papers were stacked on top of it.

"Ann, Rhonda, I'd like you to meet Juan Santiago, a recent graduate of FIU's hotel program," said Bernie. "I think he'd make a great assistant manager for the property."

At the mention of his name, Juan rose to his feet. Smiling, he held out a hand. "Glad to be here. Bernie filled me in on some of the issues. I'd like to be able to help you solve them."

I shook his hand, and Rhonda did the same.

"We need someone with a lot of energy, flexibility, and a willingness to do any job that is asked of him." As I talked, Juan nodded.

"Yeah," said Rhonda. "Someone who is honest and hard-working."

We all took seats at the table.

"I've done all the background checks when I hired him in Miami, and I'm willing to vouch for him," said Bernie.

"Tell us a bit about yourself," I said to Juan.

Juan settled his gaze on me. "I wasn't the best student at

the university because I had to work two jobs to pay for school. My mother is a single mom, and I have two little sisters."

"Did you fail any course?" Rhonda said.

Juan shook his head. "No. I did fine in class, but I don't test well. It's just one of those things. I never have."

"And yet you worked hard with both schoolwork and your jobs?" I said with admiration.

He shrugged. "I had to."

"Juan's been a good worker at the hotel, too," said Bernie. "Picks up information quickly."

"Are you willing to make the move from Miami to Sabal? Will you be leaving your family behind?" I asked.

Juan looked away and then returned his gaze to us. "My mother has a new boyfriend, and we don't get along. It will be a relief to be here." His voice held a vulnerability that touched me.

Rhonda and I exchanged silent messages, and then we nodded.

"All right, Juan. You're hired," said Rhonda.

A grin spread across his face. "Thanks."

"We'll work out final details tomorrow," said Bernie. "I gave you a broad outline of what we might offer."

Juan nodded. "It sounded good."

"Are you willing to work on the desk until morning?" I asked. "A policeman is going to remain on site overnight, as well. We'll be back around six a.m. tomorrow."

"A room here has been reserved for me," said Bernie. He smiled at Rhonda and me. "We'd better get as much sleep as we can. The next few days are going to be hectic."

"Good to have you here, Bernie. And congratulations, Juan. I think you're going to like working with us." I stood, gave everyone a little wave goodbye, and hurried out to the front desk.

Vaughn looked up. "It's been really quiet. Are you ready to go home?"

"Yes. I've got to be back here at six. Ana is meeting us then."

"No rest for the weary, huh?" Vaughn said.

I sighed and nodded. I didn't want to admit that now that we'd wrestled the hotel away from the investor group, I was nervous about pulling off all the changes we'd need to make in a timely matter—big things like the renovations of rooms and a million small things like new stationery and business cards.

At home, I quickly changed into my nightgown, the blue one Vaughn liked, and crawled into bed, both wired from the evening's excitement and exhausted from it.

Vaughn finished brushing his teeth and slid in beside me. Wrapping his arms around me, he nuzzled my neck. "I've wanted to do this all evening."

I looked at him and smiled. "Love you, honey, but I'm going to sleep. You can continue if you want, just don't wake me up."

He chuckled. "Okay, sleepyhead. Tomorrow."

I turned so that we were spooning together. Against all my worries that I wouldn't be able to get any sleep, my eyes closed, and I was soon lost in dreams.

When my alarm sounded at five-thirty, I groaned and blinked at the numbers on the clock, wishing the time away. Then I remembered all we had to do and scrambled out of bed. Vaughn mumbled something and turned over.

Later, after showering and dressing for the day, I tiptoed out of the house, careful not to wake Vaughn, Robbie, or Elena. Though her steady gaze followed me across the room, Trudy remained snuggled in her blanket in the kitchen. She was still miffed that Vaughn had kept her off our bed, where she was allowed to sleep when he was gone.

The morning air held a hint of coolness as I climbed into my car and headed for the hotel. The sun wouldn't be up for another half hour on this early November day. When Rhonda and I ran the hotel, this was the time when Consuela would be busy in the hotel kitchen making our famous cinnamon rolls. Though people might soon be working in the kitchen, the sweet aroma of cinnamon would be lacking today. It was just one of the ways the hotel had lost some of its allure.

I pulled into the front circle, parked my car at the far edge of it, and hurried up the front steps into the lobby.

Juan greeted me with a smile. "All is quiet. I've gone ahead and made a list of what rooms would be checking out today for the housekeeping department."

"Thanks. Is Rhonda here?"

"I believe she's in the back office."

I hurried to find her.

When I opened the door to the office, she looked up at me, her face flushed.

"Hold on, don't try to move that desk by yourself," I said, rushing to help her. "Where are you trying to put this?"

"In the hallway," Rhonda said. "I'm not sharing this office with anyone but you. The reservations department will have to move somewhere else. We used to handle reservations. With Dorothy's help, we can do it again."

I grabbed hold of the other end of the desk and helped Rhonda move it into the hallway. She was right. Our personal response to reservations had helped build our clientele in the past. We could do it again.

Breathing heavily, we stepped away from the desk.

"*Bonjour!*" Jean-Luc stepped into the hallway. "Are you blocking out the kitchen staff?"

Laughing, we shook our heads.

"No, but you might want to," I said. "They're due in any minute now. You'll have to decide who to fire and who to keep."

"Yes, I will know quickly who I want."

Jean-Luc helped us push the desk down the hallway to the loading dock to get it out of the way.

As we stood there, one of the kitchen staff, an older man who'd been recently hired, climbed the steps from the staff parking lot in back of the hotel.

"Come on in," I said, "and meet your new boss. This is Jean-Luc Rodin."

The man's eyes widened. "Jean-Luc? It's a pleasure. But what happened to Brian Casey?"

Jean-Luc's lips curled with distaste. "He will be gone today. As soon as he turns in his apron."

The man beamed at Jean-Luc. "This is a big change, but I like it. I'm Rick Bassett." He held out his hand, and Jean-Luc shook it.

"We'd better go," I said to Rhonda. "Ana should be here."

Rhonda and I bypassed the kitchen and hurried to the hotel entrance.

Bernie and Juan were standing together at the front desk. Bernie turned to us and said, "Ah, Ann and Rhonda, there's something you should know. Stuart apparently heard from Bree and tried to get into his office a moment ago. One of the policemen you hired escorted him out of the building. He's threatening a lawsuit, but I don't think it'll go anywhere. As I told him, he's lucky not to be under arrest. Mike is supposed to address the group of employees this morning, but, like Stuart, the real culprits are already aware of what has happened and probably won't show up for work. So, we need to talk about staffing."

"Sure. Let's go into your office. We can use it now that

Stuart is gone. Right?"

"I don't see why not." Bernie turned to Juan. "As soon as Julie comes in, you can go home."

I pulled Bernie aside. "Uh, that's not going to work. She and Stuart were working together on this."

Bernie's eyebrows shot up. "Really? She seemed like such a good worker. Who else can we get to take over for Juan?"

"The other front desk clerk working under Bree seemed fine. Let's give him a call and explain the situation."

Bernie nodded. "Okay."

We walked into Stuart's office and took a look around. From the mess on his desk, he was as unorganized as I'd always thought.

"Have a seat. I'll have this cleaned up before I leave tonight," said Bernie with a derisive snort. "You say Ana will be here to take over housekeeping?"

"Yes," said Rhonda, sitting down in a chair beside me, "but we don't want to fire the person she's replacing. Maria should simply be demoted. It turns out that Bree was blackmailing her."

Bernie shook his head. "Amazing that these things went on. No wonder George Peabody is so eager to do right by you. If word got out, it could ruin his company's reputation."

"We don't want to do that," I said. "We just want our hotel back."

"Yeah, but if they give us any trouble, I'll be glad to let the whole world know what kind of people they are," said Rhonda. "The way they treated you, us, Jean-Luc, and a lot of others is enough to make me furious."

"I agree," said Bernie, "but Ann's right. We need to make this changeover as smooth as possible, so our guests are unaware of any crooked dealings behind the scenes here at the hotel. Now, let's make that call to the front desk clerk so Juan can get some rest. I'm going to need him tonight and perhaps a couple of other evenings until we get a night auditor to replace him."

"What about Cliff Reynolds, our former night auditor? Bree dumped him in a hurry, and now we know why," said Rhonda.

"And, Bernie, we need to have a comptroller on site," I said. "I'm not going to be able to handle the financials as I used to in the past, not with my responsibilities to my family. You once told us you wanted to control the hotel. Now's your chance. Though it's our baby, you're going to be much more than a babysitter."

Bernie's eyes gleamed with satisfaction. "Good. That's the way I want it. And yes, a comptroller is a good idea. My hands are going to be full bringing the hotel functions back to a much higher level than they now are."

"But Annie and I are going to be present to greet guests and to work to bring back some of our old, more famous clients," said Rhonda.

"Those clients in government and in the entertainment business who seek privacy. Not the flashy news-seekers Bree and his crowd tried to bring in," I added.

Bernie studied us. "I think that's a good idea. The two of you work well together to promote the hotel in a way no one else can. But leave the rest up to me."

"Sounds good," I said.

"Yeah, it's getting the right people here," said Rhonda. "They don't have to be rich; they just have to be nice."

"Well, there are no promises there," said Bernie. "People are people."

Juan called on the intercom to ask Rhonda and me to come to the front desk.

We left Bernie making his phone calls.

My eyes widened with surprise when I saw George Peabody standing there.

His smile was tired when he noticed us. He stepped forward, offering his hand.

"It's been quite a night," he said, as we both shook hands with him. "But I wanted to ask the favor of being allowed to speak at the staff meeting Mike intends to hold this morning. It's important to me that staff hired under the banner of The Sapphire Resort Collection understand that we won't tolerate such behavior from anyone."

Rhonda and I exchanged glances.

"Seems fair," Rhonda said.

"Yes, I can't imagine how betrayed you feel," I added.

George shook his head. "You have no idea. Aubrey's father is ready to disown him."

Still furious by what Bree had done to my house, I couldn't hold back. "If he would stop excusing his son's bad behavior, Bree might grow up a bit."

George's blue-eyed gaze held mine, and he nodded. "He has a lot of life lessons to learn, but they will not come from working for us, no matter what Aubrey or Austin want. Period."

George had seemed stiff and cold when I'd first met him. I liked him a lot more now.

CHAPTER TWENTY-THREE

Later that morning, the staff of the hotel gathered in the dining room—some on the job, others brought in on their day off. The buzz of conversation bounced against the walls and glass windows, echoing across and around the room. Nothing like a good scandal to keep hotel staff talking.

Mike Torson and George Peabody stood together at the entrance to the room. At the sound of Mike's voice calling for attention, the room abruptly became quiet.

"We've asked all of you to assemble here today to officially let you know that Ann Rutherford Sanders and Rhonda DelMonte Grayson are now the owners of the hotel once more.

"Though you might have heard that this process had started several weeks ago, the switch in ownership is now complete, due to some nefarious activities on the part of Aubrey Lowell, Stuart McPherson, and a couple of others. We ask that you continue to work well under the new ownership until they tell you that your job is secure or ask you to leave. The goal is to keep everyone doing their job unless you, for some reason, feel you cannot continue. There will be no animosity if you decide to leave. Ann and Rhonda have always treasured their staff and treated them well." He turned to George. "And now, I turn the meeting over to George Peabody, one of the principals of The Sapphire Resort Collection."

George stepped up beside Mike. "Thank you, Mike. I wish I could say that it's a pleasure to be here, but I must confess this whole affair with Aubrey, Stuart, and others is disturbing to my partners and me. The hotel business is a tough one, dedicated to serving others and treating all with respect. Unfortunately, when one of our staff members decides to serve only himself, they not only disrespect others, but the whole idea of hospitality. We at The Sapphire Resort Collection will not tolerate behavior from any of our staff members that doesn't exemplify what we morally stand for. If for any reason you feel unable to abide by these rules, I ask you to leave now. Ms. Sanders and Ms. Grayson deserve your respect and your loyalty, as do Bernhard Bruner, the new general manager, and Jean-Luc Rodin, the new chef. Thank you."

Rhonda nudged me. "Your turn to speak. Ya know I don't like to."

I stepped up in front of Mike and George.

"Rhonda and I are pleased to have our hotel back under our control. The Beach House Hotel had a reputation in the past for superior service, excellent food, and providing our guests with a sense of elegance and discretion. We intend to reinstate those very qualities. Some of our former guests have come here with the knowledge that every staff member of ours would respect their privacy. Well-known people came to relax and to be themselves in a way they could not elsewhere. Over the next day or so, we'll be meeting privately with each of you to determine your status. As Mike said, we've always treated our staff as members of our family, and we intend to continue to do so. Welcome to The Beach House Hotel as it used to be."

As I stepped back, I realized how insulting that might have sounded to George Peabody and then decided I didn't care. The prior owners and management had continually put Rhonda and me down for our suggestions in the past. That was never going to happen again.

Rhonda grinned at me. "Thanks, Annie."

Mike came over to us and shook our hands. "Well, ladies,

this baby is yours. I'm happy for the two of you. You deserve this."

George joined us. "My apologies to both of you. I had no idea that things had gotten out of hand. Sam Logan and Austin Lowell oversaw this property. I didn't. But that's no excuse. I should have followed through on a few complaints you made. It's a shame it's come to this. The Beach House Hotel is a nice property. I'm sure you'll make it an even bigger success. Good luck with it."

As he turned to go, I stopped him. "Before you go, I want to say thanks for supporting us. It means a lot. I'm sorry that it didn't work out. We thought you all understood what we had built here."

He nodded. "I wish I had."

I turned back to the crowd in the room. "Please welcome Bernhard Bruner as your new general manager."

Some of the staffers who'd known him began to clap.

"I'm glad to be back and will be happy to work with you to make it the hotel Ann and Rhonda want it to be."

A crowd formed around Rhonda, Bernie and me.

We stood together to receive congratulations from most of the staff. I noticed Ana's look of joy and then the anger on the face of the young chef Bree had hired and realized it was a good thing we'd hired Jean-Luc. Not everyone would be happy with the new rules under Bernie's direction.

Later, after everyone had dispersed, Rhonda and I returned to Bernie's office with him.

"Any luck with the comptroller? I asked. "Will's friend backed out at the last minute."

"I've got a call into one of my manager friends in Miami. We'll see. Good news on the night auditor. Cliff has agreed to come back, though I had to promise him that he would never receive the same kind of treatment Bree gave him, that if there were any issues, we'd discuss them freely."

"Good," I said, wondering at the amount of work it would take for staff members to feel respected again.

"Bernie, we want to hire Dorothy Stern on a part-time basis. And you know about Manny and Consuela," said Rhonda.

"And we want to give Manny and Consuela the use of their old apartment again," I added.

He nodded. "I'll include them on the list. Anyone else?"

"We've put out an offer to Lorraine Grace to handle weddings for us. Maybe she can arrange a suitable wedding for Liz. Bree was making it impossible." I couldn't hide the bitterness in my voice.

"The wedding Annette and I had here at the hotel was beautiful," said Bernie smiling. "She still talks about it."

"A good thing I got you two together, huh?" said Rhonda.

His face flushed with emotion. "She's the best thing that has ever happened to me."

"We're going to use the reservations office and set it up the way it used to be. Dorothy can work in the small office nearby. Anything we need to know from you?"

"Let's meet at the end of the day. I'm sure we'll have a lot to discuss. In the meantime, I've put Amanda Collins to work on the front desk to relieve Juan. She might be a good candidate for that position."

As Rhonda and I left his office and headed for our own in the back of the house, I pulled Rhonda to a stop in the front lobby and indicated the space with a wave of my arm. "Just look at this! It's ours again!"

"You bet your ass," said Rhonda, giving me a high-five.

I laughed, loving Rhonda's spirit.

--ooo--

By the end of the day, my back hurt, my mind was spinning, and my heart was aching. Among reports and correspondence from the reservations department, we'd found some templates telling potential customers that The Beach House Hotel would no longer be accepted among The Sapphire Resort Collection, that it did not meet their high standards, and that a visit to their hotel in California might be a better choice. When we'd called Mike to inform him of this, he suggested that we withhold any legal action, that time would straighten things out for us.

Rhonda and I drafted a letter to past and future guests assuring them of a return to The Beach House Hotel's standards of excellence, but it felt, in some respects, like a middle-grader's fight of words.

"I'm pissed," said Rhonda. "Let's get Dorothy in here tomorrow. She can send these notices out for us."

"And let's bring Terri Thomas from the Sabal *Daily News* here with a photographer to showcase the hotel, talk to Bernie, and interview us."

"Okay, we've got to do something to make people understand we were the ones who threw them out," said Rhonda.

I placed a call to Dorothy.

She picked up right away. "Ann, so glad you called. The Neighborhood Association meeting regarding the rebuilding of the beach hut is scheduled for tomorrow night. Brock Goodwin scheduled it at the last minute hoping a lot of people would be unable to attend. But you've got to be there."

My sigh came from deep inside my belly. As much as I hated confrontation, I'd fight Brock for the hotel. "Okay, I'll schedule it. I'm calling you to see if you can come into the hotel tomorrow. We already have plenty of work for you to do."

"Why, my dear, I'd be delighted! I've already talked to Will about my working at the hotel again, and he's fine with it. I've missed the hotel terribly."

"Yes, I understand." One of the first things Bree did when he came on board was to fire Dorothy, who he thought was way past her prime. We knew otherwise, of course. She'd once owned her own business and was brilliant at following through on details.

As soon as we ended the call, Rhonda said, "Well?"

"Dorothy's delighted to come back to work, but Brock has scheduled a meeting with the Neighborhood Association board, and discussion of the rebuilding of the beach hut is on the agenda. We'll have to attend the meeting tomorrow night."

A look of determination settled on Rhonda's face. "I wouldn't miss it for the world."

After a brief meeting with Bernie, I raced to go home, eager to prove to Vaughn that my being at the hotel would not interrupt family life.

I arrived at our house to find Vaughn and Robbie down at the dock, cleaning the little sailboat we kept tied up there. Trudy's long body lay stretched out on the wooden slats of the dock near them.

Pleased by the scene in front of me, I hurried into my bedroom to change my clothes. Looking professional was part of the job, but it felt refreshing to strip off my dress and wiggle my toes in the soft carpet.

Sliding a T-shirt over my head, I felt some of the tension from the day's stress leave me. I pulled on a pair of shorts, slipped my feet into sandals, and rushed out the door.

Trudy barked when she saw me walking down the lawn, alerting Vaughn and Robbie to my presence. They looked up and grinned at me.

Robbie ran toward me. "Mommy! I missed you this morning!"

I wrapped my arms around him. "Mommy missed you too. Did you have a good day at school?"

"Yes. I did number three today. Tomorrow I do number four."

"Good for you." Doing numbers meant learning how to draw the numbers and count them as well.

Vaughn walked up to us. "Daddy missed you too." He leaned over and kissed me. "Glad you're home."

Not to be left out, Trudy jumped up onto my legs and barked until I'd greeted her with a sufficient number of ear scratches.

"We're cleaning the boat," Robbie proudly exclaimed.

"I see that. Good job."

"Want to take a sail?" Vaughn asked. "There's a nice, light breeze."

"Sounds great." Being on the water was exactly what I needed.

Vaughn, Robbie, and I donned life preservers, and then Robbie climbed into the boat.

"Here, Mommy. Hold my hand." He held out his hand, and I took it, impressed by his sweet action.

I stepped into the middle of the boat and sat down in the bow.

Vaughn came aboard and lowered himself onto the seat in the stern. Robbie huddled in the middle seat.

Robbie helped Vaughn hoist the sails, and then we were underway.

The steady, quiet movement of the boat through the water was a peaceful reminder that whatever troubles Rhonda and I faced, we were going to be okay. We had each other, and we had our families.

I watched as Vaughn and Robbie carefully exchanged places and Robbie took the tiller. His look of pride brightened his features, and my heart went out to this little boy who completed our family.

When it came time to come about, Vaughn guided Robbie's hand. A rush of tenderness spilled through me. His gesture was symbolic of the great father he was. I leaned back, lifted my face to the wind, and felt my worries wash away.

Back at the dock, Robbie and Vaughn worked to get the boat in order, and then the three of us, with Trudy at our heels, walked up the lawn toward the house.

While Robbie played a learning game on his iPad, Vaughn poured two glasses of wine, and we shared a few quiet moments on the porch.

"How did the day go?" Vaughn asked. "It's been a long one for you."

I filled him in and sat back against the seat cushion of the couch, feeling deflated. "We'll be busy for the next few weeks, putting things back in order, simplifying things. The running of the hotel is more about giving good service to our guests than anything else. With Bernie running the operation, Rhonda and I will be busy with guests and their issues."

Vaughn's gaze was steady. "You'll leave the running of it to Bernie, as we discussed?"

"Yes, as much as possible. I just wish we hadn't been forced to allow Bree to oversee the hotel. It's such a mess."

"A damn shame," Vaughn said.

"That's not all. Tomorrow night I have to attend a meeting of the Neighborhood Association to defend the rebuilding of the beach hut to Brock Goodwin and his cronies."

Vaughn sighed. "Guess that leaves just tonight for us. The director called. I have to return to New York."

I understood, but it didn't stop the thread of disappointment from traveling through me.

Dinner consisted of grilled chicken breasts, a spinach salad with pears and blue cheese, and carrots cooked the way Robbie liked them—with butter and a dash of brown sugar. It felt so nice to have both of "my men" share a meal with me.

Later, after I'd put Robbie to bed, I tiptoed into his room to make sure he was sleeping soundly before heading into my bedroom. I wanted nothing to disturb my time with Vaughn.

He met me at the door and pulled me into his embrace. "Ah, Ann, I've waited all day for this." He lowered his lips to mine, and I closed my eyes, savoring the touch, the taste of him.

He cupped my cheeks in his strong hands. "People in New York are still complimenting me on the gorgeous woman I brought to the charity ball."

"Do they know that I'm your wife?"

"The ones who count are well aware of that. The rest? Who knows?" He held out his hand and said in a deep, playful voice. "Come with me, wife."

I laughed and clutched his fingers.

He closed the door to our room and led me to the bed whose covers he'd already turned down. I climbed up onto it and stretched out beside him. His length, his broad shoulders, and strong features were dear to me. He shifted his body so that, facing him, I knew how ready he was. Smiling, I stared into his dark eyes, seeing our love reflected there.

"Take them off. Take them all off," he whispered, helping me out of my clothes.

After he'd quickly stripped off his, I studied him. For a man his age, he was magnificent. All of him.

He drew me to him, cupping my buttocks and fitting me to him. We lay together, kissing, showing with our tongues what our bodies would do next. Lost in the magic of our time together, I was unaware of the ringing of Vaughn's cell phone for several beats.

I pulled away. "Your phone."

"Forget it," he growled, hugging me closer.

His lips found mine, and I soon forgot about the call as Vaughn and I moved together to find the satisfaction we sought.

Later, nestled in his arms, I wondered aloud, "Who would be calling you at this time of night? You'd better check. It could be one of the kids."

He reached over and picked up the phone off the nightstand, checked Caller ID, and then sat up as he listened to a message.

"Dammit!"

"What is it?"

"It's Lily. She wants to know when I'll be back in New York."

I sat beside him, feeling the last bit of passionate heat leave me in a rush of cold. "Why does she need to know that?"

Vaughn let out a grunt of irritation. "God knows. I'm sick of this bullshit."

I couldn't stop a sigh. "It's awful—our knowing what kind of committed relationship we have and the whole world believing you're having an affair with Lily."

He nodded. "It a game for Lily, but I don't like it."

I got to my feet and tugged him off the bed. "C'mon, Vaughn Sanders. Let's go for a skinny dip in the pool."

A smile softened the deep lines of stress on Vaughn's face. "Sounds like a plan."

I handed Vaughn a towel and wrapped one around me. The

pool was heated, but the air was cool.

Outside, I dropped my towel by the pool and jumped into the shallow end, dipping my shoulders below the water's surface. Vaughn dove into the deep end and swam toward me. His long, strong arms made even strokes in the water and quickly brought him to me.

"Go ahead and do a few laps," I said, settling onto the steps of the pool, content to watch him. Swimming was a way for him to relax.

He grinned and took off.

I looked up, searching for stars. Clouds covered most of the night sky, like a shawl protecting those of us below. A few brave stars fought their way through the mistiness of the clouds and twinkled a bright hello.

I leaned back and watched Vaughn moving with a sureness I found comforting.

After doing eight quick laps, Vaughn swam up to me. "Thanks. That felt great."

He took a seat beside me on the steps and pulled me into his lap. His warm lips felt good against my cool skin as he kissed my breasts.

When he pulled away, we smiled at each other, content to be together without thoughts of New York.

CHAPTER TWENTY-FOUR

I don't know who was sorrier to see Vaughn leave—Robbie, Trudy, or I. His homecomings were always joyful, his departures sad. The three of us staying behind stood at the front door and watched the taxi cab Vaughn had ordered pull out of the driveway.

"When is Daddy coming back?" Robbie asked, slipping his hand into mine.

"I'm not sure. Definitely in time for Thanksgiving, though."

"How long is that?"

"Three weeks," I answered, fighting off panic at all that needed to be done.

Robbie nodded solemnly and turned to go inside.

Even though he couldn't see me, I gave a final wave at Vaughn and led the others into the house.

While I was giving Robbie his breakfast, Elena arrived carrying a suitcase. She'd agreed to stay at the house full-time until the holiday or until Vaughn was home.

"How about a cup of coffee?" I said to her, giving her a hug. I was so lucky to have her help, and we both knew it.

"Sounds good. Let me get settled in my room, and then I'll come join you." She took off with Trudy at her heels.

"I like Elena," said Robbie. "She's my friend."

"A special friend," I said.

Elena returned to the kitchen, and as we sipped coffee, we went over her schedule.

"I'm hopeful things will settle down into a normal routine," I said, "but for the next few weeks, it's going to be busy."

"And then Christmas and Liz's wedding," Elena replied.

"That, too. Thank goodness, it's a small wedding. But I want it to be perfect for her."

Elena gave me a shy smile. "Troy and I have finally set a date—June 7th. I hope you and Vaughn will save that date."

"Yes! Oh, Elena, I'm so happy for you!"

Elena's smile widened. "Troy and I are so excited. We're hoping we can get married at the hotel. Is that awful person handling weddings there gone?"

"Yes, and we think Lorraine Grace will join our staff. That reminds me. I'd better call her." I added a note to do so to my reminder on my cell phone. "I'd better take a shower and get going. Don't worry, if Lorraine doesn't come back, we'll find someone as talented to handle your wedding. That's one of the things the hotel used to be known for."

"Thanks, Ann. Like Liz, I want my wedding to be perfect. I know I'll never find anyone as perfect for me as Troy. It's sort of like you and Vaughn together. You know?"

Tears stung my eyes, surprising me. Vaughn and I were fantastic together. If only we didn't have to deal with all the manufactured rumors.

When I got to the hotel, Bernie was standing at the front desk with Juan and Amanda, studying something on the computer. He waved me over.

"We have a problem," he said, giving me a worried look. "A couple of cancellations have come through for today. When we tried to get in touch with them, one of the people, a friend of Bree's, told us that they'd received notice that their discounted rates had been canceled. The other person canceling did not respond."

"Part of that whole scam with Bree, no doubt. Let's be

watchful and keep track of each one. I guess he offered friends special rates. If we didn't cancel them, I wonder if the management company did. You'll have to talk to Mike about it to make sure they are the source and not Bree."

Bernie nodded. "Good idea. I thought we had control of the reservations system."

"I thought so too. And Bernie, we have to get to work on our advertising campaign to make it clear there are new owners and management. Let's call in one of the experts. Who did you use in Miami?"

"A company called Good Word. Two young guys keen on social media run it. They're expensive, but they do nice stuff."

"Interesting. Is Rhonda in yet?"

Bernie shook his head.

"I'm sure Rhonda wouldn't object to your going ahead and setting up a meeting with them as soon as possible. And after Rhonda gets here, we'll need to go through your staffing decisions with you."

"Okay," said Bernie. "Those people at The Sapphire Resort Collection have made a mess of things here."

As I headed toward the back of the hotel, the delicious aroma of cinnamon, butter, and baking bread met my nose. My mouth watered, and I hurried into the kitchen.

"Consuela! You're here!"

She looked up at me and grinned. "*Si*, Annie." She laughed as I swept her into my embrace. I loved her for so many reasons.

"It will take a while to get things right in my part of the kitchen, but I'm so happy Jean- Luc is back." She shook her head. "I was so sorry to hear about Sabine."

I quickly sobered. "Yes, she was a lovely person. We'll miss her."

Consuela scooped up one of the cinnamon rolls still warm

from the oven and handed it to me on a plate. "For you. Like old times."

"Thanks. When are you and Manny going to move into your apartment on site?"

Consuela's smile lit her eyes. "Manny and Paul are doing that today. Ana and the housekeeping crew cleaned it for us so we can move in. I can't wait. We've missed being here."

"Terrific!" Bree had insisted the apartment be used for Stuart. Sometimes justice was as sweet as this.

I sat at my old desk in our office, determined to do my best. Nibbling on the soft, warm roll, I felt a sense of hope. I took a moment to look around the office. It seemed strange, yet satisfying to be back in a space I'd once loved.

Rhonda and I had talked about sending out online letters to our former guests. I pushed aside the stack of papers on my desk, set up my computer and began to type. I had just finished a rough draft of the letter to guests when Rhonda burst through the doorway, carrying two cups of coffee.

She handed me a cup. "From Consuela. Sorry, I'm late. Rita and I interviewed one of her neighbors to help her out several days a week. I think she's going to be great. She and Willow get along, and you and I both know how important that is."

I laughed. Willow was a strong-willed little girl like her mother and was not always easy to rein in.

Rhonda sat down behind her desk and turned to face me. "What's going on? Looks like Juan and Amanda are working together at the front desk. With her reservations background, she should be good at it."

"Yes, she has Bernie's approval, and that's fine with me. We had a couple of cancellations for today. Apparently, Bree offered his friends discounts that are now not being honored. We think George is behind the cancellations, but Bernie is going to follow through with Mike on that. I'm working on a letter to our former guests."

"Good. I talked to Dorothy. She'll be in later this morning. I swear she all but cried when I told her how glad we were to have her back with us."

"Perfect." I knew Dorothy would do whatever it took to help us out.

"You work on the letter, Annie. I'll work on the list of names. I hope we can get people like Isobel Pennypacker and her sister Rosie to return to the hotel."

I felt a smile cross my face. From Palm Beach and in their sixties, Isobel and Rosie used to visit us on a regular basis, wearing bikinis at the pool during the day and changing into elegant dresses for the evening. Our former guests were like that, comfortable away from the pressures of social obligations, wanting to simply be themselves, knowing we would be discreet about who they were and what they were doing.

I went back to working on the letter. We had to be careful in how we phrased things, but we wanted to make it clear that we were recreating The Beach House Hotel of the past.

Dorothy came into the office as Rhonda and I were doing a final edit on the letter. We both jumped up to greet her. Not much more than five feet, Dorothy beamed at us. "Glad to be back, girls. Now, what can I do to help you?" Behind the thick lenses of her glasses, her eyes sparkled with mischief. "Besides what I've already done." She handed me a sheaf of papers.

"What's this?" I asked.

"Signatures for tonight's Neighborhood Association meeting, indicating they have no objection to your rebuilding the beach hut. Thought I'd beat Brock Goodwin to the punch."

"Great!" I said. Facing off with him, I'd need any help I could get.

Rhonda threw her arms around Dorothy. "That's our gal!"

"Good job!" I said, giving Dorothy a quick hug.

Dorothy beamed at us. "I can't tell you what it means to be working for you again. Any idea how dull it can get at home most days for someone like me who's had her own business?"

"I don't think you're going to be bored here for a long time," I said, patting her on the shoulder. "We've got your old desk set up right over there."

"And I've got a list of names for you to work on," said Rhonda. "Annie and I are writing a letter to our previous, longtime customers to let them know about all the changes."

"Good idea," said Dorothy. "Let's get it done." She sat down at her desk with a smile.

Rhonda and I left her working on a mailing list and went to find Bernie. He wanted to talk to us about the staff.

As we walked past the kitchen, we heard voices. We stopped and peeked in.

Rick Bassett, the older, recent hire I'd met yesterday was talking to Jean-Luc.

Jean-Luc noticed us and said, "Carl cannot come and work for us until after the high season, but Rick is more than a kitchen helper. He and I are talking about giving him more responsibility. Yes?"

Rick bobbed his head. "I'm honored to work with a talent like Jean-Luc."

"Good," I said.

"Jean-Luc and I worked together when we first started the hotel," said Rhonda. "I miss it."

"Ah *oui*, Rhonda, you may be needed again."

Rhonda's eyes lit with excitement. "I'm here for ya, Jean-Luc. No more fighting. I promise."

Jean-Luc nodded and gave me a sly smile. He and Rhonda had fought over recipes in the past. And when he'd tried to show Rhonda how to make her own mother's recipe for an

Italian soup, their relationship had almost ended.

We left the kitchen and headed to Bernie's office.

At our knock, he called out, "Come in!"

We stepped into the office to find him on the phone.

I took a seat beside Rhonda and gazed idly out the window to the front entrance. Beyond it, I noticed Manny and Paul unloading boxes from the back of his truck.

I nudged Rhonda and whispered, "Manny and Consuela are moving in."

"Good," she responded with a wink. "Can't wait to have my Manny around the house again."

I chuckled softly. Manny, kind-hearted as he was, loved the nickname she'd given him.

Bernie ended his call and smiled at us. "That was Mike Torson. He's spoken to George Peabody and confirmed they canceled the reservations. Mike said George is willing to do most anything to make things right. He's furious that the reputation of the company he's worked hard to build has been tarnished."

"I understand. How do we stand here? We've rid ourselves of Bree, Stuart, Julie, and the night auditor. Anyone else?"

"The chef. Jean-Luc told me to fire him for insubordination. Maria, the housekeeper whom Bree had threatened, is still working for us. She understands how careful she must be. Ana is back in control. Other than that, we'll get rid of the landscaping company. Manny and Paul will be heading that and the maintenance department also. We'll hire more there as needed."

"Boy, Bernie, it sure is nice to have you back," said Rhonda.

"I'm glad to be here and so is Annette. It feels like home."

"Thanks, Bernie." I got to my feet. "I emailed you a copy of the letter we're sending out to our former long-time guests. Let us know when you set up a meeting with the PR people." I turned to go.

"Annie? Good luck tonight with the neighborhood meeting," said Bernie. "I met up with Brock Goodwin last night. He's quite the ... forgive me ... the asshole."

Rhonda and I looked at each other and laughed. Bernie was no dummy.

CHAPTER TWENTY-FIVE

I couldn't help twitching nervously as I sat in a folding, metal chair in the clubhouse of a nearby condo complex. Rhonda sat next to me flexing her hands. Sparring with Brock Goodwin and his people had brought us many difficulties in the past. With the high season approaching, we wanted the beach hut restored. Sunsets along the Gulf Coast of Florida were a daily spectacle that tourists loved to witness. Sitting on the deck outside the beach hut or inside, they gathered in the evenings to have a drink and to watch the golden orb slip below the horizon, sending waves of colors through the sky.

"We can do this, Annie," said Rhonda in a stage whisper, turning the heads of people around us.

I nodded, but I hated encounters like this, especially in front of a group of people I didn't know.

Dorothy sat with two other board members at a long table in front of us. She gave us a quick wink and then turned as Brock Goodwin marched into the room with two of his cronies.

Will, sitting on the other side of me, spoke quietly into my ear. "Remember, don't let Brock's comments rattle you. Speak with authority."

I swallowed hard. Hopefully, our issue would be one of the first on the agenda, so I could make my plea and go home. It had been a long day.

An hour later, our topic still had not been raised. I stifled a yawn, torn between going to sleep and wanting to smack Brock Goodwin. He kept giving me triumphant glances, knowing very well how tired I was.

Dorothy finally spoke up. "Mister Chairman, several of us are here tonight to address the rebuilding of the beach hut at The Beach House Hotel. We need to move onto it now before people have to leave."

"Yes," called someone from the audience. "Enough talk of dogs being measured by size or by pounds before being approved by condo associations."

"That's because you have a chihuahua," said another man, and laughter erupted in the room.

"Okay, it has been requested that we move on to the question of rebuilding the hut," said Brock. "I personally have talked to the fire department. They are concerned that it might be a danger to others because of its flammability."

A woman in the audience raised her hand. "General opinion is that the structure was purposely set on fire. That doesn't make it a danger to others. It stood for several years with no problems. I say there should be no objection to rebuilding it."

Dorothy got to her feet and waved sheets of paper in the air. "I have here over a hundred signatures agreeing with her. This is an issue that should never have been brought before the board. I'm aware of your previous attempts to undermine activities at the hotel, and I say it's time to stop."

Brock's cheeks turned bright red. "What right did you have to canvass the neighborhood?"

Dorothy drew herself up as tall as possible and glared at him. "As much right as anyone who lives here. This is not a dictatorship, though you continue to try to make it one, even after being away for some time. Please stop and listen to what we in the neighborhood want."

"Do we have representatives of the hotel present?" Brock said, looking straight at me.

I had no choice but to raise my hand and stand.

"What do you have to say for yourselves," Brock said, well aware I hated public speaking.

I went to the front of the room. "We are asking for nothing new, simply for agreement that we can rebuild what had been previously approved there. As someone mentioned, we believe arson was involved, and like the previous building, we'll have the same safety protections in place. We've come here as your neighbors not for your permission, but for your agreement. You, our neighbors, are important to us. As Rhonda Grayson and I are now the sole owners of the property, we want to assure all of you that The Beach House Hotel will once again be the elegant addition to the neighborhood it once was."

"Oh, but you're not the sole owners. Not yet. I understand ongoing discussions are still taking place," protested Brock.

I shook my head. "Not anymore. It's ours."

Brock's eyes rounded with surprise.

"Okay," said Dorothy. "Let's take a vote to support this move." She held up a number of papers in her hand. "Here are the names of over one hundred people in the neighborhood who support it. How about the rest of you?"

Amid the buzz of conversation, Brock pulled me aside. "Don't think you're going to get away with canceling my contract to provide artwork for the hotel. It was clearly signed by Aubrey Lowell as the representative of The Sapphire Resort Collection."

"Take it up with them, not us," I said, knowing full well that Aubrey's signature meant nothing to the execs of that group. "The Beach House Hotel is no longer a part of that company. Issues you have should be taken up with them. But, Brock, if I were you, I'd cancel any shipments."

He gave me a venomous look before returning to his duties.

A vote was taken to support our move.

"Approved," said Brock curtly.

Amid the applause that followed, I signaled Rhonda. She came forward, carrying a large, thin box.

"We want to assure you that Breakfast at The Beach House Hotel will become an event again. To celebrate, we've brought a number of our famous cinnamon rolls for you to enjoy. Those who don't get one tonight will be able to get a complimentary one with breakfast."

Rhonda placed the box of sweet rolls on the front table. We stood back, allowing people to rush forward for a sample.

Brock came up behind me. "Cheap shot."

I didn't turn around, merely studied the looks of satisfaction on the faces of those who were happily munching away.

As I lay in bed that night trying to relax, my cell rang. I knew who it was before I even checked, and I clicked onto the call.

"Hi, sweetheart. How'd your showdown with Brock go?"

I smiled at the sound of Vaughn's voice. "Easier than we thought. Dorothy had already signed up a number of votes ahead of time. And after the vote was taken and approved, Rhonda and I passed out sweet rolls to advertise that Breakfast at The Beach House Hotel was being reinstated."

Vaughn laughed. "Who could resist that?"

"Brock was furious. He called it a cheap shot."

"I wonder how that guy can keep in business. He's such a jerk."

"He wasn't happy with me, that's for sure."

"Be careful, Ann. Brock has an ego that won't accept bruising. He'll find a way to get back at you."

"As a matter of fact, he wants us to go ahead and honor a contract he made with The Sapphire Resort Collection. But Rhonda and I want nothing to do with it. I told him to take it up with them, not us."

"Hmmm," said Vaughn. "Be sure and alert Mike to this disagreement. You might need him to help straighten things out."

"Probably," I agreed. "How are things in New York? Sorry, I can't be there with you. It'll be so nice to have you home for the holidays."

"Or before," Vaughn said. "I'm pushing for a new shooting schedule. I figure the top guys owe me a few favors."

"Good luck," I said, unable to keep a trace of bitterness out of my voice. They were behind the Vaughn/Lily rumors.

"How are plans for Liz's wedding going now that you own the hotel?" Vaughn asked.

I told him about Lorraine Grace's possibly coming to work for us and how I hoped to be able to help Liz with final plans.

"Sounds good," said Vaughn. His voice changed, became soft, teasing. "So, what are you wearing?"

I laughed. Even if he were in bed beside me, it would not be a romantic night. But I played along, loving his interest, hoping the day would never come that he'd stop caring.

CHAPTER TWENTY-SIX

The next few days were hectic as I tried to cope with duties at the hotel and perform my mommy duties at home. I was sitting in on another strategy meeting with Bernie and Rhonda when she nudged me. "What's the matter with you? Are ya listening?"

Startled, I returned my attention to the conversation at the table, trying to mentally brush away my concerns. I'd been able to pick up Robbie from school only two times that week. He didn't seem to mind, but it bothered me that Elena, not me, was the one who greeted him.

I turned to Bernie. "Sorry, you were saying?"

"As much as I hate to do it, I think we should let Amanda go. I've lost all confidence in her. She wasn't involved in the operation of it, but it turns out she knew about the manipulations and inaccuracies in the reservations system."

"Do it," I said. "We don't want anyone undermining the hotel or any of the staff who works for us."

"Yeah, we don't need someone like that here," sniffed Rhonda.

The sound of knocking on Bernie's office door stopped our conversation.

"It must be Lorraine," I said, rising.

I opened the door and let out a gasp of surprise. "Tina! What a surprise!" I pulled her to me and gave her a good, strong hug before standing back to study her. Small, but voluptuous, Tina had an undeniable appeal to both men and women. Her lovely facial features and sparkling brown eyes were offset by a carefree blond hairstyle that enhanced her appearance.

When I stood aside, Rhonda pulled Tina into a bosomy embrace. "Glad to see ya!"

"Come in. Come in," I said. "We're expecting Lorraine Grace any minute now."

"And here I am," said Lorraine approaching us.

I helped Bernie arrange the chairs in his office to accommodate our two visitors.

Bernie gave them a little bow. "Good to have you join the staff here, Lorraine. And, Tina, it's always an honor to have you as our guest."

Tina sat down next to Lorraine. "Actually, I'm here not as a hotel guest per se, but as a guest of Ann's. I'll be staying in her house here on the hotel grounds."

Rhonda and I exchanged looks of dismay.

"Uh, the house won't be ready for another two weeks, but you can stay with me, if you'd like," I said.

Tina's lips formed a pout. "But you promised ..."

"You said you'd be here at Thanksgiving," I said quietly. "I'm sorry, but a lot has been going on. Rhonda and I now have control of the hotel, and I've been diverted from following through on the house."

"I expected ..."

Rhonda shook her head. "Listen, sweetie, I know you're dealing with a lot right now, but you're gonna need to cut us some slack."

Tina's eyes widened. "Oh my God! I'm sorry. It's just that I have a lot on my mind."

Bernie got to his feet. "Why don't Lorraine and I give you some privacy."

They left the office, and I turned to Tina. "What's going on? Is it your mother and your brother?"

Tears glistened in Tina's eyes. "Not only that. I've just had a horrible fight with Nicholas."

"I'm sorry ..." I began.

She held up a hand to stop me. "And that's not all. I'm pregnant. Nicholas doesn't know, and I don't want to tell him until we settle our quarrel. It was over the dumbest thing in the world, but it's important to me."

Stunned by all the things she was dealing with, I wrapped my arms around her. "Oh, honey, I had no idea."

Rhonda came over to us and gave Tina a hug. "Good thing you're here. We'll help ya get things squared away."

"Yes," I quickly agreed. "This will be a good place for you to sort things out." Tina could be difficult at times. Having her live with me while she was upset and secretly pregnant would not be easy, but I'd do everything I could to help her. Her life was a mess.

"Excuse me," said Tina. "Is there some place I can lie down? I'm not feeling good."

"I'm sure we can find an available room for a few hours while I take care of a few things here. Will that work for you? I'll hurry with my meeting."

Tina glanced at Rhonda and nodded. "I guess. I mean, sure."

After seeing that Tina was settled in one of the guest rooms with plenty of water, ginger ale, saltines, and snacks, I left her to return to the meeting.

Lorraine smiled when I entered the room. "We've waited for you. Now we can begin."

"Thanks. We want to talk about your contract, but you wanted to talk about remodeling some areas around the hotel to make them suitable for small weddings and photo ops."

Lorraine nodded. "With a property this beautiful, there's not much to add, but I have a few suggestions I want to run by you."

We rose, and I followed Lorraine, Rhonda, and Bernie into what used to be a sizeable library. Angie had been married there, and we'd used it for many other functions.

"This room can be made more functional if we have a little stage built that matches the beautiful, dark wood of the moldings and bookshelves. The advantage of having a small platform is that musical concerts, lectures, and other events can be held here more easily. For weddings, it will give us space for harpists and other musicians.

I thought of Chad's mother who was composing a song for Liz's wedding. "Great idea. Let's go ahead with it."

"We can use the architects who worked with the conversion of The Beach House into a hotel," said Rhonda.

"Sunday afternoon concerts might bring in new business during the shoulder seasons and even in the summer," Bernie said.

We left the library and went outside to the side yard. Bernie's step-daughter, Babette, had been married there.

"The garden is lovely," said Lorraine. "My clients have loved the privacy, the lushness of this area in the past. But I think we need to add a gazebo at the far end to use in case of rain or simply for the bride to be out of the sun. What do you think?"

"I love it," said Rhonda.

"And it would still be out of the view of other guests," I added. When I'd first seen The Beach House, I had no idea how large a piece of property it sat on.

"Now let's discuss the beach hut you're rebuilding. I'd like to make a few suggestions," said Lorraine.

As I listened to her describe the soft colors she wanted to

add to both the inside and outside of what we called a hut, my respect for Lorraine grew. The hut was a charming little building, and with her suggestions, it would be even better. I realized now how lucky we were to get her.

We walked back to Bernie's office, and the four of us made a list of things we wanted to do to improve the wedding business.

"Let's discuss staff," said Bernie. "Our agreement with Lorraine said that we'd provide a part-time staff member to help her. Who did you have in mind?"

Rhonda and I glanced at each other and then Rhonda blurted out, "Annie and I think Annette would be perfect for the job. The way she handled Babette's wedding was simply wonderful."

"Yes," I said. "It was one of the best weddings we've ever had, and Annette worked with Lorraine on it."

"Annette? My wife?" Bernie blinked in surprise.

"She's lovely," said Lorraine, following my silent plea for support.

Bernie sat back in his chair and gave us a thoughtful look. "I would never have thought of it, but she'd be good. Why don't I talk it over with her and get back to you on it?"

We wrapped up other details and then I got to my feet. "I'm going to check on Tina. I'll see you later."

"I've got to leave, too. Willow has a doctor's appointment," said Rhonda. "Let me know if I can help in any way."

I said goodbye to everyone and hurried down the hallway to the guest room in which we'd placed Tina. Something more than pregnancy was her problem, and I knew it.

At my knock on the door, she called softly, "Come in."

I stepped into the room and found her lying on the bed, curled up like a toddler.

She lifted herself to her one elbow and peered up at me.

"Time to go now?"

"Before we do, let's take a few minutes to talk privately— Robbie and Elena are at the house. I want to find out exactly what's going on. I know you well enough to understand your grief. And it's not just one thing. At this moment, your whole life is difficult, and I want to help you."

Tina sat up in bed, leaned back against the headboard, and patted the space next to her.

I crawled onto the bed and sat beside her.

Tina let out a trembling sigh. "I've made an appointment to talk to Barbara Holmes tomorrow, but I feel as if I'm about to explode with all sorts of emotions. You, of all people, know how I felt about my mother. And you know how much I loved my brother. I've tried to get images of them out of my mind, but they won't go away, and I can't stop blaming my mother for Victor's death. Before the fire broke out, she'd been drinking and was passed out in bed. The only reason she kept my brother with her was that I wanted him to come and live with me."

When I put my arm around her, Tina leaned her head against my shoulder. "Everyone thinks I have such a charmed life, but you know that wasn't always true. The thing I want most is a loving family like yours."

Tears blurred my vision. I pulled her tighter to me and felt her shoulders trembling beneath my hand. Growing up, Tina had been emotionally and physically abused. She might be the most beautiful and talented movie star of the day, but, really, she was a young woman who suffered from insecurity, bad memories, and a need to be loved.

"I'm sure Barbara will help you find a way to cope with your feelings regarding the fire and your grief. What else is going on?" I murmured.

Tina's shoulders shook with sobs. "It's Nicholas and me.

224

He's the nicest guy I've ever dated. I love him. I really do."

"But?" I prompted.

"His daughter hates me."

"His daughter? I thought he had a grown child."

"She is, or should be. Emaline is twenty-one but acts like a spoiled teenager. She hates me. You know what she did? She told him *I* don't like *her* and then when he set up a dinner for the three of us, she phoned to tell me that he'd changed the time so that I was an hour late to meet them. He was furious with me, and when I tried to explain, he told me he needed to rethink things."

Tina lifted her tear-streaked face. "Emaline's a dirty, rotten liar!"

I sighed. Her words reminded me of a fight Liz had had with a friend—in middle school.

"She's nothing but ... a ... bitch!" cried Tina.

I nodded with sympathy, thinking this woman/child needed those talks with Barbara, her therapist, and a good dose of relaxation in a home full of love.

"How can I marry a man who won't believe what I say?" Tina asked, wringing her hands. "And he once told me he didn't want any other children. What about our baby? I was going to tell him after the dinner, but that didn't happen."

"When is the baby due?"

"Early May, I think. Anyway, what does it matter?"

"It matters a lot," I said. "Tina, you have your whole Beach House Hotel family to support you. Angela and Reggie are having their second baby in the spring, Nell and her husband, Clint, are expecting a baby too, and Ty and June have just found out they're pregnant. I know they'll all be willing to help you, and so will I."

"Really? That's so nice." A look of determination swept across Tina's face, changing her whole demeanor from lost little girl to strong woman. With new resolution, she climbed off the bed and faced me. "Maybe, with all of you behind me, I can have this baby. Even if I have to raise it alone."

The abrupt change in her behavior caught me off guard for a moment. But then I realized this ability was one of the reasons she was the most sought-after actress in the business.

I gave her a hug. "Ready to go home?"

She smiled and nodded.

Studying her as we headed to the car, I wondered what kind of person Nicholas was and if he knew how insecure Tina was beneath her glamour.

CHAPTER TWENTY-SEVEN

When I walked through the door into the kitchen, Robbie ran to greet me, then stopped when he noticed Tina. "Hi, Mommy!" He stared at Tina.

I drew him to my side. "This is a special friend of Mommy's and Daddy's. Her name is Tina. You probably don't remember her, but you met her at our wedding."

"Yes, I do," said Robbie firmly. "She was the good fairy who killed the monster under my bed."

I blinked in surprise. "What's this?" I asked her.

Tina laughed. "While I was staying here after the wedding, Robbie was afraid to stay in his room until I helped him get rid of a pesky but harmless monster who was just trying to find his Mommy. Right, Robbie?"

He nodded and shyly clung to my legs. "You made him go away."

"Tina is going to stay here with us for a while. In Liz's room."

Elena appeared with Trudy at her heels.

"You remember Elena, don't you, Tina?"

"Yes, it's nice to see you again," Tina responded politely.

"Tina is staying with us for a couple of weeks while my house is renovated," I explained to Elena. "She'll be staying in Liz's old room."

Elena bobbed her head. "The cleaning crew came earlier, so it should be all set."

Impatient for attention, Trudy wagged her tail and barked.

"Who is this sweet little girl?" cooed Tina, bending over to give Trudy the ear scratches she was seeking.

"This is Trudy," said Robbie. "She's my wiener dog."

Trudy trotted over to Robbie and sat down beside him, looking up at him with adoration.

"I'll show you to your room, Tina, and then help you bring in your suitcases."

Elena stayed in the kitchen while I led Tina, Robbie, and Trudy to the room Tina would temporarily have as her own.

Standing in the doorway, looking around the spacious room, Tina looked at me. "Remember how scared I was, staying with you at your house. A lot has happened since those days, but sometimes I'm just as scared. What am I going to do with a baby when I can't even manage myself?"

"You'll find a way. We all do," I said quietly.

Robbie noticed Tina's distress and patted her hand. "Don't cry."

"Oh, buddy, I'm trying not to," said Tina. She gave his fingers a squeeze. "Thanks for helping me."

He beamed at her. "Daddy says I'm a big help with the boat."

"I'm sure you are," said Tina, exchanging an amused look with me.

"We'll leave you to get settled. If you feel like a swim, the pool is heated."

"Thanks, but I think I'll just take it easy."

I returned to the kitchen to find Elena getting ready to leave.

"Have a good evening. I'll be back at seven tomorrow morning," she said.

"Is everything all right?" I asked.

"Sure ... maybe ... no. At your wedding, Tina made a big play for Troy. We almost broke up over it, and now she's back."

"Don't let her looks or behavior threaten you, Elena. You're a beautiful girl whose fiancé loves her very much."

Elena let out a long breath. "Guess you're right. But when someone like Tina goes after the one you love, not many guys would resist. As I said, I'll be here early tomorrow morning."

"Thanks." I gave her a quick hug. "Tina is hiding out here, so we don't want the news to get out."

"I understand," said Elena. "'Bye, Robbie!"

He waved to Elena and turned to me. "Is Tina a secret?"

I chuckled. "Yes, she's our special secret."

He gave me a devilish grin. "I like secrets."

I smiled, wondering how this one was going to work out for me.

After I'd put Robbie down for the night, I sat with Tina in the sunroom, filling her in on the recent activities with the hotel. "The good thing is that Bree is gone and Rhonda and I are in control again. Bernie, Jean-Luc, Ana, and others from our former staff are back."

"And you're making changes to the hotel?" Tina said.

"We're renovating the rooms with new carpets, bedspreads, and towels. And we're rebuilding the beach hut." I told her about Brock's actions to fight it and his threats to us if we didn't allow him to go forward with providing artwork for the hotel.

Tina shook her head with disgust. "Rhonda's right. He's a freakin' jerk. I can't imagine I ever thought about going out with him."

"Don't feel bad," I said. "I actually went out with him. Twice."

Tina gave me a look of concern. "How are things between you and Vaughn? It can't be easy for you with all the publicity about Lily and him together again."

"It isn't easy for either of us, but Vaughn will have to work things out. He's making noises about leaving the show and doing movies."

"He's a good actor," said Tina. "He shouldn't have any problem finding work."

"We'll see," I said. "The decision is his to make."

Tina yawned and stretched. "I'm ready for bed. Thank you, Ann, for allowing me to stay here with you. When my world came tumbling down around me, there was only one place I wanted to be, and that's with you and The Beach House Hotel."

She rose and gave me a quick hug. "I feel better already."

Tina left the room, and I turned out the lights and headed for my bedroom, exhausted from another day at the hotel and all the challenges we now faced.

As I quickly changed into my nightie and prepared for bed, I thought of Tina's situation. Jealous daughters of doting dads were not unheard of with upcoming second marriages. Did Tina have a chance of making it work?

I was still wondering at all the changes in life when Vaughn phoned. I took the call and climbed into bed.

"How are you, honey?" I said.

"Curious," he answered. "I got a call from Nicholas Swain. He knows that Tina thinks of us like family, and he was wondering if I knew where she was. I told him I had no idea. What's going on?"

"Tina's here with me until my house at the hotel is done. Then she's moving in there. But it's a hush-hush situation. No one is to know where she is. Even Nicholas."

"Trouble?"

"She and Nicholas had a fight over his grown daughter, and she needs some time to herself. She'd already made plans to meet with Barbara Holmes for some counseling."

"He sounded really upset about it," said Vaughn, "but I guess we'd better let it go."

"Yes, that sounds like the thing to do. I won't mention it to Tina. The two of them will have to work out their problems together."

"I've told the producers that I want some time off, that I'm tired of the farce with Lily, that I owe it to you and my family to end it."

I sat up in surprise. "And?"

"And I'm not sure what will happen, but I think they may have heard me this time."

"I love you, Vaughn. No one, not even Lily, is going to destroy what we have," I said with a ferociousness I meant.

Vaughn let out a playful growl. "I like it when you go all tigress on me."

"Tina said the sweetest thing. She said she wants a family just like ours."

"Considering all the factors and the people in it, our family is a little unusual, but it is a strong one. That's for sure."

We talked about the progress with the hotel staff, and then, when I couldn't hold back a yawn, Vaughn said, "I'll let you go. Love you."

"Me too," I said, and then laughed. "I mean I love *you*."

Still chuckling, we ended the call.

The next morning, I drove Robbie to school, delighting in doing this simple Mommy task, though Elena would pick him up.

"Mommy? If Tina is a secret, does that mean I can't tell Brett about her, even if he's my best friend?"

"Right. A secret means you can't tell anyone." The last time we'd tried to hide Tina at the hotel, it had turned into a publicity fiasco—something I had no intention of repeating. Especially with Rhonda's and my trying to re-establish the unspoken agreement that our guests would be met with discretion.

After Robbie climbed out of the car, he looked at me and held a finger to his lips. "See, Mommy! I can keep a secret."

"Let's hope so, buddy. It's important."

I waited until he was inside the front entrance to the school and then pulled away, intent on getting my house ready for Tina as soon as possible.

When I entered the hotel, I was surprised to see Terri Thomas, the gossip columnist from the newspaper, sitting in the lobby. I went right over to her.

"Terri, how nice to see you!"

She smiled. "I know we set up an appointment for this afternoon, but I wanted to surprise you. I often get the best news this way."

I suppressed a shiver. There was something about the way Terri studied people that made me, among them, want to spill any news I could, simply to get away from her.

"Have you had breakfast? We can talk in the dining room. Consuela is back with us and is making her cinnamon rolls once again."

Terri patted her sizeable girth. "I'd heard that, which, I confess, is another reason I decided to come early."

I led Terri into the dining room, grateful to find other diners there.

"Rhonda should be along any minute," I said, "but why don't we start? Please, order anything you like."

A young waitress approached the table. "Good morning! What may I get you besides water? Would you like coffee? Juice?"

Terri went ahead of me and ordered a full breakfast.

"Just coffee for me, please," I said.

"Now, tell me all about the takeover. I heard it was quite exciting. And then you and Rhonda got the neighborhood behind you on rebuilding the beach hut. That was a coup I'm sure Brock Goodwin didn't like." She leaned forward, eagerly anticipating any juicy tidbit of gossip I might offer.

I knew I had to play it carefully. "In both cases, things went quite smoothly."

"At midnight? Sounds like more than a smooth transition to me. I heard the manager was literally dragged out of the hotel."

"I don't know who told you that."

"It doesn't matter. I have my sources. I noticed that Bernhard Bruner is back as manager. That's a nice change—an elegant, older gentleman, not the young, smart aleck that was here. I notice these things, you know."

I nodded and sat back as the waitress served our food.

Rhonda burst into the dining room, and seeing us, hurried over to our table. "Hi, sorry I'm late. I'm still trying to get Rita settled into her new schedule."

She sat in a chair next to me and faced Terri. "I thought our meeting was scheduled for this afternoon? Did I mess up?"

"No," I assured her. "Terri thought she might get some unexpected news if she surprised us."

Rhonda nodded. "Oh, yeah, like ... Lorraine ..."

Terri bent closer, gulping like a fish reaching for a worm. "Oh? What about Lorraine? Are you talking about Lorraine Grace?"

"Yes, but you have to keep this confidential until she's ready to announce it," I said, giving her a line of malarkey. "Lorraine is moving her wedding business, Wedding Perfection, to The Beach House Hotel. She'll be handling her clients here for locals and, of course, for our many destination wedding brides."

"She did a wonderful job for my daughter, Angela. Remember?" said Rhonda.

"And, here's another tidbit," I said. "She'll be handling the wedding for my daughter, Liz. In fact, that's one of the changes that will occur here at the hotel. We'll be adding some nice features for wedding ceremonies, as well as bringing back our unique destination wedding packages."

"I hope to be invited to Liz's wedding," said Terri. "It'll be a good way to feature the hotel. Now, what else is going on?"

"The guest rooms are going to be refreshed," I said. "New carpets, bedspreads and some furniture."

"And we're doing some renovation work on the library," Rhonda added. "Adding a gazebo, too."

Terri took down notes. "And what about the two of you? With young families are you going to be back on site?"

I nodded. "We will be present for our guests, but Bernhard and our staff are most capable and will handle the day-to-day business."

"This hotel is and always will be our baby," said Rhonda. "We want our guests to enjoy it as much as we do."

Terri took a last bite of her cinnamon roll and patted her mouth with a napkin. "Okay. I've got enough for a nice article. I'll be back this afternoon with a photographer."

I stood and waited for her to rise. "Thank you so much, Terri. I'll make sure you get an invitation to the wedding. It's going to be lovely."

"Any royalty this time?" She asked with a twinkle in her eye.

My smile was forced. "No more royal weddings here." What a fiasco that had been.

"Some of our well-known guests might be around,"

Rhonda said, giving me a sly wink.

Terri stopped mid-rise from her chair. "Really? Who are you talking about?"

I smiled, though I wanted to pinch Rhonda. "We're hoping to encourage old friends to visit us again, with the understanding it will remain confidential."

"Oh, yes. That was always the attraction for some of your famous guests. I understand. But keep me in mind if there's a story I can publish."

"Right," said Rhonda.

"I'll walk you out," I said, anxious to get Terri away from Rhonda.

"See you later," said Rhonda. "I have to check on a few things in the office."

As I led Terri through the lobby, she turned to me. "What was Rhonda talking about? Was it someone other than Lorraine?"

I shook my head. "I can't imagine what it could be," I said, lying through my teeth.

Terri gave me a steady look. "Sooner or later, I find out everyone's secrets."

"I have none to give you," I said.

"How's that man of yours doing? Get home much?"

"Vaughn is fine," I replied, unwilling to play her game. "He was just here and will be back soon."

"So, it's not true about Lily?" she asked, looking disappointed.

I gritted my teeth and forced a smile. "Vaughn and I are very happy. But, so nice of you to ask."

"All right, then. I'll send a photographer over this afternoon. Thank you, Ann. Always nice to see you and Rhonda."

"Thank you in advance for a nice article in the paper. It

means a lot to us."

Terri left, and I headed for the office, fighting the urge to cry. Why were people so eager for bad news?

CHAPTER TWENTY-EIGHT

I hurried over to my house on the hotel property. Nestled among green foliage, it was my pride and joy—a perfect place for Tina to hide out.

Inside, I found the painters working on the wooden trim throughout the house. I'd kept the soft-white color on the walls and a slightly darker shade on the trim, giving the rooms a neat, tidy look that would accentuate the furnishings I'd selected with the help of Laura Bakeley.

Soon, new carpeting would be laid in all the bedrooms. And in the living room, a new area rug would sit on a soft-gray tile that was being put down instead of carpeting. Right now, the old furniture was piled in the middle of the rooms to accommodate the painters.

I went out onto the patio to phone Liz. She'd accepted my offer of the furniture, but I couldn't wait any longer for her to get it out of the way.

"Hi, Mom!" came her cheerful voice. "I just got a call from Lorraine Grace. I'm so happy. She's going to be helping us with the wedding. I said we'd meet her this evening after work. Can you do it?"

"Sure," I said, juggling dinner plans around in my mind. "Tina Marks is staying with me for a couple of weeks while the house gets renovated here. I need you and Chad to move the furniture out of the house. How soon can you do it?"

"I'll talk to Chad and get back to you. In the meantime, what do you think of an old-fashioned wedding in the gazebo you're going to build at the hotel?"

"It might be a little cool for that," I said.

"Aw, I knew you'd say that. What about a gazebo look in the library?" said Liz.

"Hmmm. That might work. We'll have to see how creative Lorraine can be. I thought you were going to keep everything super simple."

"I was going to, then I read an article in one of the bride magazines, and I've changed my mind. I want something a little more traditional. Okay?"

"Let's talk to Lorraine about it," I said, wondering at the change in Liz's plans. "See you later."

Next, I put in a call to the decorator to check on the furniture I'd ordered. After a quick conversation, we agreed that two weeks would give us enough time to have the tile done, carpeting laid, and the basic furniture in place. Decorating details would be added as they became available.

"I'll do my best. I know how anxious you are," Laura assured me.

"Thank you. I need the space. Vaughn's daughter Nell and her husband are coming for Thanksgiving." I didn't explain that Nell would be staying with us, and Tina would be the one moving into the house. As I'd told Robbie, secrets were secrets.

After checking in with Bernie and Rhonda, I went home, anxious to see how Tina's meeting went with her psychologist.

When I walked into the kitchen, I heard voices coming from the porch and the sound of Robbie's laughter. Smiling, I went to see what they were doing.

Robbie, Elena, and Tina were playing Candyland.

Robbie looked up at me with a wide grin. "Hi, Mommy! We're playing a game!"

"I see that," I said. "Who's winning?"

"I am," said Tina.

"Because she's cheating!" said Elena.

Tina laughed and got to her feet. "Okay, you two, I quit." She faced me. "Can we talk?"

"Sure. Why don't we take a walk? Give me a moment to change my clothes and then we'll go."

"Can I come too?" Robbie asked, jumping to his feet.

"Not this time, honey. I need to talk to Tina alone. You stay with Elena."

"Awww ..."

Elena stood up. "C'mon, buddy! How about some juice and crackers?" She held out her hand, and Robbie took it, satisfied for the moment.

"Ann, I'll meet you outside," said Tina, her expression troubled.

I hurried into my bedroom to change, wondering what was going on.

When I emerged, I waved goodbye to Robbie and Elena and headed out the door.

Tina was wearing big sunglasses and had tucked as much of her hair as possible underneath a baseball cap.

"Good idea to wear the disguise," I commented.

We strolled along the sidewalk away from my house until we reached a small park bench.

"Okay, what's going on?" I asked, sitting and indicating a place for Tina.

Emitting a sigh, Tina lowered herself onto the bench beside me. "It was good to talk to Barbara. Really good, in fact. But it's going to take me time to work things out. I think back to some of the things my mother did to me, and I wonder what kind of woman would do that to a child. And then I begin to think about me as a mother, and I don't think I can do it." She covered her face with her hands and then lifted her head. "I'm thinking of terminating the pregnancy."

"What? Oh, Tina, this is such an important decision. Why would you want to do that?" I held my breath.

"As I said, I don't think I'm going to be a good mother. Not when I had one like mine."

"What else is going on?" I asked gently. "Is it Nicholas? Does he know about the baby?"

Tina shook her head. "No. That's just it. He told me once that he didn't want more children. If I'm ever to get him back, I can't be pregnant."

My stomach churned. "Whoa! You're making an awful lot of assumptions. Why don't we start with first things first?"

"Like what?"

"Even though your mother wasn't the best and, in fact, was quite awful, you have the opportunity to do things your way. You've proved that already with your work. The X-rated movies are a thing of the past because *you* made that change, not your mother, not anyone else. You're bright and loving. Remember how you treated your brother? He adored you."

Tears filled Tina's eyes. "But I couldn't save him."

I put my arm around her. "You were there for him whenever you could be. Remember that, Tina."

She nodded. "I always tried."

"So, don't make any decisions about not having this baby based on that. Agreed?"

"I guess. But Nicholas ..."

I cut her off. "Stop and think what you're saying. Nicholas already has a child. How does he treat her?"

Tina's lips formed a pout that I remembered from her past. "Like she's perfect. And, Ann, she's not."

"Is that a father who doesn't love his child?"

"No-o-o." Tina gave me a thoughtful look.

"Deciding about a baby's future is the job of both the mother and the father. He deserves to know about this baby, regardless of your relationship."

"But he may not want to get back together with me ..." I raised my hand to stop her. "First things first, Tina. We need to take care of you, help

you get your thoughts and feelings straightened out, and deal with your grief. When are you going to see Barbara again?"

"In two days. Maybe after that appointment, I'll see where I am emotionally and get up my nerve to call Nicholas."

"Good. That's not something I'm going to help you with. That is between you and Nicholas."

Tina studied me a moment. "You know, I think of you as the mother I should have had, not the one I was given. Thanks, Ann. I love you."

"Love you, too. Now let's get back to that little boy of mine." I stood and turned to go.

Tina held me back. "Let me go first. I need to apologize to Elena. I think she's still mad at me for making a play for Troy the last time I was here."

I smiled at her. "Good for you."

Tina's visit among us was already bringing her out of the clouds of stardom and down to earth. I hoped it would help her make good choices.

Liz and I met with Lorraine in her new office at the hotel. She still hadn't moved all her sample and design books from her old office, but a vase of fresh flowers sat on her signature, white desk.

"Nice to see you again, Liz," Lorraine said, shaking hands with her. She turned to me with a smile. "Good news. The young woman who was working here has decided to stay on and help me. I think I can teach her a lot."

"I'm sure you can," I said enthusiastically, thinking of Lorraine's natural poise and elegance. Emily Thatcher was a pretty, bubbly young woman, but her lack of experience with elaborate weddings was a drawback to building business.

"Please have a seat. Would either of you care for coffee? Tea? Or perhaps a glass of wine?"

Liz gave me an impish grin. "I'd love a glass of red wine."

"Sounds good," I said, laughing. "To celebrate."

Lorraine smiled and poured the red liquid into crystal glasses. "I thought you might like to try this syrah. It's versatile and would do nicely with a variety of main courses."

She handed us the wine and sat down behind her desk. "Liz, you and I talked about having your wedding in the new gazebo that is being built. Is that still what you want?"

Liz shot me a glance. "Mom, I really want to be married there, with a small group surrounding Chad and me."

"What about the weather?" I said to Lorraine. "It might not be very warm."

"After I talked to Liz, I did some investigation into outdoor heaters. Because it's an evening wedding, we could place them around the perimeter of the building and use the light from them as candlelight. We can wrap silk flowers around the lampposts and build a whole garden scene around them."

Liz clapped her hands. "I love it! Don't you, Mom?"

I smiled at Liz's excitement. "Yes. It could be absolutely lovely."

Liz took a deep breath and faced me. "I know we had a dress picked out, but I've changed my mind. I want something more formal, more traditional. Can we do that?"

I turned to Lorraine for an answer.

She shrugged. "As long as the dress hasn't been worn or altered in any way, I don't see why not. They're holding the dress for you, aren't they?"

"Yes, and no alterations have been done to it," I replied.

"Okay, let's call them right now."

Watching Lorraine make the call, hearing the way she spoke to the owner of the wedding shop, I breathed a sigh of relief. A good wedding planner was priceless.

She finished the call and turned to us. "All set. You can arrange an appointment with them at your convenience. However, do it right away in case any adjustments need to be made to the dress." She leaned forward. "Now, let's talk about flowers and the reception."

I let out a gasp. "Oh, we almost forgot that Chad's mother is planning on singing a personal song for the wedding. How is she going to get music out at the gazebo?"

"I already talked to Bernie about it. The gazebo will have electricity, so Chad's mother can have access to music that way, or we can set up a temporary platform outside the gazebo for a keyboard player or a harpist."

"She wants to sing at the reception too," said Liz. "What could I say? She's very proud of what she's written for us, and Chad didn't want me to hurt her feelings by saying no."

"I understand," I said. "As far as the food goes, we'll handle that with Jean-Luc. But we need to talk to you, Lorraine, about decorating the room."

By the time, we finished, Liz's eyes were shiny. "This is going to be so beautiful! I can already see it in my mind, and now I know exactly what kind of dress I want."

She leaped out of her chair and wrapped her arms around me. "Thank you! Thank you!"

I stood, hugged her back, and turned to Lorraine. "Thank you so much. I'm so happy you're here to help us."

Lorraine nodded. "I want this to be an unforgettable occasion for the two of you."

As we were leaving the hotel, I noticed Bernie and went

over to greet him. "Liz and I have just had a wonderful meeting with Lorraine. And I'm happy to hear that Emily will be her assistant."

"Yes, we'll see how she does," said Bernie. "Are you going ahead with the idea of using the gazebo as Lorraine talked about?"

"Yes. Promise me you'll have it ready as soon as possible. Liz is thrilled with the idea, and I think other brides will be too."

He glanced over at Liz standing by the entrance waiting. "She'll make a lovely bride. Maybe we should take pictures of her for our new advertising flyer."

"Okay, but let's save that for a surprise, okay?" I didn't want Liz to know, but I was beginning to wonder if we could pull off the ceremony she wanted. Bad weather or many other factors could change everything.

The next day, however, when I saw Liz in the wedding gown she'd chosen, I knew that no matter what else happened, she would remember the way she looked in this dress.

CHAPTER TWENTY-NINE

The days flew by as Rhonda and I re-established ourselves at the hotel, working on a publicity campaign of our own for former guests. After the initial letters were sent, we received phone calls from people following up on our offer to come for a visit. And in the community, we let it be known that we were reviving the traditional Christmas Open House we'd started when we'd first opened. The prior owners had decided not to continue that event, disappointing our regular guests.

We worked with Laura Bakeley on updating the guest rooms and ordered new carpeting and other soft goods through Harold Drayton at Hotel Suppliers. The renovation, they both assured us, could be done during the normally slow time between Thanksgiving and Christmas.

At home, things settled into a more normal routine with Tina. She continued to work with Barbara on several personal matters that she kept to herself. I didn't press her, though I was anxious about her decision regarding the baby.

One morning a couple of weeks after her arrival, she padded into the kitchen wearing a frilly pink robe which barely came to her knees. She looked adorable with her tousled, blond hair and the tan she was acquiring from lazy days by the pool.

She sat down at the kitchen table and looked over at me. "Ann? I've made a decision. I'm inviting Nicholas to come here for Thanksgiving. I'll be moved into your house at the hotel, and that will give us the privacy to work things out there. Is that all right with you?"

I let out a quiet sigh of relief. "I think it's a marvelous idea. You're more than welcome to join us for our Thanksgiving celebration."

"I'd like that," she said smiling. "Any chance we could go shopping today? I want to buy some new, looser clothes for the holiday." She gently rubbed her stomach. "I don't want anyone to notice my condition. Especially anyone in the press. I'm supposed to start another movie in the spring, and I'm not sure what's going to happen when they learn I'm pregnant."

I set down my coffee cup and gave her a wry look. "Do you remember what you told me when I first took you clothes shopping here?"

"Probably something outrageous," Tina said sheepishly. "But I know now what tasteful clothes are like, and I don't want to go back to those cheap-looking, sexy clothes my mother wanted me to wear."

"Okay, it's a deal. And afterward, if you'd like, we can go to lunch."

"Sounds good. I'll use my baseball cap and sunglasses as a disguise."

I couldn't help saying, "Don't you hate all the notoriety, the lack of privacy?"

"Sometimes, I really do. Other times, not so much. It's all part of the scene."

"I'll never get used to it with Vaughn."

"How is he doing with Lily? She's not a nice person, Ann. She'll do anything to get her own way, including giving up her daughter for a juicy role on television."

"Vaughn is tired of the whole charade. He's threatening to quit the show, but he has to think of his career. He loves his work. I get that."

"Lily has made enemies along the way. If there's any justice, she'll get a good comeuppance one day."

Robbie ran into the kitchen and stopped, looking at both of us. "Hi, Mommy. I'm awake." He started toward me and then went to Tina and climbed up into her lap.

As I observed Tina hugging him to her, my worries about the future of her baby eased.

Later that morning, Tina and I went to Styles, my favorite clothing store. It was well-known for its upscale, eclectic clothing, and Christine, the owner, would keep Tina's secret, as she'd done for others.

Watching Tina try on several different outfits, I thought back to the girl she used to be—troubled, obnoxious, unsure of herself. The beautiful woman today was still struggling with so many issues, but she was a much stronger person than she knew. Maybe, I thought, it was this vulnerability of hers that made her such a respected actress given to touching performances.

"What do you think?" Wearing a sleeveless dress that showed off her well-toned arms and hid any bulge that might appear, Tina twirled in front of me. The pale-pink color of the dress suited her coloring.

"On you? It's stunning," I said, meaning it. The woman could wear anything and look fabulous.

After Tina had tried on a number of other things and selected pants, a skirt and several tops, we left the store and wandered down a side street to one of my favorite places to eat.

Seated outdoors, we each ordered a southern chicken salad with spicy pecans, fresh blueberries, and a lemony, ginger dressing. The sun tempered an on-shore breeze, keeping us warm. A few people stared at us but didn't get up to speak to Tina, for which I was glad.

Judith Keim

--ooo—

After lunch, I dropped Tina off at home for a nap and went on to the hotel to check on my house. Several days ago, Liz and Chad had removed all the furniture, the Oriental rug from the living room, and several pieces of the artwork I'd offered them.

When I pulled up to the driveway, a large delivery truck was backed up to the open garage. Pleased, I hurried inside, where Laura was directing two men placing new furniture in the living room.

"What a nice surprise! I didn't know the furniture was being delivered today."

Laura smiled. "You can't believe how hard I pushed to get it here in time. But I knew you needed it, and you're a good client. Come look at the bedrooms. We settled those first."

As Laura led me into the master bedroom and then the room that used to be Liz's, I beamed with admiration. They were beautiful—and a little pristine without all the personal items that had meant so much to me.

"I'm still waiting for a couple of the paintings we chose, but most everything will be in place by the end of the week."

I followed her into the living room. The last piece of furniture was being lowered onto the rug that Laura and I had chosen to tie everything together color-wise.

"What do you think?" said Laura.

I hesitated. "I'm not sure I like the chair in the corner. Is that the color we chose?"

Laura nodded. "But if you don't like it, we can exchange it."

I stood back, closed my eyes, and opened them slowly. *Better.* "No, I'll get used to it. I'm sure our guests will be fine with it."

"Yes," said Laura with confidence. "The grass-green color

is lovely with the tropical design of the rug. It'll be a while until we're through here."

"Okay, I'm going to run along. I'll check it later. Thanks so much." I gave her a hug. "I hope the renovation of the guest rooms goes as well."

"We'll see. We were lucky this time," said Laura.

I left her to go over to the hotel. Jean-Luc was working on the Thanksgiving menu, and I wanted to check it over before we sent it to the printers. I also needed to talk to him about Liz's wedding dinner.

When he saw me, Jean-Luc looked up from working at his desk and smiled. "I'm finally getting things organized the way I want them. Come have a seat. I've got the menu almost ready."

I sat in the chair he offered and studied him. A trace of sadness still lingered in his eyes, but there was a new energy about him. Seeing it, I was glad Rhonda and I had encouraged him to come back to the hotel.

We discussed the menu we'd planned for the Thanksgiving buffet.

"It looks wonderful. Let's go ahead and get them printed. And now, Jean-Luc, can we talk about the dinner for Liz's wedding? Though it will be the night before Christmas, Liz doesn't want it to be a typical holiday meal. Any suggestions?"

"For Rhonda's wedding, we served a prime filet of beef and glazed sea bass gently baked and sauced with a subtle blend of ginger, shallots, and cream. That might do nicely for Liz."

I shook my head. "Let's try something different from the beef with the sea bass. People are eating less red meat these days."

Jean-Luc's face lit up. "I can do something with squab. Lemon, thyme, shallots, and butter pressed under the skin of the small birds and roasted quickly, perhaps stuffed with a mushroom mixture. I will look into it."

"All right. It's such a small group you'll have the opportunity to fuss however you wish. You make it as fun and different as you want as long as Liz and Chad are pleased. We're all foodies."

"I'll get back to you with a menu to show them."

"Thanks. Is there anything Rhonda and I need to know about being prepared for Thanksgiving? We've talked to a few of our loyal customers about reviving the buffet, and they seemed enthusiastic."

Jean-Luc nodded. "Reservations are coming in. And your group?"

"We'll set it up in the library, so it doesn't interfere with hotel guests. The private dining room is twice-booked, which is great."

"Yes, people are happy to have me back at The Beach House Hotel."

I gave him a quick smile. "Not as happy as Rhonda and I. You're more than the chef, Jean-Luc, you're part of our family."

He quickly turned his head, but not before I saw the tears that sprang to his eyes.

As I was leaving the hotel, my cell phone rang. *Rhonda.*

"Hey, partner! Thanks for giving me the morning off. Tina was able to find some clothes she liked for the holidays. She wants to look nice for Nicholas. What's up?"

"I just got a call from my brother. Richie and Margaret can't make it for Thanksgiving, but they've promised to come sometime next winter. I'm real disappointed."

"Oh, I'm sorry, Rhonda. I know you were counting on seeing him. Let's plan something fun when they finally make it."

"What's new with you? Have you spoken to Jean-Luc?"

"Yes, I've just come from a meeting with him. The Thanksgiving buffet looks great. We're going ahead with printing the menu."

"Good. This morning Bernie and I interviewed two more women for our wait staff. Word is getting around that Jean-Luc's back at the hotel, and we need more good people. You all set for tonight?"

"Yes. After I check on my house, I'll go home and change and then come back."

"Like old times, huh?" Rhonda said.

I laughed. "A little hard to get used to, but we'll make it."

As we'd done in the past, when VIPs held private parties in the small dining room, either Rhonda or I would be present to greet them and oversee the meal. I enjoyed it. I'd been privy to many interesting conversations and had met many powerful men and women this way.

I left the hotel and headed for my house, where I'd left my car. Crossing the lawn of the hotel, I stopped and looked at the large, two-story, wooden garage we'd transformed into two upper-story apartments, a commercial laundry, and a small spa that Troy operated. Bree had told others they wanted to tear it down to make room for more guest rooms. I was so glad that hadn't happened.

I turned and studied the hotel, loving the fact that Rhonda and I were once again the owners. Small, private, and charming, the hotel was the perfect place for the discerning guest, not the young players from South Beach that Bree had tried to attract.

I waved to Manny and Paul, who were planting flowers by the tennis court and continued on my way, anxious to see the final results of the new furniture in my house.

The delivery truck and Laura's car were gone from the driveway. I took out my key, and feeling a little like Goldilocks opening the door to the bears' house, I inserted it into the lock and opened the door.

Pretending I was a guest, I stepped inside and gave the interior a critical look. The bold pattern of the carpet in the living room was tempered by classic furniture—a tan, oversized, leather couch, and two overstuffed chairs whose woven fabric contained many of the colors in the rug. The end tables, coffee table, and lamps were a modern mix of metal and glass that enhanced the clean lines of the furniture. The result was both artistic and classy. The oil painting of flowers that I'd brought from my grandmother's home in Boston looked classic hanging above the couch.

I wandered into the bedrooms and smiled with approval at the furniture and the soft goods in each one. The master bedroom, which had been so abused by Bree, had a fresh new floral look that any guest would like. And the guest bedroom, done in soft grays, was peaceful.

I stepped to the sliding door in the living room and checked the patio and pool. They looked fine.

Before I left, I went into the kitchen, which had been my pride and joy. The stainless-steel appliances, the tile floor, and the stove shone from the scrubbings they had received. I opened the cupboard to make sure the dishes and glasses were in order, and then checked the rest of the cupboards and all the drawers. Tina and other guests would have all they needed. We'd add things like fresh flowers and a few extra decorative pieces before she moved in.

Satisfied, I locked up and left the house.

CHAPTER THIRTY

After dressing for the VIP dinner, I kissed Robbie goodbye, waved to Elena and Tina, and hurried out to the car, eager to meet with the group. Upon receiving the notification of Rhonda's and my new ownership, a congresswoman from the Midwest had called to arrange this dinner. In the past, these kinds of meetings weren't unusual—politics, business, and personal matters handled with aplomb and discretion.

As I entered the hotel, I looked around the lobby. Some of the shine that had been missing with merely adequate housekeeping had returned to the area. Bernie took pride in his job of overseeing the place, and it showed. And Ana, as head housekeeper, was insistent things were done properly. Tonight was Annette's first time acting as a part-time hostess, and I was curious to see how she handled it.

In the library, a group of ten had gathered for cocktails. Annette was mingling with them. Watching her, I couldn't help thinking of Sabine and what an addition she'd been to our staff. But Annette seemed to be handling things well, and, like Sabine, had a certain classiness to her that couldn't be faked.

I strolled among the guests whose faces I'd memorized. Bernie had sent out an internal announcement listing these VIP guests by name and, where possible, with a photo.

Congresswoman Boyken waved me over to her. "Ann, I was so delighted to learn you and Rhonda have taken over the hotel. The last time I was here, things were disappointing. It's nice to be certain that The Beach House Hotel is once more a place I can come to with assurance of excellent service and complete discretion."

I smiled. "Of course. That's why I'm here, to give you such assurance. Please enjoy your stay. You've met Annette Bruner?"

"Yes, and thanks again."

A few moments later, word came from the kitchen that Jean-Luc was ready for them to be seated in the private dining room. I spoke to the congresswoman and then announced to the gathering, "Please follow me to the dining room. Chef Rodin has prepared your meal."

Excited murmurs followed me as I led the group to the private dining room and made sure all were seated comfortably by the two staff members assigned to the meal.

Annette watched me carefully as I gave a private signal and the staff left to get the first course from the kitchen. Jean-Luc, like most chefs, would not tolerate his food being served cold.

I stood back and watched as Annette supervised the placing of the *Coquilles St. Jacques* that had been ordered. The scallops were plated beautifully. I suddenly realized how hungry I was.

After a sauvignon blanc was poured to accompany the scallops, I turned to Annette. "You're sure you're comfortable with everything?"

She nodded. "Yes, I love doing this kind of thing, and it's nice to be part of Bernhard's world."

"All right. I'm going to leave you. I've found that when confidential matters come up in conversation in these gatherings, it's best to simply pretend you don't hear a thing. And, of course, what is spoken inside this room is never to be repeated."

"Of course," she said amicably. "I've chosen our servers for that very reason."

"I'll be in my office for a while. Then I'll return here for the dessert course."

I would have to trust our staff to do as we asked with as little supervision from me as possible. Bernie was running the hotel for us, and we had to let him do his job. I owed it to him and to my family.

When I returned to the private dining room, the conversation was brisk even as guests took last sips of coffee.

The congresswoman stood. "Thank you all for coming. We can resume our conversation tomorrow over breakfast right here in this room. My thanks to you, Ann, for the superb hospitality here at The Beach House Hotel. And thank you, Annette, for your assistance."

"It's our pleasure to have you here," I said. "Please let us know if there is anything else we can do to make your stay enjoyable."

As others were departing, one of the women in the group came over to me. "I was so sorry to hear of the breakup of your marriage to Vaughn Sanders. It always seemed like such a sweet romance to me—the hotel owner and the television star."

I felt the blood leave my face. "What are you talking about?"

The woman leaned closer. "I know I shouldn't, but I watch *The Sins of the Children* every day, along with *Hollywood Word*. Yesterday, *Hollywood Word* interviewed Lily Dorio and got her to confess she's been staying in Vaughn's apartment building in New York. When the host asked her if she was staying *with* Vaughn, Lily said, 'You guess' in such a way we all know the answer."

"But ..." I began.

"Oh, honey. I've had the same thing happen to me. My heart goes out to you." She gave me a quick hug and hurried away, leaving me so frustrated I wanted to cry.

"Are you all right, Ann?" said Annette, looking worried.

"I will be," I said firmly, filling with anger so deep my cheeks felt on fire.

I thanked Annette and went into the lobby.

Bernie was waiting for me. "How'd everything go with tonight's function?"

I forced back my anger to address him civilly. "Very well. Annette did a superb job."

A smile lit his face, enhancing his features. "Good. Annette was a bit anxious about it."

"She doesn't have a thing to worry about. She's a wonderful hostess—gracious, kind, attentive."

I left the hotel determined to settle things on the home front. I was sick and tired of Lily's insinuations regarding her relationship with Vaughn. I had a family to protect, and my feelings had been disregarded enough.

As I drove home, I rehearsed what I was going to say to Vaughn. The volume of my voice rose as I recounted aloud the hurtful incidents.

I pulled into the garage, got out of the car, and stalked into the kitchen, ready to do battle.

The lights were dimmed in the kitchen, the house silent. Figuring everyone else had gone to bed, I opened the door to my bedroom and stumbled back in surprise.

"Vaughn? What are you doing here?"

He looked up at me from the bed and gave me the crooked grin I liked. "I came home. I gave the top people at the show an ultimatum. I told them they have to get rid of either me or Lily, and until they made a decision, I was going home. They agreed I could take my six-week leave a few days early."

"And then what?"

"And during that time, they're going to decide what to do about the situation." He held out his arms. "I hate seeing you upset like this, and I don't want Robbie or any of the other kids hurt either."

I settled in his arms. "Really, Vaughn, it's so unfair to our family and to me for her to say all those things that aren't true about you and her. I'm so over it. One of our guests this evening is convinced our marriage is over. It's so embarrassing to be caught off-guard like that."

"Honey, you know that our marriage is not over. And by the first of the year, we'll know what's going to happen to my job. In the meantime, I've agreed to a telephone conversation with the producer of *Hollywood Word* to help dispel any false notions people may have. I can't just sit by and say nothing, Ann. I have to do the right thing and defend you, us, our family."

"Yes, I know." I sighed. "But I have to admit that I hate this kind of publicity when Rhonda and I are trying to rebuild the hotel's reputation."

"It doesn't help. How are things going?" Vaughn asked, rubbing my back.

"Very well considering how fast the change took place. Bernie has been working with Mike on updating contracts with various suppliers, taking over the staff, and seeing that the hotel is well maintained, like it used to be. He and Jean-Luc are working together to make things right for the kitchen, and Annette had her first job as hostess tonight and did well."

"It was a good move to bring him back," Vaughn said. "I've always liked Bernie."

"Me, too,"

Vaughn's lips curved. "But I like you even better."

Drawing a deep sigh, I hugged him. He was my rock.

Having him home with me for six weeks would be a dream come true. A dream for all of us.

The next morning, I got up early, and leaving Vaughn asleep, tiptoed into the kitchen to get a cup of coffee. At the sight of Tina sitting at the kitchen table, I stopped.

"Good morning," I said softly. "What are you doing up so early?"

"I couldn't sleep. I have both happy and sad news," said Tina, dabbing at her eyes.

I hurried over to her. "What's going on?"

Tina drew a deep breath. "Nicholas isn't coming for Thanksgiving. Emaline threw a fit about him leaving her with her aunt for the holiday, even though they normally spend the holiday together."

I felt my shoulders sag with worry. "And the news of the baby?"

"I'm flying to California later this morning. Nicholas has agreed to meet me so we can talk things over. He says he's miserable without me, but I can't live my life tiptoeing around his daughter."

"But she's in her twenties and should behave better."

"I agree," said Tina. "That's why this whole thing with her is crazy. She should be having her own life, not trying to ruin mine."

"Okay, what's the happy news?" I asked, trying to dispel the gloom that hung around Tina.

A smile curved her lips. "Liz has asked me to be an honorary bridesmaid in her wedding. It will still be only Angela standing up with her, but she wants Nell and me to be part of the wedding party in our own way."

"Oh, I didn't realize ..."

Tina cut me off. "She's doing it more as a nice gesture than anything else. We've been spending some time together while you're at the hotel, and Elena is with Robbie." Her smile was tender. "I think Liz feels sorry for me."

I reached for Tina's hand and gave it a squeeze. "Liz is a sweet girl, and she knows how much I love you."

Tina nodded and swiped at her eyes. "I'm coming back to the hotel right after Thanksgiving. Will your house still be available?"

"Of course. It should be finished by then. We're awaiting just a few decorative pieces. If you want, you can leave some of your things there."

"That would be marvelous. I want to be with your family for the holidays." Her eyes swam with tears. "I don't know if I'll be alone or not."

"One day at a time. Remember?"

Her lips curved tentatively. "Yeah. Well, I'd better go start packing."

She rose, but I stopped her. "How about having a nice, healthy breakfast? You know what airline food is like."

"Okay. I have to take good care of my baby."

"You're going to keep it?"

"Yes," Tina said firmly. "Even if Nicholas is upset, this baby was created in love."

I wrapped my arms around her. "You're going to make a wonderful mother."

"Better than mine, that's for sure," Tina said wryly, patting her stomach.

We exchanged warm smiles, already sharing a bond of motherhood.

CHAPTER THIRTY-ONE

Vaughn's daughter, Nell, and her husband, Clint, arrived from Washington, D.C. the day before Thanksgiving, filling the house with excitement. Their baby was due sometime in March. She looked adorable with a rounded stomach, and Clint was endearing as a prospective father, hastening to do any task for her. Observing the loving interplay between Vaughn and his daughter, I thought of Tina's situation and hoped she and Nicholas would be able to work things out.

While Vaughn, Clint, and Robbie went sailing, Nell and I sat around the pool. Typical of visitors, Nell lay out in shorts and a top while I sat nearby in the shade in slacks and a light sweater.

"How's Liz's wedding coming along?" Nell asked. "I haven't talked to her for over a week. Is she over the jitters?"

"Very much so," I said. "Even though it's still a small wedding, Liz has upgraded the style of the wedding from casual to more formal. Wait until you see her gown. It's almost Victorian in style. I was surprised by the choice, but it looks fabulous on her."

"It's so sweet of Liz to have me as an honorary bridesmaid, though technically my maiden days are obviously over."

At the pride in Nell's voice, my lips curved. "Tina Marks has also been given the same honor." I grew serious. "She's dealing with some family issues and has been staying here with me for a couple of weeks. After Thanksgiving, she'll move into my house at the hotel for some rest and relaxation."

"Nice," said Nell. "You are such a good friend to her." She

cleared her throat. "I've meant to ask, how are things between you, Dad, and Lily? I'm furious about all the rumors but didn't want to say much to Dad because he's really troubled by it. How are you holding up?"

"I'm angry," I confessed. "Lily knows very well that Vaughn and I are happy together. I think she finds the challenge with Vaughn amusing, though it hurts her ego to fail. She's a weird personality, like other famous movie stars who keep going from one man to another. I think it becomes a kind of game."

"Me too. I don't want to raise a child in a family where his grandfather is perceived as some kind of immoral jerk."

"Apparently, your father has given the producers an ultimatum to settle the issue, or he'll leave."

Nell sat up and turned to me. "Really? But he loves his work."

"I know. That's why I'm not saying much about it. The decision is his to make, the same as the decision to return to the hotel was mine."

Nell smiled. "I'm glad you and Rhonda are in charge again. I'm hoping to take advantage of your postpartum specials for new mothers. It's such a great idea."

"We're instituting a lot of our old programs. Can't wait for the results to be rolling in. We have to spend money refurbishing the rooms and, as usual, I'm worried about the cost of things. The nature of the hotel business can be fickle. Weather, competition, and other challenges are always present."

"I love that you haven't allowed success to go to your head, Ann."

"Success one day doesn't mean success the next," I said, sounding an awful lot like my staid grandmother.

--ooo--

Thanksgiving morning, I rose early, dressed, and slipped out of the house. A holiday for others, Thanksgiving was a hectic, busy day for every staff member at the hotel, starting with breakfast and continuing until the last, sated guest either left the hotel or went to bed.

Bernie waved at me as I walked into the lobby. The aroma of roasting turkeys enveloped me, causing my mouth to water. Jean-Luc had been preparing food for several days ahead. Turkeys, hams, and roasts of beef would be accompanied by casseroles, fresh vegetables, salads, warm breads and rolls, and every conceivable kind of dessert. People had clamored to book a coveted reservation for a good reason. Guests staying at the hotel were automatically given a reservation, but people in town were accepted on a first-come basis. A waiting list was carefully maintained, leaving a few spots open for unexpected guests.

"It smells delicious already," I said happily to Bernie.

"Jean-Luc is doing his usual thing, but I'd stay out of his way. Rhonda, Consuela, and the kitchen crew are working as fast as they can. The extra dining staff should be here soon to help set up the dining room. Annette will oversee them."

I beamed at him. "I hope you know how lucky we feel to have both you and Annette working for us. Actually, she's working for you. It doesn't seem to be a problem. Is it?"

"No, we're fine. Remember, we worked together on her daughter's wedding—probably the toughest thing a couple can do."

I smiled at the memory of them doing that, and suddenly overwhelmed by gratitude, I gave him a quick hug.

Bernie stood stiffly as was his nature, but he smiled down at me. "I love this hotel as much as you do."

I doubted that was possible, but I nodded. "Thanks for everything you do."

Juan, working behind the reception desk, called to Bernie, and while Bernie went over to him, I hurried to the kitchen.

Observing the scene in the kitchen was like watching members of an orchestra playing together. Each person was in motion—chopping, stirring, sautéing, or stuffing. Sheet pans filled with a variety of food items filled several metal racks. Rolling carts were set aside to handle roasts and other large items.

When we'd originally expanded the kitchen to suit Jean-Luc's requirements, we'd thought it was enormous. Now, filled with active people and loads of food, it seemed almost small.

Rhonda and Consuela smiled up at me from where they were preparing pies and rolls.

Flour dotted Rhonda's face, but she looked happier than I'd seen her in some time.

"Nice to have my kitchen back," she said, darting glances at Jean-Luc who was standing behind a couple of cooks at the stove.

"Better not let him hear you," I whispered, edging my way out of the room. In the past, Jean-Luc and Rhonda had fought about whose space it was.

In the office, I went through messages, updating the guest list, and responding to more requests for reservations. It was a juggling act to keep the number as high as we could without overbooking or letting seats go empty.

Rhonda came into the office carrying a cup of coffee and a sweet roll. "Consuela insisted I give this to you."

"Thanks. I didn't dare disturb you." I eagerly took a satisfying sip of hot coffee.

Rhonda took a seat at her desk and turned to me. "Jean-Luc is tough, but the kitchen is humming like a bee hive. It's so great to have him back."

"Bernie too. And Annette is working out well. She'll be here later this morning."

"How are the bookings going for the buffet?" Rhonda grinned. "I've forgotten how exciting this has always been for us. Do you remember our first Thanksgiving?"

"Indeed, I do." It hadn't been as smooth a time as I'd hoped. Back then, we'd just begun to know each other. I'd never imagined we would work together to convert her home into a hotel. "It's been quite a trip, but I'm so grateful for all that's happened. If you hadn't forced me to go into business with you, I don't know what direction my life would have taken."

"I knew I couldn't do it without you. That's what I'm really thankful for today."

I grinned. "Here's to more of us being together!"

That afternoon, I sat at a long table in the library with my family and Rhonda's, glad to be off my feet. Rhonda and I had greeted the people entering the hotel and then had helped seat them in the dining room. It felt good to have this kind of interaction with guests, but it was exhausting, and I was happy for the break.

The room rang with happy conversation as we ate delicious food. Looking around at my friends and family, I whispered a soft thank you for all I'd been given.

CHAPTER THIRTY-TWO

With Thanksgiving behind us, the rooms renovation plan shifted into high gear, and plans for our Christmas Open House began in earnest with the task of decorating the hotel. We all went to work.

In the main lobby, pine boughs and holly branches lay on the mantelpiece. Mixed among them battery-lit candles spread soft light over their greenery. Two tall, wooden nutcrackers stood guard on either side of the fireplace. Every available table surface held a small, tasteful holiday bouquet.

In the dining room, Jean-Luc placed a large gingerbread house on a table next to the entrance, and on each table, a crystal bud vase held sprigs of shiny-leafed holly, whose berries added festive color.

Outside, twinkling lights sparkled among the hibiscus lining the front of the hotel. Beside the double wooden doors, clusters of white, red, and pink poinsettias greeted guests.

When the work was done, Rhonda and I stood in the lobby, gazing around us with pleasure.

"We did it!" said Rhonda, grinning at me. "This Christmas at the Beach House Hotel is ours! Just like old times."

"It feels good, doesn't it?" I said, admiring the twelve-foot Christmas tree that Manny and Paul had erected at the far end of the front entry. Colorful glass balls in every shade, and sparkling, crystal icicles hung from its branches. A thousand tiny lights shimmered like rainbows among the green boughs and gave a halo effect to the tree's image. Admiring its glowing presence, I stood for several minutes, mesmerized by its beauty, seeing promise for the hotel's future.

"Getting ready for the Christmas Open House?" came a familiar voice behind me.

I whirled around.

Tina stood there, a wide smile creasing her beautiful face.

"You're back!" I cried, giving her a hug. "We missed you on Thanksgiving."

"Thanks, I came back as soon as I could to show you what we've done." Grinning, Tina held up her left hand. A band of diamonds sparkled on her ring finger. "Nicholas and I got married. He's out front, talking to the bellman, but I'm anxious for you to meet him." Her eyes shone with happiness. "I'm so happy. He's thrilled about the baby."

"And his daughter?"

"She's getting used to the idea that it's okay for her Daddy to have a new wife. Seriously, we had a long talk, and I've asked her to join us here at the hotel for Christmas so she and I can talk to Barbara Holmes together. I want her to be happy with me, with us."

"Sounds like a lot of good things have happened," I said as a tall, gray-haired man walked toward us.

"Ann? I'm Nicholas Swain." He held out his hand, and I took it, studying his well-defined features, the intensity of his hazel eyes. Kindness lingered in his smile. I liked him immediately.

"I understand congratulations are in order," I said. "I wish you both much happiness."

"Thank you for all you've done for Tina. It means a lot to her and to me." He put his arm around Tina and drew her to him.

I noticed the sense of peace that softened Tina's face and felt my eyes well with tears. Some things were worth fighting for.

Rhonda came into the lobby, saw Tina, and hurried over to us. "Hi, Tina! Glad to have ya back. And who is this?" She studied Nicholas openly.

"This is my husband," said Tina.

"Husband? But I thought ..."

Tina laughed and turned to Nicholas. "We decided to go to the final step, didn't we, darling?"

He nodded. "Started a family, too."

Rhonda beamed at them. "Good thing you've already worked it out 'cause I've been very good at matchmaking, ya know."

I couldn't help rolling my eyes.

Tina noticed it and laughed. "Nicholas, this is Rhonda DelMonte Grayson, Ann's partner and a dear friend of mine."

Rhonda and Nicholas shook hands. "You staying here through Christmas?" she asked.

"It's about time I had a little vacation. Not much going on at the studio, so it's a good time to be away."

"Vaughn will be glad to know you're here," I said, admiring this man who made Tina so happy.

"I was hoping he and I could get together. I have some business to talk over with him," said Nicholas. "And he's a sailor, right? I'd like to rent a sailboat while I'm here and thought he could help me."

"He's going to love that," I said. "Give him a call anytime."

Bernie joined us. "Anything I can do to help here?"

Tina and I made the introductions.

"Let's get you settled into the house," said Bernie. "I lived there at one time, and you're going to love it. You'll have as much privacy as you want."

I saw Nicholas flash Tina a sexy smile and hid a smile of my own. I wouldn't have to worry about Tina anymore. She was in good hands.

Rhonda and I left them and went back to the office. Dorothy was there, working on our guest list for the party. We'd made an effort to include members of the city council, county commissioners, supervisors, people from the neighborhood, and, of course, Terri Thomas from the newspaper. A reporter from the Miami *Herald* was also invited as well as a couple of editors of social magazines for Southern Florida. We'd been forced to ask Brock Goodwin to attend as the President of the Neighborhood Association, but neither Rhonda nor I really wanted him there.

"How are the RSVPs for the party coming?" I asked her.

"About as I expected," said Dorothy. "We're going to have a huge crowd. Everyone is excited to have you girls back in charge, and they can't wait to see you."

I returned her smile. "Good, that's settled then. Now let's see about getting the kitchen crew to help us with our famous appetizers."

Dorothy's eyes rounded behind the thick lenses of her glasses, making them seem enormous in her small face. "With so many people coming, you won't be able to make all the food for the party yourselves, will you?"

"We have Jean-Luc and Rick Bassett to help us. Rick was a pastry chef at one point in his career," Rhonda said.

"He's going to do Liz's wedding cake," I added.

Dorothy clasped her hands. "I'm so glad Liz invited me to her wedding. I can't wait to see her married to that adorable Chad Bowen. If I were Liz's age, I'd give her a run for her money for the likes of him."

Rhonda and I exchanged amused glances. Chad, with his strawberry-blond hair, bright, blue eyes, and easy grin was a handsome young man who didn't realize the effect he had on women, even at Dorothy's age.

As we left Dorothy and went into the kitchen, Rhonda

turned to me. "How many people are coming to Liz's wedding? I thought you said it was going to be small."

I couldn't help frowning. With Tina and Nicholas and his daughter added, and now Dorothy, the numbers were growing.

"I'll have to check with her. She's becoming more and more excited about it. I love that she's enthusiastic, but we can't outgrow the room after the big fuss I made about our getting it."

"I still can't believe that little prick, Bree, wouldn't honor that reservation. Heard any news about him recently?"

I shook my head. "Maybe Mike will update us at the party."

Sunday, the day of the party, was sunny and cool—perfect for a gathering like ours. Standing beside Rhonda at the top of the stairs leading into the hotel, I gazed up at the blue sky. Puffy white clouds, like dollops of whipped cream floating in the air, tempted me to create imaginary shapes of them in my mind.

Rhonda nudged me, urging me out of my whimsical state. "Here they come. The first of the mob."

The policeman directing traffic on the street waved a number of cars through the gates of the hotel. Paul and Manny directed them to the parking area beside the garage. Soon, every conceivable parking space inside the gates was filled. The small buses we'd hired to transport invitees from a nearby church parking lot began rolling through the gates.

Rhonda and I greeted guests at the door and stood back as Bernie and Annette and other staff members guided them into the lobby and to the main dining room where an array of food was displayed on a large table. In another area of the dining room, a bar had been set up. Outside by the pool, another full bar was set up, along with a keg of beer, and a tableful of appetizers and small bites.

When the bulk of the guests had arrived, I joined Rhonda inside to mingle. The smell of pine, the flickering of candles, and the holiday greenery added the perfect touch to the festive occasion. Many attendees had kept to the holiday theme by wearing green or red, and I saw more than one Ugly Christmas Sweater.

As I walked through the lobby, Mike Torson took me aside. "Great party, Ann. Thought you'd want to know I heard from George Peabody. All the final papers of the transaction are signed, sealed, and delivered. Apparently, Bree has been relieved of all duties with their company and is now out of the country at his father's house in Italy."

"That doesn't sound like much of a punishment to me," I groused.

Mike shook his head. "One of the poor-little-rich-boy scenarios. Such a shame. What he really needs is a kick ..."

"In the ass," Rhonda completed, joining us.

"Exactly," Mike said, chuckling and then quickly sobering. "I wish the two of you all the success in the world." He glanced around. "Looks like it's going to happen all over again."

"I hope so," I said, trying not to allow the old mantle of worry settle on my shoulders.

As he and Rhonda moved away, I noticed Brock Goodwin making his way into the room. He saw me and headed in my direction.

Stuck, I waited for him to approach. "Good afternoon," I said to him without my normal enthusiasm.

"Not as good as it could be," he replied. "Come now, Ann, you know I'd already ordered holiday decorations for the hotel. Why wouldn't you honor the contract for me to do so?"

I shook my head in disbelief at his persistence. "Your

contract was with the former owners, not us. And we didn't need them. We are using the decorations we've had from the beginning. I don't know what Bree was thinking by placing an order with you."

Brock gave me a hard look, his green eyes turning stormy. "I thought maybe your invitation to this party was a peace-offering, but I see now that you're not that generous."

My cheeks grew hot. I was about to answer when I felt a hand on my shoulder.

"Hello, Brock," Vaughn said smoothly. "Not up to any trouble, I hope."

Brock seemed to shrink in size. "No, no. A problem that may never go away." He gave a little bow. "I promise you that, Ann."

Vaughn guided me away from him. "Never have liked the guy, like him even less now."

Chad's mother, Sadie, came up to us. "Can't wait for the wedding to take place here. It won't be long now."

I smiled. "It hardly seems possible that it's been two years the kids have been dating. I'll be glad to see them settled down together. How's the wedding song coming along?"

Her face crinkled into a smile. "It's going to be beautiful. I've found a keyboard player to accompany me. I think the kids are going to be thrilled."

"And I know you'll like performing it," I said kindly. Sadie was a star in the local theatre group and loved being the center of attention. But she was a good singer, and it was a sweet gesture that Liz had graciously accepted.

Vaughn stayed by my side as we drifted from room to room. Lorraine Grace was talking in earnest to a woman and her daughter, hopefully pulling in more wedding business. Outside, Dorothy was sitting at a table with one of her friends, nibbling on food and talking with animation. Consuela, Ana, and other staff members were refreshing food displays on the tables. The two new bartenders we'd hired were busy crafting seasonal cocktails and pouring drinks.

"Good party," murmured Vaughn, smiling pleasantly when people recognized him. He seemed as anxious as I to dispel rumors of a troubled marriage, especially here, because he knew it meant a lot to the business of the hotel.

By the time our last guests left hours later, Vaughn looked as tired as I felt. Rhonda and I plopped down side by side on one of the couches in the living room.

"Well, partner, we did it again!" said Rhonda, giving me a high five. "Terri Thomas is doing a big spread on the hotel, and the photographer from the *South Florida Society* magazine took lots and lots of pictures. You know how people love that."

"I had a nice chat with a reporter from another magazine," I said. "Looks like we're going to get a lot of good publicity out of this."

"I saw Nicholas, but I didn't see any sign of Tina. Didn't she come?" said Rhonda.

"Over there." I pointed to a petite woman standing next to Nicholas. A hat covered most of her gray wig, and large sunglasses covered much of her face. Vaughn and Will were talking to them.

"Oh my God! I would never have recognized her. What a hoot!" said Rhonda. "Wonder what the guys are talking about?"

"Probably sailboats. Nicholas rented a nice one and is trying to get Vaughn to teach him how to sail it. Said it was on his bucket list."

"Ah, well, that sounds like a good, safe sport for the father-to-be," said Rhonda. "Will gets seasick, so I don't think he'll be joining them."

I kicked off my sandals and rose. "We'd better help the staff."

"Yeah, we may be the owners, but we know what that really means in a small place like this," said Rhonda groaning as she pushed to her feet.

In the beginning, we hadn't been able to afford much help and, realistically, though business had grown, things hadn't changed that much. Owning the hotel meant a lot of work—glamorous or not.

CHAPTER THIRTY-THREE

As we prepared for the holidays, events continued at a rapid pace both at home and at the hotel. With a four-year-old in the house, it was a fun time of year. Christmas Day was counted down by the elf who hid in secret places and left a small treat for Robbie each morning. Even Trudy got into the act, racing around the house with Robbie, wagging her tail and wearing a big red bow. In the evenings, we read holiday books and watched holiday programs together. I, like he, loved the magical idea that a jolly old man rode in a sleigh through the night sky to deliver toys. Together, we picked out a few gifts for boys and girls in need.

As it got closer to Christmas, I helped Robbie choose presents for Vaughn and Liz. He helped me wrap them, using too much tape on the packages that would nevertheless be cherished.

During this stretch of time, Vaughn and Nicholas enjoyed each other and spent many hours together on *Lucky Lady*, the thirty-six-foot sloop Nicholas had rented. Tina spent time with Liz and Angela whenever she could. Often, Nicholas and Tina joined us for dinner. When the time came for Nicholas's daughter, Emaline, to join them, they were disappointed by her sudden refusal to show up.

One night, as we were dining together, Nicholas asked me how I'd gone about becoming friends with Vaughn's children.

"Nell and I got along instantly. She knew how lonely her father had been since Ellen's death and was rooting for us to get together. I got along with Ty, too, but with his living in San

Francisco, I didn't see him as often. But both Ty and his wife, June, have been fine and supportive of our marriage. It might have gone the other way, but Vaughn let them know how important it was for him to be happy again."

His brow creased with concern, Nicholas sank back in his chair. "So, you think I should be firm with Emaline? Let her know how much Tina means to me?"

"Yes. I'm guessing you keep telling Emaline how much she means to you instead of maybe switching things around."

Nicholas cast a sheepish look at Tina.

Tina reached over and squeezed his hand. "I don't want to make it a contest, but as Barbara told me, we're supposed to be a team."

I gazed at Tina with astonishment. *This was the young girl who was a mess not so long ago? She sounded like a calm, mature adult.*

"Good thing we've had time away by ourselves, huh, Tina?"

A teasing smile crossed her face. "A honeymoon with friends isn't bad, after all?"

His cheeks reddened, and then a chuckle escaped him. "After the baby comes, we'll do something more."

Her eyes filled. "You don't understand. This is the best honeymoon ever."

Vaughn and I exchanged pleased looks.

With the slow season upon us, the renovation of the guest rooms at the hotel was finally coming together. New carpeting had been put down, draperies cleaned, and bedspreads replaced. We'd been able to use most of the furniture, though some had had to be refinished or replaced.

To celebrate, we had our staff party the week before Christmas. In addition to gifts for their children, each staff member received a bonus. The former owners may have forgotten how important each person was, but Rhonda and I were happy to show them. And as we saw the shining faces of the kids as they lined up to talk to Santa Claus or simply to watch others, we were reminded of the joy of giving.

When Ty and June and Nell and Clint came to Florida for the wedding, rooms at the hotel were ready for them. Liz had opted to "return home" for the few days before her wedding as if she and Chad weren't already living together. I loved the private time it gave me with her.

As we sat together in my kitchen, sipping coffee on the morning of her wedding, memories of her as a little girl kept intruding on the present day. She'd been a pleasant child, determined but sweet and eager to learn everything. Now, having watched her read stories to Robbie or answer one of his questions, I was certain she'd make a good mother, a good wife. I couldn't help thinking of her father and knew he'd be proud of the woman she'd become.

"Tina and Angela are going to join us at the hotel to get our nails done, and then we'll go to lunch and our hair appointments. All right?" Liz said, putting aside her phone.

"Sounds good to me. Nell and June will join us for lunch. They're enjoying the opportunity to stay at the hotel. Nell loves the charm of it."

"So, I guess the guys are going sailing this afternoon," Liz said, after taking another sip of coffee.

"Yes, they're even taking Robbie with them so we girls can enjoy this time together."

"Ah, sweet!" Liz set down her coffee cup and gazed at me with affection. "Mom, this is going to be such a perfect day! Thanks for everything. It's just like I imagined—a small, evening wedding with candlelight and everything I wanted. It will look like a twinkling fairyland."

"We have a lot of people helping us to make it perfect for you. Lorraine will be here at five to help you and the girls get dressed and then she'll leave to make sure everything is set at the hotel."

"I can't believe the weather. At this time of year, it can be awful, but it's almost like a summer day."

"A gift, I'd say. Let's not talk about how perfect everything is going to be, all right?"

Liz laughed. "I didn't know you were superstitious, Mom."

"Just cautious," I said, pushing away any bad feelings about the day.

The hotel spa filled with happy chatter and teasing as the girls and I had our nails done. Seeing the interaction between them, I was filled with joy. The day that Liz had dreamed of for so long was coming true.

As we were about to head into the dining room for lunch, Tina received a call on her cell. She lifted a hand. "Hold on! I've got to take this."

Her eyes grew wider and wider as she listened, sending alarm through me. She hung up and faced us with a look of shock.

"What is it?" I asked.

"It's Emaline. She's here. Nicholas is dropping her off at the hotel right now. I'm to meet her and keep her with me."

Knowing the story behind their relationship, we all glanced at each other with apprehension.

"I hope she doesn't ruin things," Tina said, clasping her hands. "If necessary, I'll take her home with me."

My look steady, I placed a hand on Tina's shoulder. "No, we'll work things out. This little visit may be just what Emaline needs."

"Yeah," said Rhonda. "If we have to, we'll put her in her place."

A satisfied expression softened Tina's features. "Okay."

We trooped over to the front of the hotel to await Emaline's arrival. Though I'd sounded calm, I would, in truth, be furious if Emaline destroyed the easy camaraderie we all shared.

Nicholas's rental car pulled up to hotel's entrance, and a thin, young girl with auburn hair climbed out of it and stared at us with disdain.

"Okay, I'm here. Now what?"

Her attitude was much like Tina's had been when Rhonda and I had first met her. But her style of clothing was not the same at all. Whereas Tina's outfit had been sexy—too much so—Emaline's plain white blouse and long blue skirt seemed almost prissy.

I walked over to her and held out my hand. "Hello, I'm Ann Sanders. Glad to meet you. And this is my business partner, Rhonda, her daughter, Angela, my daughter, Liz, my two daughters-in-law, Nell and June, and, of course, you know Tina."

Tina stepped forward. "I'm so surprised to see you but glad you're here to meet my friends. Actually, I think of them as my family."

I moved to Tina and wrapped an arm around her. "We think of you as family, too." I studied Emaline's look of surprise. "That's why we're all going to get along."

"Yes," said Tina, "because it's Liz's important day."

The eight of us walked into the hotel together.

Seated at a round table in the dining room, we sipped bubbly water while Liz opened the gift her sisters-in-law placed before her with sly smiles.

"What's this?" Liz asked, giving them looks of suspicion.

"Open it up," said Nell. "This kind of thing worked for me."

"And me," said June, patting her barely-rounded stomach.

We all, but Emaline, started giggling.

Liz tore the wrapping paper off, exposing a box that read Secret Success. She lifted the cover off and started laughing. "Oh my God! Chad will love it!"

She held up a short, red, see-through nightgown with two holes strategically placed in the front of it. The top was accompanied by the briefest of panties.

"We couldn't resist, dear sister," said Nell, giving her a wicked smile.

Emaline frowned. "Aren't you really stepsisters?"

Liz nodded. "Yeah, but more like sisters. Why?"

Emaline shrugged. "I dunno." She glanced at Tina and then away.

Conversation continued easily among seven of us. Emaline remained quiet and standoffish, even when I tried to engage her.

At one point she said to me, "So who at this table isn't pregnant?"

"Liz, the bride, and Rhonda and me. Why?"

She slid a glance Tina's way. "I guess I'm not ready to become a stepsister." She paused. "Or a stepdaughter."

"You're a lucky girl to have Tina for a stepmother. She's been through a lot and is caring about others. And you can see how much fun it can be to be a stepsister, a daughter-in-law, or anyone in a good family."

Tina smiled and leaned toward us. "What are you two whispering about?"

Emaline stiffened. "Nothing."

I let it go and turned to Angela sitting on my other side. Tina and Emaline would have to work things out themselves.

Following lunch, we moved as a group to Hair Designs downtown for an afternoon of primping. Malinda and her

crew were waiting for us when we arrived.

"Nice to have you here." Malinda studied Emaline. "Who do we have here?"

Tina spoke up. "Emaline Swain, my stepdaughter."

Emaline's body went rigid, but she remained quiet.

"Love the color of your hair," Malinda said. "Ever had any thoughts of cutting it shorter, doing something a little more contemporary? I'd love to try it."

"Yes," said Liz, and the others joined in.

"Okay, I guess," said Emaline, and a round of cheers broke out.

Three hours later, the eight of us were ready to leave.

I checked my watch. "We still have some time before getting ready for the wedding. Anyone need something from Styles? Different dress? Anything?"

Emaline glanced at me.

"Emaline, do you want to change up your dress to go with your new, stunning haircut?" I said boldly.

She smiled and nodded.

"Let me buy you something," said Tina. "It'll be my treat."

"Okay," said Emaline. "I didn't bring much with me. Didn't think I'd be staying long."

"I love Styles," said Nell. "Maybe I'll look for something for after the baby."

After paying Malinda and the rest of the stylists, I followed the others to my favorite clothing store.

Watching the girls pick through the clothes, Rhonda and I talked quietly.

"Seems like Emaline is becoming less of a brat," said Rhonda. "She reminded me a lot of Tina when we first met her. Sweet justice?"

I laughed. "It's ironic, all right. Let's hope shopping therapy helps. Amazing how a new hairdo can help boost a girl like her. She's pretty."

"Bet she doesn't think so, next to Tina."

I gave my partner a smile. "Of course! That's got to be part of it."

A few minutes later, Emaline modeled an emerald green dress for us. When we all clapped and exclaimed over it, a smile spread across her face and lit her hazel eyes.

"You look beautiful," said Tina. "Your father will be so proud to see you in it."

"Really?" said Emaline.

"Of course. We both will. Now, how about strappy sandals?"

"What size shoe do you wear?" Liz said. "Looks like you're my size. If so, you can borrow a pair of mine."

Emaline looked startled. "Okay. Thanks." She faced all of us. "Thanks so much for everything."

"All right, everyone. Ready to go to my house to change? The men should be back by now. I've asked them to go ahead and get ready, so we can have the rest of the house to ourselves."

Rhonda shook her head. "Sorry, Annie. I just got a call. Angie and I have to get home. Will and Reggie are taking care of the kids, and they're sending signals for help."

"But, Liz, I'm coming back to join you as soon as I can," amended Angela.

"Me, too, darling," said Rhonda, giving Liz one of her bosomy, heart-felt hugs.

As I drove into the driveway of my house, I was surprised to find Vaughn's car missing.

"Where's Vaughn?" Liz said. "I thought they were supposed to be back by now."

"Maybe they're running a little late, cleaning up the boat or something like that. Why don't you give him a call while I get everyone else inside?"

I ushered Nell, June, Tina, and Emaline into the house and led them to two of the bedrooms in the back. Ordinarily, we'd use the Bridal Suite at the hotel, but we'd had to book it for another group—a paying group. As we offered in the suite, I'd loaded the bathrooms with plenty of perfume, lotions, and makeup for everyone to use.

When I returned to the living room, Liz waved me over. "I tried Vaughn's cell, but there was no answer. And Chad didn't answer either." She grabbed my arm. "Mom, I'm worried about them. Really worried."

A thread of unease crept through me, turning me cold. "Me too."

CHAPTER THIRTY-FOUR

Nell approached me. "Where's Dad?"

The others followed behind her.

"What's going on, Annie?" Nell persisted. "I thought you said Dad and Clint would be here."

"And where's *my* dad?" said Emaline. "He told me he'd be back before four o'clock."

"I tried to call Nicholas earlier, but he didn't pick up the call," said Tina, looking worried.

I held up a hand. "Let's each try to reach our loved ones again. Then we'll determine what we're going to do."

"I hope nothing went wrong with the boat," said Tina. "Nicholas is learning to sail, but he's still quite new at it."

"Vaughn is an excellent sailor," I quickly said, trying to tamp down the hysteria rising within the group.

"Ty knows how to sail," said June, attempting a smile. "If I didn't like sailing, I wouldn't be his wife today."

We tried to reach the men by phone, but no one answered.

"Don't panic," I said. "I'm going to call the marina to see if they've docked yet."

I called their number and waited for what seemed hours for someone to answer. Finally, a voice said, "Waterside Marina."

I told him who I was and that we were awaiting word from anyone aboard *Lucky Lady*, the boat Nicholas was renting. "Can you please check to see if they're back. It's important. We have a family wedding taking place soon."

As I waited, the other women gathered around me.

"Yes?"

"No sign of them. It's a clear day, so I suspect they're probably just out of cell range."

"Can you send someone out to check on them?" I asked.

"Sorry, I don't have anyone available to do that," he said.

"Oh, but ..."

"Look, if you don't hear from them in the next half-hour, I'll try to find help. Or you can go ahead and call the coast guard and give them a heads-up. But they won't send someone out unless it's an emergency."

"Thanks." I ended the call more worried than ever.

"Well?" said Liz, her eyes filling.

"The guy at the marina thinks they're just probably out of cell range."

"But, Mom, look at the time! How long will it take for them to get in cell range and then back to the marina?"

I gulped. "I don't know."

Tears spilled from Liz's eyes. "I'm scared. I can't lose Chad."

"Let's not panic," I repeated. "We'll wait a little while and then we'd better go ahead and get dressed for the wedding."

"But what if the wedding is late?" Liz wailed. "Will it ruin everything?"

"Not necessarily," I said. "I'll go ahead and call the hotel to explain the situation to Jean-Luc, so he can plan ahead."

Fighting my own panic, I went into the kitchen to make the call. It would be devastating if something awful happened to Robbie and the men on the boat. The thought made me nauseous. I sank into a chair next to the kitchen table and made the call to Jean-Luc.

Jean-Luc was understanding, but he asked me to give him more information as soon as possible.

My nerves were doing a tap dance inside me. Knowing I

had to keep myself together, I called the one person who could talk me down.

"Hello? Annie? What's up?" said Rhonda.

"It's the men on the boat. They're not back, and none of us can get in touch with them. I'm sick with worry but trying my best to hide it from the girls. Rhonda, you know what it was like when I thought I'd lost Vaughn. What if I lose him again? Or any of the others?"

"Annie? I'm on my way."

"Thanks," I said in a wobbly voice.

"Well?" Liz said when I met up with the group on the porch.

"Jean-Luc was nice about it, but we'll need to keep him informed. Right now, all we can do is sit and wait."

Emaline started to cry softly. "If anything happens to my dad, I don't know what I'll do. He's been so disappointed in me."

Tina sat on the couch beside Emaline and rubbed her back. "Your dad loves you. I'm scared too, but let's try for positive thoughts. Your father might be a new sailor, but he's very smart. I trust him to do his best to get back home safely to us."

"You do?" Emaline said.

Tina nodded. "He's a good man, and I love him."

Emaline leaned into Tina and began weeping. "I'm sorry, so sorry ..."

"I know." Tina hugged her. "It's okay. We're going to be okay."

Observing them, so close in age, so far apart in maturity, I thought it was a good thing that Emaline had come to Florida after all.

Rhonda and Angela arrived together.

"Any news?" said Rhonda.

We all shook our heads.

"Maybe no news is good news," said Rhonda in an unconvincing voice.

"Don't worry about the wedding," Angela said, hugging Liz. "It's going to be beautiful even if it's late."

Liz gave her a bleak look. "What if it doesn't happen at all?" Her voice quavered.

"It's going to happen all right," said Rhonda. "C'mon, girls, make a circle and hold hands. We're going to send good wishes their way."

Rising, we formed a circle and took hold of each other's hands.

I said, "Think only good thoughts now."

In the quiet of the room, I could sense people praying.

Moments later, the shrill sound of my cell phone broke through the quiet, startling us.

"Get it!" Liz shrieked.

I ran to the table and picked up my phone. "Hello? Vaughn? Oh my God! Where are you?"

The group gathered around me as I put him on speaker.

"Ann? We were becalmed on the water, and when we tried to turn on the motor, we discovered something was wrong with it. We couldn't call because we were out of cell phone range. The minute we could, we called the marina, and they sent someone out to tow us in. Tell Liz we're sorry, but we're going to be late."

"Vaughn? I don't care if you're late as long as everybody is all right."

"We're fine, just sorry this happened. Is Liz there? Chad wants to talk to her."

"Hi, darling!" came Chad's voice. "I'm so, so sorry. Are you going to be really mad at us?"

"No, goofy," Liz said, though tears were running down her

cheeks. "I'm just glad you're okay. Hurry up, though, because like Rhonda says, our wedding is going to happen. I'm not letting you get away."

He laughed. "We're on our way."

They ended the call, and then Liz turned to me and gave me a fierce hug. "They're okay."

Nell, June, and Tina all held phone conversations of their own. I tried not to listen, but I couldn't help hearing Tina say, "Now, Emaline wants to speak to you."

Tina and I exchanged smiles as Emaline said, "Hi, Daddy! I'm so sorry for the rough time I gave you and Tina."

"Nice job," I said to Tina, giving her a hug.

"Being part of the Florida family has made all the difference to me." Tina squeezed my waist. "I love you all so much."

After everyone had concluded their phone conversations, I beamed at them. "Okay, ladies. Lorraine is due any minute. Time to get dressed for a very special wedding."

CHAPTER THIRTY-FIVE

The small group of us, family and friends, stood in a circle inside the gazebo waiting for Vaughn and Robbie to escort Liz down the white cloth runway Lorraine had arranged.

An assortment of white flowers filled a huge, crystal vase on top of the makeshift altar. Strings of them, like fat leis, were strung from the ceiling, making it seem as if we were immersed in a garden. White poinsettias in silver pots sat on both sides of the altar, adding a holiday flavor to the festive occasion. Tiny, white lights sparkled among the lattice work surrounding the base of the gazebo and hung from the high ceiling beams, creating the fairyland effect Liz had wanted. Soft, classic, love songs played in the background, adding a touch of romance to the scene.

I gazed at the people standing with me. Nell and June, both pregnant, shone with happiness and the unmistakable, iridescent glow of impending motherhood. Tina looked beautiful, though she wore almost no makeup. Standing between Nicholas and Emaline, she seemed to anchor that small family. The men, I noticed, had sunburned noses, a small price to pay for what might have been a disaster.

My gaze swung to my hotel family—Bernie, Annette, Dorothy, Manny, and Consuela—and my heart filled with gratitude for them.

Rhonda and I exchanged glances, well aware of how much we meant to each other. Will, standing beside her, had his arm around her shoulders and was quietly talking to Angela and Reggie.

The sound of the wedding march had us all standing taller. Chad, between his mother and the minister, shifted his feet with nervous anticipation.

I held my breath.

Then I saw them—my family. Tears blurred my vision as I observed Liz in the white dress she'd chosen. With her blond hair done up in a mass of curls behind her head, she was breathtaking. In a cloud of silk and lace, she seemed to float toward us. On either side of her, Vaughn and Robbie looked like the proud father and brother they were. My heart filled with love for them.

As she climbed the stairs to meet her groom, Liz smiled at me, her eyes shining with happiness. Then her focus turned to Chad and remained there.

Emotion washed his fine features and filled his eyes as he gazed at her with what could only be called adoration. As I witnessed their obvious love for each other, tears rolled down my cheeks. But I didn't care. This was the Christmas Eve wedding Liz had always dreamed of, and she fit the part beautifully.

Vaughn came up beside me, slipped his hand in mine, and gave me a quick kiss. I wrapped my free arm around Robbie's shoulder and drew him to me. He looked up at me with shiny dark eyes and grinned.

The simple service began.

I listened to the words being said, lost in memories of my own wedding on the beach here at the hotel, and hoped my daughter would find the happiness I knew.

After vows and rings were exchanged, I clapped along with everyone else as Chad kissed his bride, my little girl, all grown up.

Soft music began to play. Chad's mother moved to the bride and groom and began to sing the romantic song she'd written for them. Her musical notes soared above us like a private blessing. Spontaneously, we all formed a circle and held hands, surrounding Liz and Chad with the love we had for them.

When the song ended, Chad and Liz exchanged kisses with his mother and came over to Vaughn and me.

"Thank you, Mom," Liz whispered in my ear before kissing me and turning to Vaughn, who was shaking hands with Chad.

A moment later, Lorraine announced, "The bride and groom will now lead you into the hotel, so that you may celebrate with them."

Hand in hand, Liz and Chad descended the stairs and headed toward the hotel.

Vaughn pulled me aside. "I haven't had the chance to tell you about the Christmas gift I have for you."

At his teasing smile, I arched an eyebrow at him. "You bought a boat?"

Vaughn laughed. "It's better than that, although I'm not giving up on that idea."

"Oh?"

"Yeah, I figure it will be a fun way to spend my time when I'm not working in New York." His grin turned impish.

I gazed up at him. "Vaughn, what aren't you telling me?"

His smile grew wider. "I got a call from Roger Sloan. Seems like they took my ultimatum seriously. Right after the new year, Lily is off the show. And by the way, I've agreed to do an interview with Terri Thomas for the local newspaper just so there's no mistaking how much I love you."

"Really? That's fantastic!" I gave him a joyous hug.

Vaughn held out his hand. "Shall we go inside, Mrs. Sanders, and celebrate our daughter's wedding?"

"Yes, indeed," I replied, wrapping my fingers around his.

As we walked into the hotel to join our group of family and

friends, it pleased me that everyone seemed happily settled for the moment. Liz and Chad were married, Tina had her new family, and Angela, Nell, and June would soon hold babies in their arms.

Inside the small, private dining room, I caught Rhonda's eye. She winked at me and dabbed at her eyes. This day meant so many things to each of us. For Rhonda and me, among other things, it meant a return to working together to make The Beach House Hotel all it could be.

My eyes welled with gratitude for all I'd been given. The holidays were not about gifts, but the people you loved, and I was so very, very lucky.

"Merry Christmas," said Vaughn, squeezing my hand and looking down at me with such tenderness my heart raced, drumming in my chest with happy beats.

"And Merry Christmas to you, my darling," I said, thinking any time with him, my family, and friends was treasured, but this Christmas at The Beach House Hotel was the best of all.

Thank you for reading *Christmas at The Beach House Hotel*. If you enjoyed this book, please help other readers discover it by leaving a review on Amazon, Goodreads, or your favorite site. It's such a nice thing to do.

Enjoy an excerpt from my book, *Finding Me - A Salty Key Inn Book*, (Book 1 in the Sullivan Sisters Series), which was published in February 2017.

CHAPTER ONE
SHEENA

In early January, Sheena Morelli sat with her two sisters in a conference room of the Boston law office of Lowell, Peabody and Wilson, waiting to meet with Archibald Wilson himself.

"Do either of you have any idea why we're really here?" said her youngest sister, Regan. "The letter from Mr. Wilson said something about a reading of a will. But that doesn't make sense to me. I didn't even know Gavin Sullivan."

"Me, neither. He's probably some rich uncle leaving us a lot of money," teased Darcy, the typical middle sister, who was always kidding around.

Sheena laughed with her. The three Sullivan sisters had no rich relatives that they knew of in their modest family. They were hard workers who relied on only themselves to make it through life. *Well,* thought Sheena, *maybe Regan wasn't as reliable as she and Darcy.* As the baby of the family, Regan had always been a bit spoiled. At twenty-two and eager to escape her old life in Boston, Regan wasn't about to spend too much time with the family. This time, though, at the formal request of Mr. Wilson, Regan had dutifully left New York City to come to "Bean Town."

As Sheena waited in the conference room for Mr. Wilson to show up, she studied Regan out of the corner of her eye. With her long, black hair, big, violet-blue eyes, and delicate Sullivan features, she was a knockout—a Liz Taylor look-alike.

Darcy sat on the other side of Sheena in a stiff-backed chair. Studying Darcy's blue eyes, red hair, and freckled nose, Sheena thought of her as cute...and funny...and maybe a little annoying, though everyone seemed to love Darcy's sassy attitude. At twenty-six, Darcy claimed she hadn't found her true calling. Whatever that meant.

Sheena had found her calling in a hurry when she got pregnant as she was starting college, where she'd planned to take nursing courses. Ironic as it was, her wanting to become a nurse and getting caught like that, had changed many things for her. Now, at thirty-six and with a sixteen-year-old son and a fourteen-year-old daughter, she still hadn't recovered from losing her dream.

She straightened in her chair as a tall, gray-haired man entered the room carrying a file of papers.

"Good morning, ladies. I'm Archibald Wilson, the lawyer representing Gavin Sullivan. I'm pleased you all could attend this reading of his will," he announced in a bass voice. He looked the three of them over critically. "Which one of you is Sheena Sullivan Morelli?"

She raised her hand. "I'm Sheena. Do you mean the 'Big G' Sullivan?"

Wide-eyed, her sisters released loud gasps. The name "Big G Sullivan" had been mentioned in the family on rare occasions, and only when her father and his two other brothers had had too many beers. And then it was never kindly.

Mr. Wilson nodded with satisfaction. "Yes, that's my client.

Sheena, though all three of you are beneficiaries, I will address you on most of the issues, as it pertains to the specific language of the will."

Sheena sat back in her chair, her mind spinning. This scene seemed so surreal. Their father had broken his relationship with his brother years ago. He'd always said his brother was a loser, someone he could never trust.

"He's left something for us?" said Darcy. "I was only teasing about such a thing."

The lawyer studied Darcy a moment, took a seat facing the three of them on the other side of the small conference table, and opened the file he had carried in.

He began to speak: "I, Gavin R. Sullivan, of the State of Florida, being of sound and disposing mind and memory, do make, publish, and declare this to be my Last Will and Testament..."

Certain words faded in and out of Sheena's shocked state of mind. Though her sisters might have been too young to remember him, she had a clear image of the big, jovial man who'd captivated her with his smile, his belly laughs, and the way her father grew quiet when they were in the same room together. On one particular visit, the "Big G", as he was known, gave her a stuffed monkey that she'd kept on her bed for years. It wasn't until the fur on the monkey was worn off that she'd noticed a seam was tearing. One day, while she was probing the hole, a gold coin fell out.

Sheena showed the coin to her mother, who snatched it away and whispered, "Don't tell anyone about this. It's very valuable. Someday you'll need it. Until then, I'll keep it safe for you. Your uncle loves you very much." As her father walked through the doorway, her mother held a finger to her lips.

Until now, Sheena had forgotten all about the coin.

Archibald Wilson's voice brought her back to the present.

"Sheena, you, Darcy, and Regan are now the legal owners of the Salty Key Inn, but you, Sheena, will be in charge of taking over the small hotel in Florida, as your uncle directed in his will. Is that understood by the three of you?"

Sheena and her sisters dutifully bobbed their heads. The bewilderment on her sisters' faces matched her own feelings. How in the world were the three of them going to run a hotel?

"Remember," Mr. Wilson warned them, "the hotel may not be sold for a period of one year. And the three of you must live there together for that entire time if you are to have a share in the rest of his sizeable estate, the details of which will remain undisclosed until the end of your year in Florida. You have just two weeks to prepare. In conversations I had with him in setting up the will, I believe Gavin Sullivan intended for this to be a life lesson for each of you."

"Whoa! Wait a minute! What about the lease on the condo I share with two of my friends? I can't just walk away from that," said Darcy.

"And mine?" said Regan.

The lawyer nodded. "Read over the conditions of the will. Any expenses like that will be taken care of by Gavin's estate. All expenses as you settle in will be handled through me. But, beware, there will be hidden tests for you throughout this entire process. Tests that could make a lot of difference to each of you."

Sheena exchanged worried glances with her sisters. She wished she'd asked their mother for more information about the uncle she was never to mention. And now it was too late. Their mother had died a little over a year ago.

"Live together in Florida for a whole year? Was Uncle Gavin crazy when he set up this deal?" exclaimed Darcy. Her indignation was understandable.

Mr. Wilson stood. "I realize you all have a lot to talk about, a lot to think about. And let me know if you need any further clarification of the terms of the will. You are welcome to continue using this conference room, and please feel free to help yourself to any of the refreshments on the side table." His lips curved with a touch of humor in what had been a mostly expressionless face. "Enjoy the challenge."

After Mr. Wilson left them, Sheena sank back into her chair. Her mind raced at the thought of suddenly leaving Boston to go live with her sisters in Florida for an entire year. How could she do that? It would be difficult for her on many levels. They were sisters, after all, and like sisters everywhere, being together for too long sometimes caused battles to erupt. More than that, she had a family. And her husband, Tony, wouldn't like the idea at all. Her children even less.

"What a joke," said Darcy, shaking her head. "Living with the two of you for an entire year? Running a hotel? No way. And, Sheena, Tony would never allow you to do something like this. You're what he calls 'the Mrs'. And what about the kids?"

Sheena glared at Darcy. "Wait a minute! What did you mean by that 'Mrs.' remark?"

"Don't take it the wrong way," urged Regan. "It's just that your family depends on you for everything. Especially Tony."

Deep in thought, Sheena remained quiet. Tony was a good man who prided himself on always doing the right thing. And he expected her to fulfill what he thought was her proper role.

Though their relationship was still new when she got pregnant, Tony had stepped right up and offered to marry her to prevent her mother's conservative church friends from counting on their fingers how long it took for their first baby to appear. It helped that their son, Michael Morelli, had started his life in the outside world a little late. Still, Sheena had always appreciated Tony's consideration.

A worried sigh escaped her. She knew Tony wouldn't support her being away from their family for an entire year. That would be going against his idea of her in the proper role of taking care of their family. And yet, with his business recently doing poorly, it might be an answer to their prayers— though Tony's fragile ego might prevent her from actually saying so.

"What about you two?" Sheena asked. "You'll have to quit your jobs. What then?"

Regan shrugged. "I don't care. My job is boring—answering phone calls, greeting people and all. They'll just find another receptionist to take my place."

Darcy shook her head. "Receptionist? You were so much more than that. More like some kind of hostess with all those special meetings you helped them with. When I visited you in New York, I witnessed how it was—you serving them drinks before they went out to some business dinner."

"What about you, Darcy?" Sheena asked. "You've got a very good job working in IT."

Darcy grimaced. "Actually, I don't like it very much. Working with numbers and codes all day isn't that exciting. Mom was always so proud of me and my job that I didn't dare tell her I wasn't happy there. But, with her gone, I've been thinking of doing something else." She smiled. "Maybe this whole thing isn't dumb after all. Maybe this will be the beginning of something new for all of us."

Sheena returned her smile. Put this way, it sounded wonderful. If, only...

Following lunch with her sisters, Sheena took the Red Line on the T to return to Davis Square in Somerville, where Tony, she, and the kids shared a duplex with his parents. When they'd moved into the house as newlyweds, she and Tony had thought they'd live there just long enough to save for a small place of their own. But Rosa and Paul, Tony's parents, were so pleased with the idea of the families living side-by-side that Tony agreed it was best for them to stay there, where everyone was available to help each other out. And with two young babies to take care of, Sheena had thought it was a good idea. Later, after Tony set up his own plumbing business, they decided to keep on renting their unit while they tried to build his business. It was very convenient not to have to worry about a mortgage payment and taxes.

It turned out to be a good decision. A lot of the houses the same size in their neighborhood were now selling in the high six figures—something they couldn't afford. And with Tony being a plumber, they'd added a couple of bathrooms to the building, which made the house even more valuable in this close suburb of Boston.

Studying it now, Sheena supposed she was stuck there until the children were grown and gone and Tony's parents gave up the house.

As Sheena walked up to her front door, Sheena's mother-in-law opened the door on her side of the building to greet her. "Everything all right? You were standing outside looking at the house for a long time."

Sheena smiled. "How are you, Rosa?" If she had just one word to describe Rosa it would be warmth. Short and on the well-fed side, Rosa exuded maternal, protective feelings.

"Fine, fine. Just worried about you," Rosa answered. Her dark eyes were filled with concern.

"No need to," Sheena said cheerfully, though she sometimes felt trapped by the idea that she couldn't do much of anything without her mother-in-law knowing. But she'd never tell that to anyone. Rosa had been sweet to her from the time they first met. And after Sheena had produced not one, but two grandchildren to dote on, Rosa became even more of a supporter of hers.

When Sheena walked into the house, Meaghan jumped up from the couch in the living room. "Where were you, Mom? You said you'd go shopping with me for a dress for the Valentine's Dance at school." She narrowed her hazel eyes. "Remember?"

"I had an appointment downtown and was delayed. Honestly, Meaghan, you'd think I was hours late, not just twenty minutes behind schedule."

"I know, but Josie and Lauren have already picked out their dresses. There will be nothing good left for me if we don't get busy." A pout that was becoming familiar spread across her face.

Sheena sighed. "The dance isn't for another five weeks." Her stomach clenched when she remembered she wouldn't be around for the dance. Not if she was in Florida. Two weeks and she'd be gone. Meaghan had been looking forward to this dance all school year—especially after Tommy Whitehouse had invited her to it.

"Well? Are you ready now?" Meaghan said in a demanding tone Sheena found irritating.

Sheena frowned. *When had Meaghan become such a brat?* she thought and immediately felt bad about viewing her teenage daughter this way. She tried to keep things smooth between them.

"Give me a minute to get out of these good clothes and I'll be ready to go," Sheena said and hurried into her bedroom to change. She wanted to be comfortable. Shopping with Meaghan could take hours.

Sheena was emerging from her bedroom when Michael came into the house. "Hey, Mom! I need you to wash my uniform. It has to be ready tomorrow morning. Can I borrow the car? I have to go to B-ball practice."

"Put the uniform in the laundry room and, no, you can't have the car. Meaghan and I are going shopping. Hurry and get ready. I'll drop you off."

"Mom!" wailed Meaghan. "We need to go now!"

Sheena drew a calming breath. "Michael, hurry up. We can't wait forever."

"Geez. Give a guy a break!" he said. "I just got home. Did you get those cookies I wanted?" A taller version of Tony, with his dark eyes and dark, curly hair, Michael's voice even sounded the same.

Exasperated, Sheena shook her head. "No, I haven't had time to go to the grocery store. I've been busy."

Michael rolled his eyes at her.

"Don't go there," Sheena said, a little sharper than she'd intended.

He blinked in surprise. "Gawd! Why is everyone uptight?"

A tense few minutes later, the three of them piled into Sheena's Ford Explorer.

After dropping Michael off at his basketball practice, she and Meaghan headed out to the Natick Mall.

As Sheena drove, she glanced at her daughter. Her fair skin, auburn hair, and Sullivan features had mixed with Tony's darker tones and features to produce a lovely-looking young girl. Though pleased with her daughter's appearance, Sheena was becoming more and more distressed by Meaghan's feeling of entitlement. Tony worked hard, and they lived well, but this idea that everything was all about Meaghan was beginning to wear thin on her.

"Let's see if we can pick up something on sale," Sheena said. "You got a lot of nice clothes at Christmas."

Meaghan's lips thinned. "Mom, this dance is important. I

don't want everyone to think we're poor."

"Meaghan, buying something on sale doesn't mean you're poor," Sheena said evenly. "It means you're being careful with your money. And, in your case, you don't have any money of your own to speak of. You haven't babysat for months."

"How can I babysit if I'm studying for good grades? And if Tommy calls, I want to be available."

"I have no complaints about your grades. You're doing well. But for extra money, you could babysit on the weekends from time to time. Just saying."

Meaghan let out a long sigh. "I don't need to work. Dad's doing okay."

"We'll talk about this another time," Sheena said, telling herself to let Meaghan's attitude go. "Let's just have fun. Okay?"

Meaghan smiled and nodded.

Shopping with Meaghan was fun until Meaghan found the perfect dress—for four hundred dollars. When Sheena told her no, a ferocious creature emerged from the body that used to be her sweet daughter. Meaghan begged and pleaded and threatened her for the dress, but Sheena remained firm.

Tearful and angry, Meaghan followed Sheena out of the mall, stomping her feet like a two-year-old.

Sheena had planned to surprise Meaghan with dinner, but that idea was ruined by Meaghan's behavior. Sheena got behind the wheel of the car and waited for Meaghan to get in and buckle her seatbelt.

As they drove along, Meaghan sulked in her seat, mumbling under her breath when she wasn't staring sullenly out the window. Then, when Sheena continued to ignore her, Meaghan muttered, "I hate you, Mom."

Hurt by her words, Sheena gripped the steering wheel of the car even harder and stared straight ahead. She wasn't about to get caught up in another fight with her daughter. Especially after the day she'd already had.

"Mom? I'm sorry I said that," Meaghan said in a soft voice. "I didn't really mean it."

"Thank you for the apology," Sheena said. "Let's put this shopping day behind us. We'll try again tomorrow."

"Okay. Maybe we can find a dress on sale just like the one I wanted."

Sheena doubted it, but she'd give it a try.

When Sheena walked into the house, Tony looked up at her from the couch where he was watching the news on television. "Where you been?" The dark eyes that had drawn her in from the beginning now focused on her.

"Shopping with your daughter," Sheena said. "Did you put the casserole I left for you in the oven like I asked in my note?"

"Yeah. Earlier, Mom knew I was here alone and invited me for dinner, but I told her I'd wait for you." He grinned, lighting his strong features, exposing the small dimples he hated but she loved.

Sheena couldn't help smiling. "Let me get the table set, and then I'll sit with you for a few minutes. Did Michael get a ride from practice?"

"Yeah. He called me, and I went and got him."

"Good," Sheena said. "There's something I need to talk over with you later after the kids have left us alone."

Tony's eyebrows lifted. "Serious stuff?"

"Yes, and very surprising." She turned to go. "Want another beer? I'm going to have a glass of wine. It's been quite a day."

Tony rose and followed her into the kitchen. "You okay, hon?"

Sheena turned to him, too full of turmoil to know how to answer him.

He drew her into his arms. "It can't be that bad, can it?" He rubbed her back in comforting circles.

Sheena rested her head against his broad chest, grateful for his comfort. "It'll be all right. It's got to be." Earning a sizeable sum from Uncle Gavin's estate would help ease the worry of being able to give their children a good education. Tony's attempt to succeed in business was a struggle from time to time.

They'd no sooner sat down to dinner than Tony got an emergency call. He grabbed a few bites of the chicken casserole she'd made, and left.

Sheena hid a groan. So much for telling Tony she was leaving him for a year.

About the Author

Judith Keim was born and raised in Elmira, New York, and now makes her home in Idaho with her husband, her long-haired dachshund, Winston, and other members of her family.

"Growing up, books were always present—being read, ready to go back to the library, or about to be discovered. Information from the books was shared in general conversation, giving all of us in the family a wealth of knowledge and a lot of imagination. Perhaps that is why I was drawn to the idea of writing stories early on. I particularly love to write novels about women who deal with the unexpected with strength and open their hearts to finding love, because no matter what our circumstances, we all need to love and be loved in return.

"I hope you've enjoyed this book. If you have, please help other readers discover it by leaving a review on Amazon, Goodreads, or the site of your choice. And please check out the Hartwell Women Series, the Fat Fridays Group, and the other Beach House Hotel books. ALL THE BOOKS ARE NOW AVAILABLE IN AUDIO! So fun to have these characters come alive!"

Ms. Keim can be reached at www.judithkeim.com And to like her author page on Facebook and keep up with the news, go to: https://www.facebook.com/pages/Judith-Keim/184013771644484?ref=aymt_homepage_panel

To receive notices about new books, follow her on Book Bub - http://bit.ly/2pZBDXq

And here's a link to where you can sign up for her periodic newsletter!
http://eepurl.com/bZoICX

She is also on twitter: @judithkeim; LinkedIn; and Goodreads.

Acknowledgements

I wish to thank the people who edit my books for me—Lynn and Peter—making my books better than they would be without them.

BOOKS BY JUDITH KEIM

The Talking Tree (The Hartwell Women –1)
Sweet Talk (The Hartwell Women – 2)
Straight Talk (The Hartwell Women – 3)
Baby Talk (The Hartwell Women – 4)
The Hartwell Women Series – (Boxed Set)
Breakfast at The Beach House Hotel –1
Lunch at The Beach House Hotel – 2
Dinner at The Beach House Hotel – 3
Christmas at The Beach House Hotel – 4
Fat Fridays (Fat Fridays Group – 1)
Sassy Saturdays (Fat Fridays Group – 2)
Secret Sundays (Fat Fridays Group – 3 – (Coming soon!)
Finding Me – A Salty Key Inn Book – 1
Finding My Way – A Salty Key Inn Book – 2)
Finding Love – A Salty Key Inn Book – 3 (Winter 2018)
Finding Family – A Salty Key Inn Book – 4 (Autumn 2018)
Winning BIG – a little love story for all ages
For more information: http://amzn.to/2jamIaF

CHILDREN'S BOOKS BY J. S. KEIM

The Hidden Moon (The Hidden Moon Series – 1)
Return to the Hidden Moon (The Hidden Moon Series – 2)
Trouble on the Hidden Moon (The Hidden Moon Series – 3)
Kermit Greene's World
For more information: http://amzn.to/2qlqKMI

Made in the USA
Middletown, DE
23 October 2017